I0599705

# Everything Good

# That

# Happened

# Everything Good That Happened

# Happened

### A novel

## Michelle J. Mann

This book is a work of fiction. All of the characters, names, organizations, places, and events in this novel are either products of the author's imagination or are used fictitiously.

Copyright © 2025 by Michelle Mann
All rights reserved.

No part of this publication may be reproduced, distributed, or transmitted in any form or by any means, including photocopying, recording, or other electronic or mechanical methods, without the prior written permission of the author, except as permitted by U.S. copyright law.

Book Cover Design by Katriona Jaspersen

ISBN 979-8-9924683-0-4 (ebook)
ISBN 979-8-9924683-1-1 (paperback)
ISBN 979-8-9924683-2-8 (hardback)

First Edition: 2025

This book is dedicated to Mike.
Thank you for giving me a better life than
I deserve.  I love you more.

# Acknowledgements

Thank you, Mike M. for giving me the motivation to write this book and making me believe I was capable of doing it. Thank you to Katelynn L. for being my "manager" and attending our daily debriefs at 5:00PM sharp to discuss the progress on the book. Thank you to Justin and Courtney M. for being yourselves. Thank you to Amy A. for driving me in the snow at night with only one headlight. It changed my life. Thank you to Lesli R. and Jamie D. for understanding and supporting my "winging it" method. Thank you to Erica Ramos for your endless encouragement, suggestions, and valuable critique of my draft. Thank you to Sarah McMurray for providing feedback on parts of my draft. Thank you, Darrell G., Brenda G., Mike G., and Linda L., for giving me the motivation to always do my best. Thank you to my editor Ramona Mihai and to my book cover designer Katriona Jaspersen.

# Everything Good That Happened

## Happened

**A novel**

# Chapter 1

## *Sydney*

### As luck would have it...

Everything bad that has ever happened to me has been my own fault. At least, that's the motto I've lived by for years. I'm known for doing things first and thinking about it later. Sometimes my spur of the moment ideas turn out to be a disaster, but every now and then they work out in my favor. Is everything bad that ever happened to me my own fault? Well, let's see. Am I missing the end of my right thumb because I had a temper tantrum when I was seven years old and slammed a door on it? Yes, that was my own fault; however, it has been a great conversation piece. Have I had to show up at work looking like a kindergartener with bangs that were way too short because I cut them with dull cuticle scissors instead of waiting three days for my hair appointment? Yes, that was my own fault. Oh, and let's not forget that time when I had to go around looking like I was flipping everyone off because my middle finger was sticking out in a splint after my own dog bit me when I tried to take a chicken leg out of his mouth. My fault again.

"Everything bad that has ever happened to you has been your own fault." I don't recall what the exact conversation was about, but I'll never forget being told that by somebody that I thought was my friend. I must have done something stupid, made one of my iconic spontaneous decisions that didn't turn out well, who knows. Those words have stayed with me, and I repeat them whenever something goes wrong.

…..

It was one of those rare days when the wind was surprisingly still, and the sky was free of brown hues. Instead, the sun shone brightly against a pristine, blue backdrop. The February air carried just a hint of sharpness, perfect for the fresh start I was embracing. I envisioned the day as a sensational, liberating break from the confines of the past few years. As I reflected on my former life, I couldn't help but wonder if I might eventually revert to my old self.

I took the morning off from work to finalize my divorce. Looking at the passenger seat, I felt a sense of relief at the sight of the divorce papers sitting there. I wasn't even sad about this chapter of my life being over. Though we'd had some good times in the beginning, our relationship had been over for a long time. Finally, it was official, and I could move on with my life. For the first time in years, I could be optimistic about what the future held for me. I told myself I was a strong, independent woman and I was going to be ok, better than ok, on my own.

The only problem was, I didn't genuinely believe that. My plan was to wing it and hope for the best, only I had a reputation for winging things that should not be winged. Yes, I'd been doing most everything on my own for years, but I'd also had the cushion of Jeff's income. And there had been those few and far between occasions that he was useful for something. He was at least another person here during the night in case something happened, or God forbid, somebody tried to break in.

I'd spent the past few years in an emotionally and verbally abusive marriage. After Jeff completed his master's degree and began his new career, his behavior worsened further, and he became more arrogant than ever. I often had the pleasure of hearing all about how stupid and worthless I was.

There was one glorious day when I had a shining moment after I'd had enough. I'm not sure what I'd done to make him mad, but he had looked at me with so much disgust in his face.

"You aren't even worth the mud on my boots," he'd said, looking at me from top to bottom as if I were the equivalent of a dead, decaying rat carcass.

I normally wasn't this brave, but that day it pissed me off enough that I had one of those "act now and think later" moments that I'm so famous for. It was before he graduated and still worked outside with a construction job. After he went to sleep that night, I'd taken his work boots and put them in the freezer so they would be nice and cold the next morning, which so happened to be in the dead of winter and icy outside.

Lying in bed the next morning, I pretended to sleep while he searched for his boots. There was no way he would think of looking in the freezer for them and he was going to be late for work. Panic set in with the realization that I would have to let him know where they were because things were going to get terribly ugly if he was late for work due to my antics.

"Sydney, where are my boots?" he'd asked, clearly agitated.

"They're in the freezer," I blurted out, not knowing what else to do, then waited for all hell to break out.

Silence.

He retrieved his frozen boots, actually put them on, and left for work without saying a word to me.

I'd spent the whole day worrying about what would happen when he got home, but he never brought it up again for the entire rest of our marriage. It was the only time I'd had any kind of spunk in me to do something like that and I was proud of myself for it. I faced no consequences, though I never quite understood why, and I still find myself giggling when I think about it today.

The first time I filed for divorce was a couple years ago, but I changed my mind after he gaslit me into believing I was the reason for all our problems, and I wasn't giving the marriage a fair chance. Finally, his affair made the decision easy for me. He tried to deny that he was cheating on me, even after he accidentally butt dialed me. I heard him telling his coworker about his girlfriend and how they went on a whole vacation together without me knowing about it. I thought he was on a work trip, never even had a suspicion that he was cheating on me. This was one thing that I could not be blamed for, although he tried to as narcissistic cheaters tend to do.

Being away from Jeff for the past few months, I was gaining a bit more confidence. I was used to putting a new outfit on only to have him say, "Do you actually think you look good in that?" Then I'd change back into jeans and a T-shirt instead of trying to look nice. I still struggled with this sometimes, but today I felt good about myself and the way I looked in my new outfit that I'd bought just for this occasion. I didn't have to listen to him say, "Those jeans make you look fat, have you gained weight?" or "Don't wear your hair like that again, it looks ugly." Considering Jeff didn't waste any time moving to Colorado with his girlfriend after I filed for divorce, he wouldn't be here to insult me anymore.

He hadn't had any contact with me since he'd moved. I'd tried to text him or call him about some things that we still had to handle, but he usually ignored my calls, or he would respond with a vague text. He never committed to anything.

I worked as a leasing agent at Green Ridge Townhomes. Not the best paying job, but it paid the bills if I was careful and exercised some will power. I'd become skilled at budgeting and making my paycheck stretch without forgoing any real necessities. I could maneuver the coupons on the grocery app like a trained professional. Lately, my heroes were the extreme couponers that I saw on TV.

Recently, I'd been offered the management position after my former boss retired. It would have been a bump in pay, but I wasn't able to be on call 24 hours a day. Without a college degree and not the best work experience, I couldn't find anything that paid much more than what I was already earning.

I'd wanted to go to college, but I put it off and then it seemed impossible once I made the poor decision to marry Jeff. Then, once I had the kids, I didn't know how to make it work out. Instead, I supported Jeff through obtaining his master's degree. He couldn't, or wouldn't, make himself available to help with the kids so that I could go to school. My success and future were of no importance to him. Maybe someday I'd have my chance, but it wasn't going to happen right now.

My stomach was growling, so I got lunch before heading to work. My go-to order from The Crunchy Chicken, a classic chicken sandwich and a large diet lemonade, would hit the spot. I opened my app and found that I hit the jackpot. I'd accumulated enough reward points that the whole meal was free this time. Nothing beats a freebie.

Now that I could eat whatever I wanted without having to sneak it or justify it after being caught, it tasted better. I'd spent the last few years having to apologize for being disrespectful enough to eat away from home without Jeff, even if it was at my own parents' house. Eventually, I simply started lying about it even though it's stupid to have to lie to your husband about eating. He had this absurd idea that he should be invited anytime I would be eating anything, and if he wasn't there to partake, then I shouldn't be eating either. He would even search through my car, checking for any hidden food contraband. If he discovered that I ate something without him, then I would be punished by not being allowed a blanket if I slept in bed that night. It was a punishment that did not fit the crime, but whatever. It was fine. I got used to sleeping on the couch with a throw blanket which I would rather do anyway.

I pulled up to the red light and took a moment to embrace the unfamiliar sense of freedom. It was a peculiar yet calming feeling. As a naturally high-strung, Type A personality, I'm always on edge and prepared for the worst.

The left turn arrow turned green, and as I pulled out into the intersection, I froze as I saw a white, older model van barreling toward me, too fast to stop. It was too late to do anything about it.

"No," was all I remember saying to myself. Of course, it happened the one time I wasn't prepared for tragedy.

.....

I heard the sound of loud machine-type noises, maybe a saw, that seemed to be doing something to my door as I could feel the vibrations of it. My head had been at an odd angle, and I wondered if I'd been sleeping. There was a crowd of people in uniforms at my window. Discombobulated, I didn't know who they were or where I was. In front of me appeared to be a large black dashboard that was too tall to see over. This couldn't be my car. It looked like an airplane cockpit but why would I be in an airplane? There was blood on me, but I didn't understand why because I didn't feel any pain. Only semi-conscious, I didn't have the capacity to be worried about whatever was happening to me. I really just wanted to go back to sleep.

The noise stopped and something bent my door open.

"Ma'am? My name is Lance, I'm a firefighter. You were in an accident. There's an ambulance here and they will take you to the hospital. Can you tell me your name?"

"Sydney Gillison. Why do I need a hospital? And why am I on an airplane?" I asked, sluggishly, as he unlatched my seatbelt.

"You were in a car accident, ma'am. Don't worry, we will take good care of you. Just stay still and let us get you out of here."

"I'm sorry but I have to cut off your jacket," someone else said to me. I had worn that brown leather jacket for years. I loved that jacket, but I didn't protest as they cut it.

People were talking to me, but I didn't understand or even pay attention, and I seemed to doze off and on. Blood was dripping onto my hands and into my lap, but I wasn't concerned about it. Was I even hurt? I still didn't feel anything.

"Where are my kids?" I asked in a moment of clarity.

"What kids? There are no kids in the car, ma'am."

I went to sleep again.

When I woke up, it was bright, blindingly bright, and it felt hard and sterile. Now there was a new group of people, this time they were in scrubs. They were cutting off the rest of my clothes, my brand-new outfit. If I had been more coherent, I would have thought about this being what people must have been talking about when they said, "Make sure to wear clean underwear in case you are in an accident."

I heard somebody say I needed a tetanus shot. Being terrified of shots, I wanted to tell them no, but nothing came out and I felt the thickness of the medication as it went through the needle in my arm anyway. Somebody seemed to be on top of me, putting a tube down my nose, and I started to gag and vomit. I tried to fight but my arms wouldn't move as if they were held down. My long hair was wet with blood and pieces of glass were removed from my head. Apparently, I was going to need stitches. "Sweetie, I think we can get it without shaving any of your hair," a nurse said to me.

I realized I was crying and couldn't seem to stop. It was all making sense now. I remembered the white van and realized it must have hit me. But where were my kids, Elsie and Micah? Did anyone know I was there?

It wasn't long before my family started showing up. My grandparents, Mimi and Pop, were the first to arrive. I still do not know how they knew I was there.

Mimi was already making plans for the kids. She was always ready to jump into action and help. "Elsie and Micah are in the waiting room with your mom and Raymond. Elsie is having the best time dancing and singing!" She was talking so fast it was overwhelming me.

She continued, "Don't worry about them, they can spend the night with us tonight. We will get the puzzles and the colors out and they will have a good time!" The realization finally hit me that the kids were with them all day, which is why they weren't in the car with me.

Elsie, at the age of two, made it her mission in life to be the center of everyone's attention, a task made easier by her lively and somewhat bossy disposition. Not to mention, she was the cutest little thing and looked like a cherub with her chubby cheeks and bright blue eyes.

Micah was five and was much calmer than his little sister. He had the same dark blonde hair and blue eyes as Elsie and looked adorable in his little glasses. He felt most comfortable in small groups of familiar people and was the kind of kid who was consistently on his best behavior in public. Older women often referred to him as 'precious,' a nickname he wasn't particularly fond of at all.

Having no babysitting experience before Micah was born, I was completely clueless when he arrived. It seemed odd that at sixteen, I'd had to take my driving test four times before being allowed to drive a car unsupervised, yet I was allowed to take a tiny human home with absolutely no test questions to answer. If there was anything completely perfect that came from my marriage, it was Elsie and Micah.

I had the kind of family that all pulled together when somebody needed help. If Mimi and Pop couldn't take care of the kids while I was in the hospital, somebody else would be right there to take over. My family has been my support system for the past few years, especially in the past year. There were many times that the kids and I spent the night with either my parents or my grandparents when Jeff and I were fighting, except for the times when he took my car keys and my phone so I couldn't leave.

By the end of the day, I was moved upstairs to a regular room, but still couldn't have a pillow, and lying on the flat mattress was making the back of my head hurt. The nurse said they were waiting for test results before I could have a pillow. My mother turned the TV on to distract me, and I saw my wrecked car on the local news. My white sedan was unrecognizable to me. "27-year-old female, hospitalized with serious injuries." It hadn't registered in my mind yet that my car was a total loss, and I had nothing to drive. I couldn't afford to buy another vehicle, and the divorce had ruined my credit rating.

"The police said you're lucky to be alive," Raymond, my stepdad, was saying to me. After talking with the police officer, he learned that the van ran a red light and hit me which caused my car to spin around in the intersection and hit four other cars before landing partly in a fenced backyard on the corner.

Raymond had already been to the wrecking yard to get my things out of the car and assess the damage. He was always the one to think of things like that. He'd pried my shoe from where it was wedged against the side of the floorboard and retrieved my blood-splattered divorce papers from the passenger seat.

I felt the sores on my neck from my seatbelt and thought about how I'd probably be dead right now if this had happened when I'd been in the car with Jeff. I wasn't allowed to wear a seatbelt when he drove.

"Take your seatbelt off," he used to say.

"What if we have a wreck, though?" I'd always ask him.

"If you wear your seatbelt then you don't trust my driving," he would say.

I always hesitated which would be followed by him saying, "Take off your seatbelt or get out of the car."

I was disappointed in myself for being so stupid. I would always take off my seatbelt just as he instructed even though looking back at this now, I could have gotten out and found a ride home. I don't know why I never realized that I didn't have to put my life at risk simply because he told me to.

My younger sister, Kennedy, stood at the side of the bed staring at me. In her hand was a CPR and first-aid manual. "I know CPR if you need it." Kennedy was 25 years old and had an autism spectrum disorder and was fixated on anything medical. She had taken first aid and CPR class in high school and kept the training manual. She was waiting on her time to shine if she ever got to use her training and she brought out her manual anytime any of us were sick or injured, just in case. She'd been hoping for the chance to get to do an emergency tracheotomy, but she hadn't had any luck finding anyone who needed her services.

"Thank you, Kennedy. I think I'll be ok, though." Kennedy could be a handful, but she had such a good heart. She was independent in many areas, but not enough to live on her own, so she still lived with my mom and Raymond.

I was asleep when my dad visited. My mom told me he didn't want to wake me, but he left a red teddy bear, which he put in my bed with me. He also brought a vase of colorful flowers and a card. It was my favorite gift, and it was the one gift that made my eyeballs leak.

"What's this tube actually for and when can I get it out?" I asked the nurse when she came in to check my vitals. She explained that the tube going down my nose was called a nasogastric tube, and it was pumping out any contents of my stomach. It was uncomfortable and the tape was causing a sore on my nose. What was worse, the tube was clear. The mini chocolate donuts I ate for breakfast were on display in their partially digested form for my visitors' viewing pleasure. They would all have PTSD from this clear tube and never think of chocolate donuts the same way again. I wondered what kind of psychopath decided these tubes should be clear.

My left side was decorated with various bruises and scratches, but fortunately, nothing was broken, although my left leg and shoulder felt like it. My head was the worst of it. Dried blood made my blonde hair hard, matted, and red. I watched another blob of chocolate donut make its way through the tube.

So much for this being the grand day of new, fabulous beginnings.

Everything bad that has ever happened to you has been your own fault. I think of those words over and over and wonder if there was something I could have done that would have changed how this day turned out.

# Chapter 2

## *Sydney*

### A month later...

The month following my wreck had its share of challenges, but overall, I'd recovered well. After leaving the hospital, the kids and I spent the first couple of nights at my mom's house. Kennedy had a field day with that. She set up a "hospital bed" for me on the couch and monitored my vitals regularly. She taped a toothpick to my arm for an IV, for dramatic effect.

When I went back to work, Pop drove me, but I only managed one day. I couldn't remember how to turn off the security system or how to log into my computer. The contracts were too blurry to read, and I was also dizzy and nauseated. After my dad took me for a CT scan, we found out my concussion was still present, so I stayed home from work for a few more days.

Gradually, everything returned to normal, the scar at my hairline where my stitches were was barely even noticeable, unless I had my hair up.

I'd been looking forward to a rare quiet evening hunkered down in a blanket. With two little kids, "me time" is scarce. My plan was to relax on the couch reading a book or maybe start The Office from season one again. One truly can't watch The Office too many times. My mom offered to take the kids for the night, so I had the place to myself. This was a golden opportunity that didn't come along often, and I intended to take full advantage of it.

But then the phone rang.

It was Leanne, my cousin. "Ok, picture this. Me. You. Night out. It will be fun."

Leanne was hard to resist. She was truly one of the sweetest humans on the face of the Earth and would do absolutely anything for anyone. It's no surprise that she was the best social worker that had ever graced the halls of Meadow View Nursing Home.

"I don't know. I'm already in my pajamas so I'm pretty much in for the night."

"Come on," Leanne pleaded over the phone. "I promised Brayden I would go out to see him tonight, and I don't want to go alone," she said, and paused for a moment. "And besides, he may or may not have a friend," she added. Brayden and Leanne had been together about two months. He liked to hang out at the Karaoke bars, so Leanne was spending more time in bars than she was used to. I wasn't crazy about that.

Being more of an introvert, I felt out of place in bars, clubs, parties, and basically anywhere too "people-y." I had no good excuses tonight though, other than the fact that I was already clad in pajamas. I was healed up from my accident so I couldn't use that either; although, it did come in handy for a while.

"Okay, fine. I'll go," I said, letting out an exaggerated groan. Besides, I felt protective of Leanne, and I didn't like the thought of her hanging out in a bar by herself. I didn't know Brayden yet, and didn't know how trustworthy he was. I may look innocent, but he won't want to mess with me if he hurts her.

"I'm only going on your behalf as your emotional support cousin and not to meet any *friends* that Brayden may or may not have. Remember, I want to be living the single life a while and have no intention of finding anyone new, especially at a bar."

The simple fact that I was a package deal with a two-year-old and a five-year-old would send them running anyway. I felt like guys my age would be more interested in a girl with an STD than getting involved with me, a mom of two little kids.

"Yay! I'll pick you up in half an hour, it will be good for you to get out into civilization." We didn't have any other option than to take her car since I still had nothing to drive after my accident. I'd had a lot of driving-induced anxiety since my wreck, and I would just as soon let Leanne drive anyway, even if I did have a car.

I'd been borrowing Pop's old silver Cadillac to get to work, but I'd been avoiding driving anywhere else if I could help it. My dad offered to let me drive his extra car, but it was a standard, and I didn't know how to drive it. I'd tried to learn to drive a standard a few years ago, but I'd failed miserably, and I was too nervous now to try again.

It was unseasonably cold for March. I switched from my beloved pajamas to a blue and white striped sweater, jeans, and my favorite ankle boots. I wasn't used to going out to bars, so I literally had no idea how to dress to blend in. Since I wasn't trying to impress anyone, I didn't put much time into hair and makeup; only straightened my hair and put on a little mascara. I was going to try to lay low and not draw any attention to myself anyway.

I could see Leanne's little red car leaving her driveway and then stirring up dust as she headed toward my house. She lived down the street, five houses down from mine. We lived in the country in the somewhat small town of Willow Creek, Texas. We rarely got any rain, and the dirt road was bone dry as usual with tumble weeds stuck into fences along the road.

As Leanne and I walked into the Iron Bar, it was loud and people-y. I looked around to scope out the situation. It was a small bar. The stage with the karaoke equipment was set up in the front. Next to the stage was a small dance floor where a group of middle-aged women were getting their line dance on.

Before I had time to look around anywhere else, a short, balding, middle-aged man with a beer gut approached us and proceeded to get down on his knees and bowed to both of us as if we were royalty. People were staring. So much for not drawing attention.

Amused, we looked at each other while he awkwardly got back up.

"You two ladies are the most heavenly looking little things I've seen in here in a long time. I'm buying you both drinks, what'll it be?" he said, obviously drunk.

"Nothing for me, thanks. We are just here to see my boyfriend," Leanne told him, walking away.

He looked at me and raised his eyebrows. "Well, *you* aren't here to see a boyfriend?"

"I don't need one," I said and followed Leanne, leaving the man staring after us.

Leanne spotted Brayden next to the stage and hurried over to him. Brayden was quite tall, probably over 6 feet, and towered over Leanne's petite frame. He didn't fit the profile for the type of guy she normally dated, which was usually more preppy. Brayden had dark, wavy brown hair that almost hit his shoulders, a short beard, and a snake tattoo wrapped around his arm. She met him at work. He used to visit his grandmother in the nursing home until she recently passed away. Leanne told me his grandmother loved to hear him sing, so he would sing for all the residents. That's what first attracted her to him.

"Brayden, this is my cousin Sydney," Leanne said as she gestured to me.

"Hey there, Sydney. It's good that you two could come out tonight. I saved y'all two seats at the first table by the dance floor. I'll be over in a minute."

"Next up, we've got Brayden! Brayden, come on up!" the DJ announced.

Leanne and I clapped when we heard Brayden's name. We watched as he got up on stage and took the microphone. People whooped and hollered, then started gathering on the dance floor as he started to sing. Brayden seemed to feel quite comfortable on stage and it was obvious he enjoyed the attention. When he was through, the crowd cheered as he made his way to our table. It appeared that everyone knew Brayden, and he was somewhat of an Iron Bar celebrity.

"Sydney, we should sing something together!" Leanne yelled over the noise, excited.

"Have you completely lost your mind?" I laughed, shocked that she would even suggest it. "You go right ahead, or maybe sing with Brayden, but I'm sure these people haven't done anything bad enough to have to listen to me sing." I couldn't imagine singing in front of anyone at all, much less a whole crowd of people. I used to sing in the car with Jeff when we first got married, but he started quickly turning the volume down and I'd still be belting out the song before I realized the music was off. One time, he smirked and said, "You actually think you can sing, don't you?" I never sang in the car or anywhere else again after that. The only people that had heard me sing since then were Elsie and Micah, but they didn't judge.

Leanne and I both ordered light beers even though neither of us were beer drinkers. As the waitress handed out our beers, the DJ motioned for Brayden. They spoke for a few minutes, occasionally glancing over at our table, then walked back to our table together.

"Leanne and Sydney, this is my friend Will. He's the DJ here tonight." Will was slightly shorter than Brayden, but more muscular. He had a tan, short dark hair, and deep-set greyish blue eyes. Those eyes though… they were the sincerest eyes I'd ever seen. Not that I was paying attention. He wore a baseball cap, jeans, and boots and looked like the kind of man that was rugged and tough, but approachable and sweet at the same time. Exceedingly masculine. He reminded me of one of those guys that people refer to and say, "Oh, he's just a big teddy bear."

After saying hi to Leanne, Will turned to me and smiled. "It's nice to meet you. Are you having a good time so far tonight?" he asked me. There was something familiar and oddly comfortable about him. I couldn't figure out where, but I felt like I knew him from somewhere.

"Hi! Yes, I am," I said, still trying to place where I recognized him from.

"Let me know what you want me to play. I'll even sing anything you want. I can't promise it will be good, but I'll sure try!" He laughed.

"I'll let you know if I think of something." He struck me as the type to have a damn good singing voice. "But I think I know you from somewhere. I don't know where from, but do we know each other?" I asked, wondering if maybe we went to school together.

"Oh! That sounds like a pickup line to me!" Brayden said as he and Leanne both laughed.

My cheeks flushed instantly. Fumbling to find a response to Brayden's comment, I looked at Will awkwardly. "No need to worry, I am not hitting on you." I was in no way coming on to him and mortified that it appeared that way. I was genuinely curious about whether we'd met before, and in the unlikely event that I ever did try to flirt with somebody, it certainly would not be in front of an audience.

Will chuckled. "Well, that's a relief! I've got to get back to work, but do you want another drink?" Was he flirting or was he just being nice? Surely just being nice.

"I've been drinking beer, but I'm really not much of a beer drinker," I said, pulling the label off the bottle.

Will called the waitress over, "Lyndsay, can you bring this pretty lady a margarita, please?" he said as he walked back to the stage. Ok, he said '*pretty.*' That qualifies as flirting, doesn't it? I noticed he had an old-fashioned gentleman quality, the kind I didn't see often with younger men anymore. That's neither here nor there, I wasn't trying to meet men, not even the gentlemanly kind.

Leanne and Brayden were staring at me. "I think he likes you," Leanne said matter of factly.

"Do I need to remind you that I am here only because you practically begged me to come, and not to pick up men?" I asked. "And just because he is nice doesn't mean he likes me. He's probably required to make sure everyone has fun; he is the DJ after all. Don't they get paid on commission or something?"

"Trust me, I've known him for about a year, and I've never heard him call anyone else here '*pretty*' and he *definitely* doesn't ever buy anyone drinks. Ever." Brayden said.

My margarita arrived, and I drank it as Leanne and Brayden danced. I hadn't had a margarita in forever and I'd forgotten how much I loved them. Much better than beer, but the bar tender was way too generous with the tequila, and I was starting to get a little buzzed. It didn't take much since I almost never drank. Will came back to the table for a short break, carrying another margarita. He handed it to me as he pulled up a chair and sat next to me with his bottle of beer. I could smell his cologne. He smelled good... *really* good. But that's still neither here nor there. Not paying attention to all that of course.

I sat up straight and announced, "I want you to play 80s music," as if it were the most important thing I could have said. "My favorite music is the oldies, 60s, 70s, and 80s." I was much more relaxed now that the alcohol had kicked in. I stopped myself as I tend to ramble when I drink.

"Anything you want, you have good taste in music! I like the oldies too." He laughed.

The beer-gutted bald guy that bowed to me and Leanne earlier came to the table and held out his hand to me. "Now will you dance with me?" I noticed he had a tan line on his finger where a wedding ring was supposed to be.

"No, thank you," I told him. This guy just couldn't take no for an answer, apparently.

"Oh, come on," he said still holding out his hand. "Please? I made a bet with my friends over there that I could get you to dance with me. Come on, just this once, as a favor," he pleaded with me. What? He was literally telling me that he needed to dance with me to win a bet. I was shocked.

Will reached over, grabbed my hand, and held it on top of the table. "She's with me, and she said no. Now leave her alone," Will said to him. Instant butterflies, I hadn't experienced that sensation in years. I didn't say anything but sat there, looking at his hand holding mine as if it were the most natural thing for us to be doing, like we had done this a hundred times. I reminded myself again that I wasn't in the market for meeting men. Besides, he probably wouldn't be interested anyway if he knew all that dating me entailed.

"Thank you," I told him after the man left and I took my hand back.

"No problem. That was Barry. He's a regular here and he can be a little persistent with the women. I've heard him use the ridiculous pick-up line before and I don't know why he thinks that will work." He rolled his eyes and smiled.

We talked for a few minutes until Will stood up and started to pull me onto the dance floor.

"Oh, I don't know. I can't dance," I said, hesitating and pulling back.

"It's ok. I'm not great either."

"Uhh… Ok… but don't come crying to me when it's a disaster." I hesitated and let him pull me out onto the dance floor. This would be one of those things I winged when I shouldn't wing it.

Dancing with Will wasn't the end of the world. It had been years since I had danced, but Will didn't try anything fancy. To my surprise, I was able to keep up and we did okay together, not well, but definitely okay. Not once did I step on him or trip which was truly a miracle, especially with me being somewhat impaired from alcohol. There was no denying that I liked how it felt with Will's hand on my waist and my hand in his other hand. He had rough hands, but I liked that.

After the song was over, Will returned to his place on stage to get another singer going as I sat back down with Leanne and Brayden. However, he didn't introduce a new singer, he picked up the microphone, sat on the stool, and started singing one of my favorite songs. He had a spectacular voice, the kind that should have been on the radio. I was expecting him to be good, but dammit, he was exceptionally talented, and I couldn't take my eyes off him.

"Damn!" I said to Leanne, surprised. "He can really sing. Like, *really* sing. There is just something so freaking hot about men who can sing."

"Yea, men in uniform and men who can sing. He's *good*," Leanne agreed. Then she looked back and me. "So, you *do* like him!"

"I like his singing, yes."

When the song was over, Will smiled at me and winked as he walked back to his station with the equipment. Winking was a thing? I hadn't been winked at in probably my entire life. That was definitely flirting.

And of course, Leanne caught the wink and stared at me with huge eyes. "Mmmm hmmm?"

"Damn it," I said to myself, smiling back at him but definitely not returning a wink. I wondered if I should rethink my whole *I'm-not-going-to-start-dating-yet* strategy, but at the same time, I knew I wasn't ready either. What if he wasn't actually as nice as he was letting on right now? Jeff was nice when I met him, and he didn't stay that way.

As promised, the oldies that I requested started blasting through the speakers. Apparently, I wasn't the only one that loved them because that got the crowd going more than ever. Will seemed to be a pretty good listener so far.

It got late and we decided it was about time to go. Will noticed we were getting our jackets on and came over to say bye.

"Are y'all leaving already?" Will asked me, looking disappointed. We watched as Leanne and Brayden walked outside to bid their farewells in private.

"Yea, it's getting late, Leanne normally doesn't work on weekends, but she needs to go in the morning for a while. It was good to meet you though, I had a good time tonight. Thanks for the dance lesson!" I told him.

"Ok, well I had fun hanging out with you. I hope you plan on coming back soon. We can do another dance lesson," he said and smiled as he started slowly walking back toward the stage, looking back once like he wanted me to stop him.

I watched him walk away, slightly disappointed. I wanted to stop him and say, "Wait! You forgot to get my phone number!" But I didn't. Instead, I simply said, "Ok, see you later." I didn't need to give out my number to anyone anyway.

"Sydney, stop being stupid. You aren't ready for this, just let him go," I told myself out loud as I walked out to Leanne's car.

After Leanne and I got into her car and started the drive home, she looked at me and said, "So? Do tell. What do you think of Will?"

"He seems nice," I said and quickly changed the subject. "You and Brayden are cute. I had no idea you could dance like that. You're getting good with the fancy dance moves!"

"I think you and Will would be so good together! Yall seemed to click with each other, and you looked so cute together when you were dancing!"

"Will isn't really my type." I lied. "And you know I just want to be by myself for a while, I'm not ready to jump into the whole dating scene." Dating was literally the last thing I needed to be doing.

"If you're not into Will, there is this really good-looking guy that I'm friends with at work. I totally trust him with you, and I can set you two up on a blind date! Either way, we are getting you out on a date with somebody. I think it's time." Leanne, it seemed, was going to take the matters of my love life into her own hands.

"You make me sound like a shelter dog seeking a good home with a nice family. And it really isn't time, I'm fine the way things are right now."

The truth was that I was scared. I couldn't deny that I was attracted to Will, but that didn't mean I needed to jump into dating already. Not to mention, I'd basically only known him for four seconds, and it probably isn't the best idea to judge anything by what happens in a bar. There is probably an unwritten rule stating what happens in a bar, stays in a bar.

Even if I was going to jump into dating, I was afraid I would disappoint him if he got to know the real me. He didn't know that I had two kids, that I was complicated, that I was a little messed up.

I was getting myself worked up over this man that I had no intention of even seeing again. Aside from the fact that he probably didn't even like me, the hand holding incident may have been more of a damsel in distress rescue mission, except I didn't need a hero. The winking and dancing, though? The beer was probably behind that. People act differently in a bar. Just because they have fun together when they are drinking and dancing, doesn't mean they would have any fun together anywhere else.

# <u>Chapter 3</u>

## *Will*

### A week later...

I finished loading the last of the tree stumps into the trailer. It was a busy day, and the trailer was loaded almost to the top. We had more tree trimmings and removals than we usually did on a typical day. Since we worked later than normal, it was too late to drop the load off at the city landfill. We liked to use the city landfill because they recycle the wood into mulch to use in places like city parks and botanical gardens. It was Friday, so I would have to keep the trailer until I could drop the load off Monday morning.

I live in Fairwater, a small town right outside of Willow Creek. It was a 30-minute drive from town. While I drove, I thought about the previous weekend at the Iron Bar when I met Sydney. She was on my mind all week. When I first saw her with Leanne, I thought she was one of the most beautiful women I'd ever seen in my life. I figured she was way out of my league, but I wanted to meet her anyway. I asked Brayden to introduce us even though I was sure there was no chance in the world that she would give me the time of day.

I could tell she was uncomfortable when Barry tried to get her to dance with him and I was glad I was there to handle it for her. Helping her out with that felt so natural, simply taking her hand and telling him she was with me. I wish it had been true that she had actually been there with me, but she probably wasn't interested in somebody like me.

Self-confidence isn't something I had an abundance of. People didn't typically give me a reason to have much of that. I'd failed at almost everything I'd tried since I could remember. I didn't have a lot of money, and I worked two jobs for what little I had which paid for the dump of a house that I lived in. There is no way I could have somebody like Sydney over at my house. She was probably used to nicer things. I didn't have much to offer and she probably had her pick of a lot of guys that were more in her league than I am.

Relieved to finally be home, I pulled the truck and trailer as far into the driveway as I could get it. I lived in a mobile home park and the houses were extremely close together with the driveways in between them. I drove a blue and white one ton pickup. It was huge, old, and used up gas faster than I could afford to fill it back up, but I loved it anyway. It was probably the only thing that I owned that I was proud of. The truck, along with the trailer, was a tight fit in the narrow driveway. It would be inconvenient if I needed to go anywhere, but I was too tired and cold to deal with it right then.

My neighbor, Ethel Beasley, was sitting on her porch bench diligently keeping an eye on the neighborhood. Ethel was 86 years old and still surprisingly independent. She didn't drive anymore, but she tried to do as much for herself as she could. Last week I saw her balancing the leaf blower on her walker, blowing her leaves out of her driveway. The neighbors and I all tried to find ways to help her out without implying that we thought she needed it. Keeping an eye on Mrs. Beasley seemed to be up to the neighbors and me because there wasn't any family coming to check on her.

I waved to her. "Hi, Mrs. Beasley! It's too cold out here, you need to get back inside before you get sick!" I usually called her Mrs. Beasley rather than Ethel because it seemed more respectful. She seemed to like it.

"Oh, I'm fine! I have my blanket on me. What are you doing getting home so late? I was starting to worry!" she hollered back. She always kept track of the neighbors' comings and goings. We considered her our neighborhood watch system. She even kept a pair of binoculars on her living room windowsill. Sometimes I'd see her peering through the blinds with them.

"Just a busy day at work. Well, I'll see you later, Mrs. Beasley. Have a good evening and stay warm!" I said as I walked up the steps to the door.

"Oh, Will? When the cold spell is over, do you think you could help me get my tulips out of the greenhouse so I can plant them in my flowerbed?" For the past few years, I'd helped Ms. Beasley with her greenhouse. She had more of a green thumb than I did, but I was able to help her with potting and getting the plants into the ground.

"Of course I will! Have a good night!"

I went inside and threw my coat down on the couch. The house was a disaster as usual. Working two jobs kept me so busy that I hadn't found the time nor the motivation to clean. I survived mostly on macaroni and cheese, frozen pizza, and ramen noodles. The kitchen was full of dirty dishes with caked-on food. The fish aquarium hadn't been cleaned in way too long, and half the water had evaporated. Somehow, the fish were alive and adapting to their shrinking living space. Half the lightbulbs in the house were burned out and there was an odor that I couldn't quite place. I wasn't proud of the way I'd been living lately, but I'd been in such a slump that I hadn't actually cared enough to do anything differently and didn't see a reason to try. I could only imagine what my mother would say if she saw this mess. Fortunately for me, there wasn't much risk of any company popping by.

I'd always tried to be a good person, do the right thing, and help others out when they needed it. However, it seemed like no matter what I did or how hard I'd tried, I never seemed to be good enough for everyone. I'd spent most of my life trying to prove myself but always falling short and living in the shadows of my older siblings who seemed to both be the picture of perfection.

Once, when I was in high school, I landed a solo in the spring choir concert. This was the biggest concert of the year, and I was so excited. I'd attended every practice, sang in the shower, in the car, anywhere I had a chance. I wanted it to be the performance that everyone would remember. That night, I drove myself to the school's performing arts building because I needed to be there an hour early before the concert. My clothes were perfect and ironed, my hair was cut, and I was fully prepared to wow my family. The only problem was nobody in my family went to my concert. Instead, they all went to my sister, Lilly's, dance recital. She was the star of her dance team and of course, they could not miss that. Later that evening they apologized profusely and said they had forgotten about my concert, and it was an oversight with so many events that were going on in the same week, but I knew it was more of a priority to see her than me. They would have never forgotten about my brother or sister.

Another time my dad needed help installing the dishwasher. I tried to help him and was doing fine. I'd done it before.

"Well, I'm not sure if this is right." Even though I was one hundred percent certain that we were doing it right. "We'd better call your brother to be on the safe side."

Those types of things happened consistently and made me eventually stop trying.

Fortunately, I had found a purpose in helping Mrs. Beasley. I had grown to love her as if she were my own grandmother. I'd also discovered a non-profit down the street and I'd done some volunteer work for them. They'd even asked me to participate in some fund raiser events. I'd developed a good rapport with even some of the more challenging individuals there, and I looked forward to seeing them. Mrs. Beasley and the volunteer work were unquestionably the only things that kept me going lately.

I'd barely finished my pizza and started trying to find something on TV when my phone rang. The caller ID showed it was Brayden. I wasn't in the mood to talk but answered anyway. Brayden and I were friends, but we usually only spoke at the bar when I was working.

"Hey Brayden, what's up?"

"I know you aren't working tonight, but are you planning on coming out to the bar?" he asked.

"Absolutely not, Brayden. I worked late, I'm tired, and I still have a full trailer that I couldn't dump today." I couldn't imagine anything that would make me want to leave the house that night. I was exhausted from running chain saws and stump grinders all day.

"I think you need to change your mind and get out here," he said seriously.

"I already said no. I'll talk to you later, Brayden," I said impatiently. I was already at the bar enough when I was working. I didn't want to be there when I was off work. Brayden didn't understand that because he loved being at the bar and he didn't have to associate it with work.

"Leanne will be there with her cousin, Sydney," he said, knowing he was delivering important news. I sighed, not knowing quite what to do considering my truck was hooked up to the trailer and I didn't have what I needed to unhook it. It was heavy with a ton of huge tree stumps that I'd chunked into it that day.

"Will, Leanne said she's been trying to set Sydney up on a blind date. She said Sydney hasn't agreed to go yet, but if you don't get out there tonight, it may be too late. I saw how you were with her last weekend, and you don't want to mess this chance up."

He was right. I had to figure this out because Sydney was the first girl that I could picture myself going out with since me and Tabitha broke up last year. We'd been engaged, but she broke up with me three months before our wedding, saying she wanted more than I could give her.

I remember Tabitha with that guilty look in her eye. "I just wanted more out of life. I wanted to travel and have a nice house, be able to buy the things I want without having to worry about whether or not we can have groceries. I'm sorry, you're a great guy, I just think I can find somebody who can give me the kind of life I want." Then, she'd taken her ring off, put it on the coffee table, and walked out. As much as that hurt, she did me a favor by leaving when she did.

I could easily back the trailer out of the driveway, but turning the trailer around with such a long truck was not an easy task with such limited space. Wiggling back and forth, I was able to get it backed up into the driveway in the right direction. The trailer didn't have a jack on it, so I got the bumper jack out and lifted the trailer off the hitch. I searched around until I found some cinder blocks in the backyard, carried them over to the trailer, and stacked them underneath the tongue to hold it up. By then, it was freezing outside and snowing. I raced to take a shower and change clothes. All of that took about half an hour and I still had the half hour drive to get to the Iron Bar.

Once I finally got there, I spotted Leanne, Brayden, and Sydney sitting at a table near the back. Sydney looked gorgeous. I noticed she wore a little makeup this time, and her blonde hair was fixed in loose waves. She was a petite little thing, probably just barely over

5 feet tall and couldn't weigh more than one of the tree stumps I'd thrown into the trailer that day.

"You made it!" Brayden yelled when he saw me. There was an empty seat next to Brayden, conveniently right across from Sydney.

"Hi, Will!" Leanne said. "Sydney and I risked our lives and limbs to come here tonight! We drove all the way here in the snow with only one headlight!" From what I'd heard about Leanne, this was out of character for her. I thought she was normally more safety conscious than that. Brayden said she was always fixated on whatever worst case scenario tragedy might occur.

"Well, we didn't realize the headlight was out until we were already halfway here," Sydney explained.

"Um… Brayden, you might want to drive them home tonight." I didn't like the idea of the two of them driving back home like that, it wasn't safe.

We all talked, laughed, and had a few drinks. Brayden and I both sang a couple of songs, and we danced with Sydney and Leanne. Brayden was a better dancer than I was, and he was teaching Leanne some complicated dances that I didn't know how to do. Sydney, it seemed, was a true lightweight when it came to alcohol and probably wouldn't be up to learning anyway. This was obvious when she began rhyming.

"Will takes a pill to chill when he pays the bill," she rhymed, seeming pleased. "I am a poet, and I know it," she added, smiling at me. Even with the ridiculous rhyming, she was hot, especially when she smiled at me with those blue eyes.

"She doesn't get out much," Leanne apologized for her suddenly poetic cousin. "We are putting a limit on your drinks next time, Sydney."

After a while, we decided to go next door to the 24-hour diner. Nothing else was open at that time of night and we were all hungry. Again, I sat across from Sydney.  The restaurant smelled of a mixture of coffee, pancakes, and hamburgers. The brown booth seats were too short for the table, making Sydney and Leanne look like children sitting in it.

"I'm getting pancakes and a fried egg. I'll beg for an egg," she said and giggled. Apparently, the alcohol hadn't worn off yet but maybe getting some food in her would help.

"Like I said before, she doesn't get out much and almost never drinks." Leanne laughed.

"Why don't you get out much, does somebody keep you hostage most of the time?" I asked her.

"Well, I'm not exactly in a hostage situation, but I'm a single mom with a two-year-old and five-year-old. I spend most of my free time at home with the kids. I had never even been to a real bar until last weekend, this is only my second time," she explained, then added, "Oh geez, that's embarrassing. Please omit the part about the bar from your memory."

Ok, well, that wasn't what I was expecting her to say, but for some reason this new information didn't scare me like it probably should have. I also liked knowing that she wasn't into the bar scene. I didn't like being in bars much either. I only worked in one because the money was good for a part time job.

"Kids don't scare me. When I was in high school, our next-door neighbor's kids moved in with us for about a year because their mom was in a plane crash. It was a miracle that she lived. I've babysat more than most people my age."

"Will you marry me?" she joked. I'm sure she was used to guys my age being immediately turned off when they heard the word "kids." I didn't know how old she was, but she had to be about my age, and I was 26, which was an average age to have kids. So, this certainly wasn't unheard of.

"I think it's about time to head home," Brayden said, looking at his watch after everyone finished eating. "I don't think you two should drive home in your car since the roads are slick, especially with only have one headlight," he said to Leanne and Sydney. "I can drive y'all home and we can pick up your car in the morning."

I looked at Sydney and said, "I can drive you home if you're ok with that."

"Well, I mean, I just live right down the street from Leanne. I'd hate for you to drive all the way over there when I could just ride with them."

I looked at her seriously. "I promise you, I do not mind, and you don't want to be a third wheel, do you?" I asked. I wanted to get to know her better without Leanne and Brayden around.

She thought about it for a second. "OK, I guess, if you don't mind," she said and put on her jacket.

We waved to Leanne and Brayden as I opened the passenger door to the truck and let her slide in. Since the truck was so old, it had a bench seat all the way across instead of having a console in the middle, but she sat all the way to the other side, right next to the door. I thought about what it would be like if she were to one day be sitting next to me in the middle, where I could drive with my hand on her leg, holding her hand, or putting my arm around her shoulder.

"You can drop me off at Leanne's house because I have my things over there anyway," she said. I wondered if she was being cautious and didn't want me to know where she lived.

On the drive to Leanne's house, we got to know each other a little better. She was easy to talk to.

"One thing I must know about you is how do you pronounce coupon? Do you say coo-pon or q-pon? This is particularly important," she asked me.

"Coo-pon."

"Crap. You're a coo-pon person… I'm going to try to not hold that flaw against you," she said, and it made me laugh. She had a great sense of humor.

I learned that she was 27, just a year older than me. She also shared a little about her past marriage. It infuriated me to think of what she has been through. I hoped I would never meet her ex-husband because I wouldn't be able to force myself to be cordial to him.

I also learned that there was no risk of her going on a blind date with the guy Leanne knew. Apparently, Leanne had brought it up, but Sydney quickly shut that idea down.

She put her phone number in my phone and texted herself with it so she would have my number. "For our records," she said, smiling.

When we turned onto the long dirt road toward Leanne's house, I was glad they weren't driving Leanne's car. The road was muddy from the snow, and I didn't want to think of the two of them stranded in the ditch out in the country at night.

When we stopped in Leanne's driveway, I looked at Sydney, hoping she would want to see me again for a real date or at the very least, just come back to the Iron Bar. I just wanted to kiss her, but I knew it was way too soon for that. I didn't want to even risk it with a hug because she was giving off a vibe of not wanting to be touched. So, I kept my hands to myself. "I had fun tonight; I'm glad Brayden let me know you were going to be there."

"Me too! It was fun. Thanks for driving me home tonight." She looked at me for a few seconds as if she wanted to say something else. Then seemed to change her mind and opened her door. "Remember, you have my number," she said and smiled as she closed the door.

# <u>Chapter 4</u>

## *Sydney*

### Speak now, think later...

Several weeks had passed since my accident; although, I still had headaches occasionally and a few more pieces of glass recently surfaced on my head. I couldn't see them to get them out myself. Leanne, always prepared for the worst, told me to go to the doctor in case it got infected. I knew my cousin, Ashley, would be thrilled to pull something out of my scalp. She had this odd fascination with DIY medical procedures. She and Kennedy had that in common. Once, she removed a mole on her husband's arm with a pocketknife. She should have been a doctor, but instead she was a legal assistant. Sure enough, she was more than willing to help.

"Hold still," she ordered me as I started regretting not just doing it myself.

"If it starts to bleed, just stop and I'll wait for them to push through more on their own!" I told her.

"Settle down, you're fine," she said, pushing around on my scalp to feel where the glass was. Ashley was 8 months pregnant with her first child and she looked like she could pop at any second.

She dug around on my scalp with a pair of tweezers until she finally pulled out two pieces of glass.

"Alright, I think that's it!" she said, seeming pleased with her work. I looked at the pieces that she collected from my head, surprised at how big they were.

"Thank you, Doctor."

"So, have you heard from Jeff? He hasn't seen the kids at all since he moved to Colorado, has he?" she asked. This had been an ongoing issue with him. He hadn't spent much time with the kids when we were married, but he hadn't seen them at all since he moved out of town. I wasn't even surprised.

"I haven't heard from him at all since the divorce has been final. Elsie hasn't even asked about him and Micah has only asked about him a few times. That shows how involved he's been with them, when they are barely phased by the fact that he's not here."

"Wow, that's bad. He's going to regret that one day. At least they have an amazing mom. You've done a fabulous job with them," she said.

"Thank you, Ashley, I'm not perfect by any means, but I do my best with them."

"My beard has grown back," she announced, changing the subject and pointing to her chin to show me her small amount of fuzz. We always referred to the peach fuzz on our faces as our beards. "We are way past due for spa day. We should do it tonight so we can be beautiful for Easter tomorrow!" Ashley loved at home beauty treatments just as much as she loved performing DIY medical procedures. Her spa treatments tended to be quite painful, and it wasn't uncommon for one or all of us to end up bleeding, swollen, or have patches of hair missing where it shouldn't be. Even with all that, Leanne and I continued to subject ourselves to the torture, but usually ended up enjoying it almost as much as Ashley did. This was mainly because we all shared a rather warped sense of humor.

"Oh yes! We can do that tonight. I still need to get things ready. I haven't even been to the store yet."

This morning, I had googled "easy recipes." It seems most people's ideas of easy recipes differed greatly from my idea of an easy recipe.

My meager food contribution for Easter would have to be homemade macaroni and cheese. I was able to find an easy four-ingredient recipe. My cooking skills were minimal, and people were usually hesitant to eat whatever I cooked. Typically, I was put in charge of paper products or drinks. I also had to get things from the "Easter Bunny" for Micah and Elsie's egg hunt.

After Ashley left, I cleaned the house and started working on a spring wreath for the front door while the kids played in Micah's room. I wanted everything to look nice when my family came over. It was the first time they had been to my house since my divorce, and I wanted them to see that the kids and I were all getting along fine on our own... even though we'd truly been on our own for years. Jeff wasn't ever here, and when he was, he wasn't doing anything for us. One of the main differences now was the finances. Another was the absence of emotional abuse in our home, which finally gave me the peace to start rebuilding my self-worth and confidence.

I was always the one who handled everything around the house. Jeff never lifted a finger. Nothing had actually changed; I was the one who planted all the shrubs and trees outside, painted the kids' bedrooms, built the shelves in the laundry room, and even poured our sidewalk all by myself while Jeff sat indoors watching football, not even bothering to peek outside.

The hardest part of the sidewalk by far was getting the bags of concrete out of the trunk of my car by myself. I could have asked somebody for help, but that would have made Jeff mad, and it wasn't worth it. Those bags were extremely heavy, and I developed a system for prying them out of the trunk and dumping them onto a wheelbarrow positioned next to the car. Once it was in the wheelbarrow, it wasn't too hard. I did the best I could at it. The sidewalk didn't look as good as it could, but it served its purpose, and we didn't have to walk in the mud to get to the house.

One of my biggest weaknesses was I was afraid to let anyone know that I was a flawed, messy, person who had trouble keeping up with the demands of everyday life. My house was never spotless. I wasn't always organized, but I did try.

When I was planning on having company, I felt like I had to make the house look like nobody really lived in it. Heaven forbid, people know that we have an overflowing laundry basket full of dirty laundry or unmatched, dollar store towels with holes in them. So, I cleaned, and scrubbed, and put out the nice towels that I only put out when company was coming, and I hid all the evidence of how we normally existed. What they saw was actually just a big lie, but I was too afraid to let people see the real me.

As I worked on the house, I thought about Will. I'd given him my phone number when he drove me home, but I'd regretted it immediately. Honestly, I wasn't ready for that. I liked him, he seemed like a great guy, but I couldn't just jump into another relationship. I could see us being good friends, but it needed to just stay a friendship. At least for a while. I didn't want to lead him on.

The phone rang, and as if he could read my thoughts, it was Will. "Hey there, what are you up to?" This was the first time he had called me.

"Oh! Um... Hi!" I stammered. I hadn't had a man call me since before Jeff. "I'm trying to get some things ready for Easter. We always have it at my house and my family will all be here." I was nervous as if I'd never spoken on the phone before.

"Sounds like fun!"

"What are you doing for Easter?" I asked him.

"I'm not doing anything. My family doesn't do anything for Easter anymore."

"Oh." I paused for a moment. "Leanne is bringing Brayden. Do you think... I mean, you can totally say no if you don't want to... but we will have plenty of food if you want to come?"

Wait, what did I just do? I immediately panicked. I'd just asked him to come to my house on a holiday even though we'd basically known each other for five seconds. I tended to have what my brother and I called diarrhea of the mouth, where words just kind of spilled out of my mouth before I had a chance to think about what I was saying.

"Sure! I'd love to come!" he said, much faster than I expected him to.

Well, dammit, now what was I supposed to do?

"You do understand that my entire family will be here. My kids, Elsie and Micah, will be here too of course," I told him, just as Elsie ran through the kitchen, laughing, with a toy raccoon tail attached to the back of her pants. Micah ran after her in a football helmet.

"I'm ok with meeting your family. Thanks for inviting me. Can I bring anything?"

"No, just yourself! See you around 12:30." I hung up and realized I had a huge smile on my face even though I knew I was getting myself into a predicament.

I heard the kids giggling way too hard from Micah's bedroom. I walked in to find that both Micah and Elsie were engaged in a suspicious activity on the other side of the bed. I peered over the side to find Elsie vigorously coloring the carpet with a red crayon and didn't appear to feel the least bit guilty about it. Micah was just watching her, laughing.

"Look, Mommy! We're coloring the carpet!"

A few hours later, after I'd dealt with the red-carpet fiasco the best I could, Ashley and Leanne came over for "spa treatments." Ashley spread the supplies out on the kitchen table and plugged in the wax warmer. She brought waxing supplies, tweezers, an epilator, and even a laser hair removal machine that none of us knew how to use. "OK, who is the first victim, I mean client?" she asked, anxiously waiting to get started. Leanne and I looked at each other, waiting for the other to volunteer.

I hesitantly sat down in a kitchen chair and pulled my hair out of the way as she draped the cape around me. Without even giving me a chance to finish preparing, she was already spreading on the hot wax. It seemed like the wax was a little too hot. "This may hurt just a bit," she said and ripped the wax off the side of my face.

I screamed as my fuzzy facial hair, along with some side pieces of my hair, came off with the wax. Ashley laughed loudly at my misfortune as she showed us the long strands of hair on the wax strip that weren't supposed to be there, then started spreading it on the other side. She also did my eyebrows, and we experimented with the other equipment she brought. When my turn was over, I had no hair left on my face except for my eyebrows. My legs, and one forearm were also hairless. But my face was swelling, and I could feel whelps beginning to develop. This was all just part of the spa experience and was expected.

Leanne was next with a similar experience, although she also ended up with one eyebrow that was too short. "Oh, it will be fine. Just draw it in with a pencil," was Ashely's solution. Ashley and I laughed so hard at Leanne's eyebrow that I had to get my asthma inhaler out. Leanne and I took turns with Ashley, but we were much more careful with her than she was with us, since she reminded us that it would be cruel and unusual to inflict pain on a person in her "delicate condition" as she called it.

"Now you will look stunning when you are in labor," Leanne told her. But truthfully, Ashley always looked stunning, no matter what she was doing. She had a classic, glamorous look, the kind of person that looked good in every color and could pull off every style effortlessly. Leanne and I had always been envious of her.

"I kind of invited Will for Easter," I told them. They both looked at each other, surprised.

"What? He had nowhere else to go and Brayden will be here anyway, so it all makes perfect sense," I tried to explain.

"Thank goodness, you are finally coming around. I thought you just wanted to be friends with him," Leanne said and turned to Ashley. "You will like him, Ashley. He is so nice, kind of old fashioned and gentlemanly. And he can sing!" Leanne said to her sister, trying to sound more positive.

"Oh, hmmm," Ashley hummed.

"What?" I asked.

"I'm just worried that everyone is going to think you are jumping into things since it hasn't been that long since your divorce. You know how our family can be with all that. Plus, they might worry about the kids," Ashley said.

"Calm down, it doesn't mean anything. He was going to be alone because his family won't be doing anything for Easter and since Brayden was coming anyway, he can just tag along and get some good food. No big deal," I said.

"It isn't like there is a time frame on how long she needs to be flying solo instead of just getting out there and dating again. I mean,

Will is perfect for her and she's all I-just-want-to-be-friends," Leanne told Ashley.

"Plus, it's none of anyone's business what I do. I'm 27 years old; I'm not a kid. And I'm not going to do something stupid." I started to get defensive.

"True," Ashley said.

"Actually, who gives a flip what anyone thinks? It's hardly scandalous to invite a friend for Easter," I said, finally. My family was incredibly protective of me, but I didn't want anyone to give me their opinion. I was a grown-ass woman and fully capable of making my own decisions. There was going to be a man at Easter, big deal. He's Brayden's friend, it isn't newsworthy.

"Honestly, I don't think anyone is going to think anything of it. Somehow, this conversation spiraled downhill." Leanne laughed.

Micah walked into the kitchen carrying a plastic tub of tractors. He'd been obsessed with them lately. "Mom, I'm hungry," he said to me.

"Me too, Mommy," Elsie said, following right behind Micah. "I want beans." Elsie had developed an obsession with pork and beans. She wanted them at every meal.

I looked at Leanne and Ashley and laughed. "Well, I've got beans to make. Thanks for beautifying me, hopefully the swelling goes down by tomorrow!" I scoffed and smiled.

After dinner, the kids took their baths and watched Toy Story again. That was their current favorite movie, and we watched it almost daily.

My phone dinged.

Will: **What are your thoughts on potato salad?**

Me: **I have good thoughts about potato salad.**

Will: **Ok, good. Goodnight, sleep tight, and don't let the bed bugs bite.**

That line brought back so many sweet memories and reminded me of when Pop used to tell me the same thing when I was little. Ugh, why did Will have to be so damn sweet?

# <u>Chapter 5</u>

## *Will*

### Easter...

Brayden, Leanne, and I all arrived at Sydney's house together. Sydney and Leanne belonged to a family that was what Leanne called "particular." Apparently, there were rules to follow which Leanne quickly debriefed us on. I was here as Brayden's best friend whom she invited. Under no circumstances would there be any mention of going to bars, working at a bar, or singing karaoke at a bar.

If I was going to have any chance with Sydney, I wanted to make a good impression on her family. The hardest to please would be Leanne and Sydney's grandfather, Mr. Richardson. Nobody was good enough for his daughters or his granddaughters and if he decided he didn't like Brayden or me now, it would be almost impossible to win him over later. It seemed that once his mind was made up about somebody, there was no changing it.

Several cars were lined up in Sydney's dirt driveway. We had to park in the ditch along the front fence across from a pasture. I was immediately impressed with Sydney's yard. The grass was freshly mowed. There were pink and purple pansies planted with fresh black mulch in the flowerbeds. Along the front of the house were neatly trimmed boxwood shrubs. I could see bulbs coming up in front of them. By the looks of her yard, she had it together more than I did, and she had two little kids to take care of all by herself.

Willow Creek weather could be snowing one day and warm the next. It was warm that day and when Sydney walked out to greet us, she was wearing shorts that showed off her toned leg muscles that I kept my eyes locked on a few seconds too long. Just as she said "hi," the wind blew my hat off my head. I ran out to catch it where it landed in the middle of the road. A dark-haired man walking up the driveway watched with a smirk on his face. Embarrassed, I dusted it off and held onto it until I was safely inside the house which smelled of barbecue and a hint of pine scented cleaner.

"Hi y'all! I'm glad you could come!" she said to Brayden and me as we went into the house, which I noticed was already full of people. I was suddenly nervous and wondered why I thought coming to her house on Easter and meeting her entire family was a good idea.

"Lovely eyebrow, Leanne," Sydney said, smiling, as Leanne scowled at her. I looked back at Leanne to see what she meant. There was definitely something different about her eyebrow, but I couldn't figure out just what it was.

"Where should I put this?" I held up the bowl of potato salad.

"Oh, wow! This looks so good, Will," she said, taking it from me.

"It's my own recipe. I hope you like it." I'd tweaked my potato salad recipe until I finally got it about as good as I could. It was my go-to dish for gatherings and people seemed to like it.

Sydney's house was not particularly large or expensive looking, but it was spacious with plenty of room for everyone. There was no clutter anywhere, and it looked like she was particular about the neutral décor. The sunlight coming from the large windows was ideal for her impressive assortment of plants. Near the window stood one of the largest monstera plants I'd ever seen. It had a sign sticking into the soil that read "Big Bertha." Mrs. Beasley would be impressed with that one.

In the corner of the living room was a small child's size table with two tiny chairs that were painted to look like cows. I guess I'd imagined that there would be toys piled in corners everywhere, but instead, everything looked incredibly organized and clean.

"Do you mind if I use your bathroom, Sydney?" Brayden asked.

Sydney pointed towards the kitchen. "It's right through the kitchen, the middle door."

A few seconds later, we heard what sounded like an elderly woman scream, followed by Brayden shouting, "Oh no! Ma'am, I'm sorry! I'm so sorry!" We ran over to see what the commotion was. Brayden stood wide eyed, face bright red, and a small cut on the side of his forehead.

"Brayden! What happened?" Leanne asked.

"I didn't know anyone was in there! The door wasn't closed all the way. I knocked to see if anyone was in there, but nobody answered, so I walked in," he said, holding his hands over his face.

"Did she attack you or something?" Sydney asked him, looking at the cut on his head.

"No... when I turned to get out of there, I hit my head on the door frame," he said, touching the knot forming on his head.

I looked toward the bathroom and saw a tiny, white-haired woman who had to be at least 90 years old coming out of the bathroom holding onto a walker. Someone was asking her if she was ok.

"A strange long-haired man just walked in! Just about scared me to death!" the elderly woman said. "He hit his head, serves him right," she added.

Sydney and Leanne looked at each other and gasped. "Oh no, Brayden! You walked in on Grammy? She can barely hear so she probably couldn't hear you knock," Leanne said to him. Both girls started laughing.

"Um, it isn't all that funny. Remind me to not drink anything, I'll be holding it until I get home," he said, looking traumatized.

While Sydney got Brayden a bandage, Leanne put her fruit salad on the kitchen counter and properly introduced Brayden to her Grammy and apologized for the mishap. Then she introduced both of us to the rest of the crowd. Everyone seemed friendly, except for the one guy from the driveway when we came in which I later learned was Sydney's brother. He seemed annoyed that Brayden and I were there.

Leanne came up to an older man whom I assumed to be Mr. Richardson.

"Pop, I'd like you to meet Brayden and Will. Brayden and Will, this is my granddad Rusty Richardson," she said to him, and we both shook hands with him. Mr. Richardson wore jeans, western boots, and a trucker hat with a farming co-op logo on it. He used a cane, but I imagined he wasn't one to ask for help if he needed it.

Mr. Richardson nodded at both of us. Then, in a gruff voice that I figured was probably due to many years of smoking, said, "Which one of you is dating my granddaughter?"

"I am, sir, I'm Leanne's boyfriend," Brayden spoke up.

"Oh, you're the one who walked in on Grammy," he said. "What do you do for a living?" he asked Brayden.

"Sir, I'm a software consultant at Alliance Virtual Technology," he said, ignoring the comment about the bathroom incident.

"I have no idea what that is," Mr. Richardson said, seeming unimpressed. Without giving Brayden a chance to try to explain it, Mr. Richardson glanced at Brayden and Leanne and walked away into the living room to sit down. A little girl wearing a white floral dress ran to sit on his lap. That had to be Elsie, she looked just like Sydney.

I overheard Mr. Richardson saying, "That boy needs a haircut."

I recognized Sydney's grandmother, Mrs. Richardson, immediately because I'd seen her many times over the years at Willow Creek National Bank before they finally got a drive through. She always seemed so grouchy, but now I realized she was just a sweet little lady who took her bank teller position a little too seriously. She finally retired last year.

Sydney yelled from the kitchen, "OK everybody, the food is ready!" The crowd began lining up, Grammy in front and younger people in back as if this line had been formed and rehearsed countless times before. I watched Sydney fix two plates, carry them to the little cow table, and then go back to the end of the line to make her own plate. Leanne, Brayden, and I lined up behind her with Leanne's sister, Ashley.

"The food looks amazing!" I told them.

"Yea, we always have plenty of food. I just made the macaroni and cheese because most people don't trust my cooking." She laughed. "My brother, Eric, smoked the brisket and the sausage. His cooking is top notch." That was good to know, maybe if I compliment him on his brisket, he will soften up a bit.

A girl walked up to Sydney, carrying a book. She looked just like Sydney but maybe a little younger and she was wearing a T-shirt that was way too big and had a monkey on the front of it. "Did you wash your hands when you made the mac and cheese? We don't need any food borne illnesses around here." Wow, that caught me off guard.

"Yes, Kennedy, I observed all food safety guidelines. It's safe to eat," Sydney told her. "Will and Brayden, this is my younger sister, Kennedy."

"Hi Kennedy, it's nice to meet you," I said and tried to shake her hand, but she didn't take it. I noticed the book she was holding was a CPR and first aid manual.

"He's trying to shake your hand, Kennedy," Sydney said to her, politely. Kennedy took the cue and shook my hand. Then she walked off.

"I'm sorry. She has autism and we have to prompt her sometimes." I had suspected that. She reminded me of some of the individuals that I volunteered with.

We ate in the living room with the parents and grandparents. Sydney's macaroni and cheese was much better than the boxed kind with the powdered cheese packet that I always ate. I knew I was invited over just as a friend and Sydney didn't seem to be wanting anything else, but I couldn't keep my eyes off her all day.

Mr. Richardson caught me looking at her. "Will, what do you do for a living?" he asked me while we ate.

"I work for a company called Gerald's Fence and Tree. We build fences and do tree removals, tree trimming, and chimney sweeps." I left out the information about my part time job since Leanne prohibited any talk of bars.

For some reason, that sparked Mr. Richardson's interest, and he seemed to approve of my job, even though he didn't seem to be impressed at all with Brayden's higher paid, more professional career.

As Mr. Richardson and I talked, I learned that he was a rancher when he was younger. He also had great carpentry skills and admired people who could work with their hands. We talked about hunting and fishing, and he skilled me on buying in bulk in order to prepare for a possible doomsday occurrence. It turned out we had a lot in common with the exception of doomsday survival prep. By the time we were through talking, he told me I could call him "Pop."

"What the hell?" Brayden asked me after Mr. Richardson left. "He already doesn't like me, but you two are best friends now?"

Eric walked over and asked if I would help him carry some boxes to his truck.

"That brisket was incredible," I told him as we walked out.

"Thanks," he said shortly. I guess he can't be won over with compliments of his smoked meat skills.

Once we loaded the boxes, Eric stopped and said, "Look, I'm not stupid and I know you're here because of Sydney because I've seen you staring at her. I don't know if you know all this, but she's been through a lot. I don't want to watch her go through that shit again. I can be one of the nicest guys you'll ever meet until you hurt my sister." Judging by the look on Eric's face, he was serious. I was skeptical about the part about being one of the nicest guys I'd ever meet.

"Look, we're just friends. And I'm the last person you need to worry about, trust me. But if anyone messes with her, they're going to have to deal with you and me both." Her brother wasn't going to be an easy one to win over, but I respected that. I was the same way with my sister.

After most of the family was gone, Ashley, Leanne, Brayden, and I all sat around the living room while Elsie and Micah looked through their Easter basket loot.

There was a moment of awkward silence. "So… anyone heard any good jokes lately?" Leanne asked.

"Sydney, why don't you tell Will and Brayden your lawyer joke!" Ashley exclaimed, smiling.

"Um, maybe not that joke," Leanne said, rolling her eyes.

"Yea, that's going to be a no," Sydney said firmly.

"Just tell it," I said, curious. Sydney didn't strike me as the type that told jokes.

"Me, Ashley, and Eric are the only ones in all humanity that think it's funny," Sydney said but started to giggle. "Dammit. Ok, fine. But I promise, you won't think it's funny either."

"The only funny thing about it is that she thinks it's so funny. It's the only joke she tells, and she has been telling it for years now," Leanne said.

"OK, here it goes." She took a deep breath. "What did one lawyer say to the other lawyer?" she said, already trying to hold back her laughter.

"What?" I asked. Ashley and Sydney were laughing already.

"He said..." More laughter. By then, Sydney was laughing so hard she couldn't get any words out.

"Uh huh?" I said, as Brayden and I looked at each other, waiting anxiously for the punch line.

"Ok. I can do this," Sydney said, taking another deep breath and trying to compose herself. "He said, we are both lawyers!" Then she completely lost it and she and Ashley were laughing so hard they couldn't even make any sounds.

Brayden, Leanne, and I all just looked at each other confused. But seeing them laugh so hard at this completely unhumorous joke made the rest of us laugh too. She was a difficult one to figure out. Serious a lot of the time but laughing so hard she was crying at jokes that weren't even a little funny.

Sydney was wheezing and coughing by then. "That joke always gives me asthma," she said, getting her inhaler out of her purse but still giggling.

"Are you ok?" I asked her, still curious how that joke could make her laugh to the point of an asthma attack.

"Oh yes, it happens all the time. No big deal," she said, and she stopped wheezing and coughing quickly.

After we all settled down, Elsie came to sit on Sydney's lap and almost immediately vomited all over the front of Sydney's shirt. We all stared for a minute and then everyone, except for Sydney and Elsie, burst out laughing again.

"I frew up," Elsie told everyone, looking pitiful.

"Somebody ate too much Easter candy," Sydney said, as she and Elsie went to change clothes. I'd never seen anyone look so calm and collected while covered in vomit. That's probably a skill that isn't perfected until one becomes a parent.

While Sydney and Elsie were getting cleaned up, Brayden and I played tractors with Micah on the floor. I had only heard him say a few words the entire day, but he started telling us everything there was to know about those tractors. At five years old, he knew more details about them than most adults probably did.

There was a small stuffed elephant next to the chair and it reminded me of something.

"Have you ever been to the circus?" I asked Micah.

"No," he said.

That was too bad. One of my best childhood memories was at the circus. I was about five years old, Micah's age, when I got to be King of the Circus. I was so proud to get to wear a special hat and lead out the parade when the circus started. The elephants and all the circus performers were behind me while a performer held my hand, walking with me as I made my way around the Colosseum. My brother and sister didn't get to do that, they had to stand with my parents, waiting for me. I thought I was a superstar that day because all eyes were on me. I hope Micah and Elsie get to do something fun like that while they are little, something that will give them a good memory to hold onto forever.

When Sydney and Elsie returned, all fresh and clean, Elsie seemed to have made a miraculous recovery. I got on the floor with the kids and gave them both rides on my back, played tractors some more with Micah, and read three books to Elsie.

When it was time to go, Sydney walked us outside to the truck. Cows were grazing in the pasture across the street, right next to the fence.

"That's Penelope." Sydney pointed to a black and white cow that stood looking over the fence at us. "She's my favorite; she loves it when I give her apples." She walked over to Penelope and scratched her on the head. Leanne went over and petted Penelope, too.

"We were raised around farm animals," Leanne told me and Brayden.

"Yea, I love bulls mostly. Our granddad used to be a rancher, and we had cattle growing up. Longhorns and Brahma bulls are my favorite. I feel bad for them, being branded and having hooks stuck in them. I'd love to go to a cow cuddling farm, but I can't find any near here."

"You know, when I first met you, I'd never even imagined you would be a bull loving, cow cuddling, joke teller." I laughed. Even though Sydney lived in the country, everything about her gave more of a city girl vibe: how she dressed, talked, even decorated her house. I'd never expected her to love cattle so much, but I liked that about her.

Sydney and I walked around to the driver's side of my truck. "My mom asked if you are my boyfriend and lectured me on already having a new man around my kids," she said to me.

"Boyfriend, huh? Your brother threatened me, thinking the same thing. But your granddad likes me enough to let me call him 'Pop.'" I laughed and took a step towards her, leaned down and attempted to kiss her. Huge mistake. Sydney just turned her head and stepped back.

"Well, thanks for coming, the potato salad was wonderful!" she said, changing the subject.

Trying to hide my disappointment and pretending to not have just made a fool of myself, I responded, "Thanks for the invite. I had fun." I gave her a hug, thinking this wouldn't be as offensive as me trying to kiss her, but she stiffened up suddenly. She was extremely difficult to read.

"Well, I need to get back in to check on the kids. See you later!" she said, waving as she walked back to the house.

I wish I could take back the last five minutes and not try to kiss her. I probably ruined everything.

It was obvious that Sydney wasn't into me like I hoped she was. She didn't even want to be hugged, much less kissed. As much as I hated to believe it, she wanted us to be on a friend's basis and nothing else.

# Chapter 6

# Sydney

I went back inside and collapsed onto the couch, confused and disappointed in myself. What the hell did I just do? Will tried to kiss me and I simply turned my head. No explanation, nothing. He probably had his feelings hurt and I hated that. I panicked. I hadn't kissed anybody in so long, I just freaked out. And was I even ready for that? I wasn't sure. I didn't want my heart broken and I didn't want to lead him on if I couldn't handle a new relationship.

Aside from my thoughts about Will, I was completely worn out. It was mentally and physically exhausting for me to host get togethers at my house. It took so much work for me to get things ready and I certainly wasn't the best host. It didn't have to be so hard, I just made it that hard because my expectations for how things needed to be were unrealistic for what I was able to do. Truthfully, I was most likely the only one that even noticed whether the floorboards were scrubbed, or the bathtub faucet was shiny. Not only did my family have a false impression of me, so did Will. He probably thought I always lived in a spotless, organized home with homemade macaroni and cheese.

I didn't know how to stop playing superwoman. It was exhausting, and I knew it would be easier to just let things go and relax, but that wasn't exactly my strong suit. Maybe it was because, for the past few years, I'd been made to feel like a failure, always pushing myself to do better just to prove that I wasn't.

I put up the Easter leftovers that had been donated to my kitchen. I'd bought some TV dinner type containers, and I made individual dinners with the leftovers to put in the freezer. This way we had several dinners ready to heat up later. There was enough for us to freeze and eat for the remainder of the week. Saving money has been my hobby lately as I was still getting used to making ends meet without Jeff's income.

Will left his bowl of potato salad. It was almost gone but I scooped out a little for a snack. This was some seriously good potato salad. I'd never had anything quite like it, he did it more like mashed potatoes and I loved the creamy consistency. I put the lid on the bowl and put it in the refrigerator.

I'd have to get his bowl back to him. Maybe I'd send it with Leanne when she went to see Brayden again at the Iron Bar. I didn't need to make it a habit of seeing Will too often. We were friends, that's it. No need to get it all complicated and messy.

My phone rang, it was my mom.

"I forgot to tell you; Raymond and I are going to Boston for a week in August. Can Kennedy stay with you?" she asked.

"Yea, that should be fine. I'll find some fun things for us to do." I'd have to work, but she could stay home alone during the day. Mom wasn't comfortable with her staying alone all night by herself, though.

"Oh, and don't forget about Wacky Wednesday this week," she said. It was an event that a non-profit in town put on once a month. I promised Mom and Raymond I would pick up Kennedy and take her to it after work. They would show a movie, serve pizza, and have games and activities. She had a couple of friends from high school that went to that sometimes too.

That was another thing I always kept in the back of my mind. Even though Kennedy had many skills, she would most likely need to live with somebody else for the rest of her life. Now, it was entirely possible that something would change but until that happened, we had to have a plan in place. Our dad and stepmom were both pilots and were away from home too much for it to work out for Kennedy to do well there. Out of all the rest of the family, Kennedy did best with me, and I would most likely be the one she would live with if anything happened to our mom.

That was also something I had to think about when I started getting back into dating. Jeff hadn't been ok with Kennedy potentially living with us one day. But it also wasn't something we discussed until after we were married. I learned my lesson there. Whoever I was with not only had to be ok with the fact that I had two small kids, but they also had to be ok with Kennedy.

The wind had picked up throughout the afternoon, and now it was in full force, rattling the windows with each powerful gust. When I glanced outside, I saw that the loose section of the fence had finally given way, toppled by the storm.

"Dammit, how am I going to get that back up?" I said out loud to myself.

I texted Leanne. **Can you run over here and help me put a section of fence up really quick?**

Leanne: **Do we know how to do that?**

Me: **No.**

Leanne: **Be right there.**

She showed up a few minutes later, still in the dress she wore for Easter. We went outside to survey the damage and found what I already knew. The fence panel was down.

"Do you have any screws?" she asked.

"No, I just have finishing nails. Do you think we can wire it back together? I just have floral wire, but surely it would work if we did it really tight? Oh, and I have a container full of bungee cords."

"I don't see why that wouldn't work," Leanne said, looking at the fence with her hands on her hips, as if she were a fence repair expert.

I went inside and came back out with the wire and bungee cords. I had the kids stand on the porch where I could see them.

"Ok, lets pick it up and then if you'll hold it still, I'll start hooking it back up," I said as we picked it up. It was much heavier than we thought it would be, especially against the wind but we were determined.

Leanne tried to hold her dress between her knees to keep it from flying up while we worked but wasn't working.

"Here, try these short bungee cords," I told her.

She wrapped a short bungee cord around each leg, and it held her dress down perfectly. "It works!"

Once the panel was upright, I connected a bungee cord through the side pickets of the tops of both sides, then I put two more on the bottoms and one in the middle for good measure. Once they were all secured to the posts, I wrapped some floral wire around the hooks of the cords then onto the fence posts to make sure they didn't come off.

"There! That ought to hold for now at least," I said as we both stood back and admired our handiwork. Not bad for two strong, independent women using our creative minds for a free fence repair.

"You realize Will builds fences for a living, right?" Leanne asked, still staring at the fence.

"Yes, I do. But we fixed it, right? It's fine. I don't see it blowing down tonight. I'll get some screws, and we can fix it the right way later. I don't need anyone coming to my rescue."

"You know how to fix it the right way later?" Leanne looked at me with her eyebrows raised up.

"I'm pretty sure it's self-explanatory, Leanne." How hard could it be? It seems like you would just drill some screws in and if that doesn't work, the bungee cords will probably hold.

I took a picture of the fence because, who else has a bungee corded, floral wired fence? It would be a conversation piece for future social gatherings. In a moment of weakness, I could always text this photo to Will and see if he might want to come take a look at it. What is it about men fixing a fence that is so sexy? And would seeing Will fixing my fence make me want to do a replay of the awkward non-kiss and maybe not turn my head this time?

"Brayden and I had an argument after we left. He's all mad because Pop likes Will more than him," she said.

"What the heck? So, how did that turn into an argument?" I asked. He was beginning to sound like Jeff.

"He said I should have tried harder to make him look good."

Oh, please, I thought to myself. How ridiculous. If that's how he's going to act, they might as well break up right now. I didn't have the patience for that kind of crap anymore.

"Well, I'm not sure what to say about that, but I hope you worked it out," I said, and decided I no longer cared much for Brayden.

I took the kids inside and warmed up some leftovers for dinner. While I ate, I texted a picture of the fence to Will. I thought he might find it intriguing.

Me: **New and innovative way to repair fence panels.**

Will: **Is this your handicraft?**

Me: **It is, I have a gift for repair work.**

Will: **I could have come over and fixed it.**

Me: **I know, just showing you a new method you may want to try...**

Will: **I left my bowl. I can come pick it up.**

Me: **No need, I'll send it with Leanne to the Iron Bar.**

Okay, I've got to stop. I don't want to lead him on. I'm still trying to figure out how to navigate a friendship with a man without him thinking it's something else. I'd never had guy friends when I was married to Jeff. Actually, I didn't even have female friends when I was married to Jeff, other than my cousins and one of my coworkers.

Another big gust of wind shook the house. I hesitated to look, half afraid my carpentry skills weren't as solid as I'd hoped. But curiosity won out, and to my surprise, my fence panel was still standing tall and proud.

# Chapter 7

## *Will*

### *Wednesday...*

I'd been working on a pool deck all day. I cleaned up the work site, put my tools away, and headed home.

The last time I heard from Sydney was Sunday when she texted me a picture of her fence repair. She was resourceful, if anything. She'd somehow managed to do a fence repair in the wind with bungee cords and something that looked like thin green wire. But she was also stubborn. I could have fixed it for her if she had let me, but I also admired her determination to do things on her own.

I'd tried to use the potato salad bowl as an excuse to go back to her house, but she wouldn't let me do that either. She was making this difficult and I was starting to think she just wasn't into me like I thought she was. I wasn't going to push myself on her if she wasn't interested. Maybe I needed to just distance myself and see where things went when she was ready to start dating again.

I took a shower and headed over to the Willow Creek Baptist Church. The church was hosting the Wacky Wednesday event tonight. It was a monthly event that was held on the last Wednesday of the month by Shell's Place, the non-profit company that I volunteered for. I'd recently learned that Shell's Place's name came from a girl named Shelby that had autism and had wandered off from her aunt's birthday party. She was found after drowning in a nearby lake. Her parents started a non-profit in her name for individuals with intellectual and developmental disabilities. Although I'd volunteered several times at the regular facility, this was my first time going to Wacky Wednesday.

When I got there, I went to the front desk and asked where they needed my help.

"Anything you want to do is just fine. Pizza will be here in a minute if you want to pass it out, or you can just hang out and play games with everyone. We're just happy to have some help!" the lady at the desk told me. She had a sticker on her shirt that indicated her name was Hazel.

I walked into the activity center and surveyed the area. There were tables set up with puzzles, games, and crafts. A pool table was set up on one end, and a large TV was showing a movie. One of the guys recognized me and wanted me to play a game of checkers with him. When the game was over, I smelled the pizza and decided to help pass that out.

"I know about foodborne illnesses, and you're supposed to wear gloves." I heard a familiar voice saying.

When she turned around, I saw that the voice was Sydney's sister, Kennedy.

"Hey there, Kennedy! I didn't know you came here. Do you remember me? I'm your sister's friend, Will. I was there at Easter."

"Yea," was all she said, seeming uninterested.

"Do you always come to Wacky Wednesday?" I asked her.

"Yea," she said and looked away. I needed a way to spark up a conversation with her.

I looked at Hazel, who was now stationed at the pizza cart. "Can I help pass out the pizza?" I asked her.

"Sure! Everyone gets one piece to begin with and then we'll see how much is left for seconds," she said.

I started to take the cart, but Kennedy stood staring at me disapprovingly.

I stopped. "Ma'am, do you happen to have any gloves? I wouldn't want to pass my germs around."

Hazel gave me a look that told me she knew exactly why I was asking. "We sure do! Let me go get them. I'll be right back." And she hurried off.

"You can't be too careful, right, Kennedy?" I asked her.

"Did you know that Listeria is the third leading cause of death from foodborne illness in the United States?"

"Wow! I had no idea," I said as Hazel returned with two pairs of gloves. She gave both me and Kennedy a pair.

"If you get listeria, you'll experience fever, muscle aches, nausea, vomiting, and diarrhea," she continued as we pushed the pizza cart into the activity center and started passing it around.

"Well, I sure don't want that then," I said, happy to have found a way to communicate with her.

"Can I have two pieces, please?" a girl at the craft table asked Kennedy.

"One piece per customer," Kennedy said sternly, and dropped her plate down on the table in front of her, almost making the pizza slide off the plate.

"You're really a no-nonsense assistant, aren't you?" I asked her, impressed by her attention to the rules.

"Rules are rules, Will," she said as she continued to make her way around the table.

Between Kennedy and I, we passed the pizza out quickly and efficiently and then found a table to sit at to eat our own piece of pizza.

"You're better at passing out pizza than the other people are. They never wear gloves and sometimes they give people more than one piece even though they aren't supposed to," she said.

"Oh, that's not good. I hope I can volunteer here again and maybe I can be on pizza duty with you again. We made a good team." I think I may have made a friend in Kennedy.

When we finished eating, Kennedy went to the puzzle table and worked on a puzzle with a couple of girls she seemed to know.

By the time the event was wrapping up, I walked around with a trash can collecting the last bits of trash left behind. I saw Kennedy walking toward the door and went to tell her goodbye.

"See you later, Kennedy!"

"Bye, Will!" she said, opening the door.

"Will's here?" I heard Sydney's voice. I looked back and saw her walking into the church wearing wide legged jeans, a New York T-shirt, and a baseball cap. What was it about Sydney dressed down that was so damn attractive? She was holding Micah and Elsie's hands and scanning the room for who I hoped was myself.

"Hey!" I walked over to her. "Hi, Micah and Elsie!" I told them as they both smiled at me.

"Hi... What are you doing here?" She looked at me confused.

"Just volunteering. Kennedy and I were on pizza duty together. She runs a tight ship," I told her.

"I'm confused. Did you know Kennedy came here?" she asked. Did she think I was stalking her or something?

"Nope. I've been doing some volunteer work at Shell's Place for a couple months and they asked me if I wanted to help out here tonight. Honestly, I enjoyed it so much that I might make this a regular thing."

She stared at me for a moment with a blank look on her face.

"You volunteer at Shell's Place? And now you volunteer at Wacky Wednesday? Seriously?" She looked dumbfounded.

"Yes, that is correct," I said, not sure why this was so difficult to understand.

"Wow. I mean… that's great!" she said. "Huh, that's actually really great..."

"Are you sure? You seem a bit confused," I said.

"Oh, no, it's wonderful! It's just unexpected, that's all."

"Well, I better get back in there and get the rest of the trash picked up. Bye everyone!" I waved and walked away. I wasn't sure how to interpret the look on Sydney's face, but she definitely had some thoughts going on about my volunteering here tonight. Surely, she didn't disapprove of my volunteering. I can't imagine why she would have a problem with it, but maybe I'm reading her wrong. Sydney isn't exactly an easy one to figure out.

After I got out of the shower, I noticed I missed a call from Sydney. I also had a text from her. **Can you give me a call when you get a chance?**

This was the first time she had ever called me. Nervous and excited at the same time, my heart raced as I called her back.

"Hi, Will. Sorry to bother you, I'm sure you're about to go to bed," she said, sounding nervous.

"You're not bothering me at all! What's up?"

"I didn't mean to act weird about you being there tonight. I was just surprised. A lot of people are uncomfortable around people with special needs, and it just caught me off guard."

Sydney and I spent hours on the phone, talking about everything from the frustrations of our jobs to the places we dreamed of visiting. We debated the proper way to cook a steak, whether mushrooms belong on burgers, and if spices are truly essential in any recipe. Apparently, Sydney thinks steaks are burned if they aren't red, she doesn't like burgers but loves mushrooms, and she will gladly cook a meatloaf without so much as a sprinkle of salt in it.

We discussed our relationships with our families, our preference of dogs versus cats, the joy of Bluetooth speakers, and whether or not school lunches should be free. We also talked about the many uses for bungee cords and floral wire, which seem to be an effective means of holding a fence panel up.

About 2:00 AM, I finally decided it was safe to ask the question I'd been wanting to ask before we hung up.

"Are you busy Saturday? If not, do you think you'd like to maybe go out to eat? Get to know each other a little better?"

"Sure! I'd like that. Um, is this a date, or are we just meeting up as friends?" she asked shyly.

"How about let's not put a label on it and see how things go?" The last thing I wanted to do was put Sydney in a situation she wasn't ready for. We could see how things played out. I'd been paying attention, and I planned to make this unlabeled eating engagement something she was going to love.

"That sounds perfect, Will."

Four hours later, my alarm went off and I had to get ready for work. I was tired, but it was worth it.

# Chapter 8

## *Sydney*

### The next day...

Looking at Ashley's huge, protruding abdomen made me wonder how she could possibly make it to her due date. Leanne, me, and the kids were at Ashley's house for our annual turkey ball making party. Turkey balls were a family favorite, and we turned it into a big production when we made them. We usually did it after Thanksgiving, but we thought it would be fun to do it early and then Ashley and her husband, Antonio, could have turkey balls in the freezer ready to just heat up instead of having to worry about making dinner with a newborn baby.

After being awake until about 2:30 this morning, I wished we had planned our party for the weekend instead of after work on a Thursday. I'd been awake all night talking to Will. I still couldn't believe he was volunteering at Wacky Wednesday and Shell's Place.

Kennedy had been talking about him the whole drive home. She had extremely high standards and he received her seal of approval, so that should tell me something.

So much for my rule to keep to myself and not start getting involved with men yet. I'm not sure if I'm ready to start dating again, but I'd find out soon because I'd agreed to go out with Will this Saturday. He said we don't have to label it as a date, but I'm not stupid. This is a date. A date that I have agreed to go on. Will is just being patient and giving me an easy out if I need it. With two young children to think about, I have to be much more careful about dating than I was before I got married. Is Will truly as good a man as he appears to be? He literally seems almost too good to be true. My opinion is that when things seem too good to be true, they probably are, but I hoped that wasn't the case with Will.

We'd been texting off and on today and I hope I wasn't on the verge of losing my phone number privileges.

"Ciao, I'm off to work," Antonio told everyone and leaned over to kiss Ashley. "Keep Luca in there until I get back home," he added, patting her stomach. They'd decided to name the baby Luca, after Antonio's brother who died in an apartment fire. That is what inspired Antonio to become a firefighter. His work schedule required 24 hours on, 48 hours off rotation and he was on duty today until 6:00 PM tomorrow. We'd been checking in on Ashley when he was gone because Luca could be making his big debut at any second.

Ashley's house was impeccably clean, and I wondered if she'd be able to keep it that way after the baby was born. She had a knack for creative decorating that I'd always admired. She could turn just about anything into a beautiful décor piece. We were about to make a huge mess all over her tidy kitchen, though.

Leanne and I set out the ingredients. We always did it in an assembly line and over the years, we had turned it into an art form. I was always in charge of spreading out the crescent rolls because I was the pickiest about the formation. Nobody seemed to enjoy it when I hovered over them inspecting their work. Then Leanne would plop the turkey/cream cheese mixture in and form the ball. Ashley rolled the ball in the crushed croutons. Micah and Elsie were given jobs this year and were responsible for putting the foil wrapped balls into the freezer. Under the table, Ashley's miniature dachshund, Weenie, sat up on his hind legs begging for a sample.

"I've been having Braxton Hicks contractions all afternoon," Ashley said, rubbing her stomach.

"I think we should take you to the hospital to be checked, in case it isn't Braxton Hicks. You are almost at your due date," Leanne said.

"Nah, I'm fine. I'm sure I'll know when it's real labor," Ashley said, inspecting her finished turkey ball. She was always care-free and didn't panic about much at all.

"I'm going out with Will Saturday," I told them, changing the subject since Ashly's mind could not be changed. They looked at each other surprised.

"I thought you were swearing off dating for a while," Ashley said.

"Well, you know, things change," I said.

"At least he's a whole lot better than you know who," Leanne said, referring to Jeff.

"Anyone would be better than you know who," I agreed.

Ninety-seven turkey balls later, we finally ran out of ingredients. We always made a lot of them, so we had plenty to divide between the three of us. Ashley looked uncomfortable the entire time and paused her turkey ball rolling every few minutes. Leanne and I both noticed, but we knew better than to say anything because Ashley always said she was fine.

"What's wrong with Weenie?" Leanne asked. Weenie was walking around with his tail between his legs, panting and whimpering. He was a high anxiety kind of dog.

"I don't know. That's what he does when it rains." Ashley looked out the window. It was a little cloudy, but it wasn't raining.

Being around Weenie always made me want my own dog. My family always had at least one dog growing up, none with thunderstorm anxiety as severe as Weenie's though. I hadn't had one of my own since I moved out of my parents' house.

As I put some balls in the oven for us to eat for dinner, the alerts on our phones went off. Severe thunderstorm warning. I groaned. We never had any rain all year until spring, then most of the rain we did get was from severe thunderstorms. Most of Willow Creek had new roofs from the storms we had last spring, mine was one of them.

Ashley was getting the plates out and made a growling noise as she held onto the kitchen counter.

"Ashley? Everything ok?" I asked. I legitimately believed she could be in true labor.

"I think I'm ok. Even if it is real contractions, it's my first baby so I'll be in labor a long time. My doctor said to go to the hospital if the contractions are five minutes apart. I don't think these are that close together."

I texted Leanne even though she was right next to me.

**Me: We need to get her to the hospital.**

**Leanne: I know. I already tried and she won't go.**

**Me: Let's keep trying. This is ridiculous.**

The rain started and there was a big flash of lightning followed by a crack of thunder so loud that it shook the house. Weenie was in full panic mode by then, shaking, panting, and pacing around the floor. I picked him up and tried to calm him, but he was too far gone to be consoled.

Ashley looked in the medicine cabinet. "Oh no, I forgot to refill Weenie's anxiety pills that he takes when it rains." Poor Weenie looked pitiful, shaking with his head hanging low.

Leanne turned the TV onto a local station to watch the weather. There was large hail up to baseball size coming, but it was about half an hour away. Right now, it was just heavy rain. Maybe we would get lucky, and the storm would go around us, I hoped so anyway, I didn't have the money for another home insurance deductible.

"Ashley, let's go ahead and get you to the hospital right now because we won't be able to get out once the hail gets here. Come on, we need to leave right now; we can be there in ten minutes," Leanne pleaded with Ashley.

"We have time. It will be hours before anything happens anyway. Everyone I know has been in labor for at least 8 hours with their first baby. I'll wait until the storm is over, and then I'll call Antonio to come and get me if I need to. They're already prepared at the station for him to be out a while."

"Um, I've had two kids, and I promise it doesn't always work that way. Come on, let's go before you have the baby right here!" I cannot even begin to imagine having to be responsible for delivering Ashley's baby. What if there were complications?

Another alert on our phones stated the National Weather Service issued a tornado watch, including Willow Creek. We didn't think much of that because we had tornado watches with almost every thunderstorm, there was almost never a warning, though. Willow Creek hadn't had a real tornado in decades; they were always in the nearby counties instead. If by chance we happened to actually have a tornado, we would go to Ashley's basement.

By the time our turkey balls were out of the oven, the storm intensified. Hail beat down on the roof and windows. It looked to be golf ball-sized at least, maybe larger. Wind speeds increased to about 70 miles per hour. Leanne had to turn the TV volume up to hear over the storm.

Ashlley moaned loudly from the kitchen, holding onto the table.

"That's it. I'm calling Antonio," I told her. I had zero intentions of suddenly becoming a mid-wife. I called him, but there was no answer, so I had to leave a voicemail.

"Tornado warning for Willow Creek!" Leanne yelled from the living room. "Everybody to the basement!" I took the kids and Weenie downstairs, and Leanne helped Ashley.

Fortunately, Ashley's basement had a few comfortable chairs. Leanne helped her into one of them. I had Micah and Elsie both sit in another one. I found a notepad, and some pens for them to draw on to keep them occupied.

Leanne called Mimi and Pop to make sure they got into a safe place while I called my parents to make sure they knew about the tornado warning.

"Oh no, Will told me last night that he lives in a mobile home! I don't know if they have a storm shelter there!" I said worried.

I texted him. **There is a tornado warning so make sure you get out of your house! Do you have a storm shelter to go to?**

Ashley was sweating now. "My water just broke," she said, and this time, she did look like she was terrified. "The contractions are closer together now and more intense!" Crap! Leanne and I looked at each other, trying to appear calmer than we were.

"Ok, everything's fine, nobody panic." But I was seriously panicking. There was a tornado warning, it was too dangerous to drive in this storm, and we were going to have to call 911.

"I'll call Antonio again. Leanne, you call 911, we can't drive in this storm." I tried Antonio again, still no answer.

Ashley screamed, "I feel pressure!" She cried, with a death grip on the arms of her chair. "It hurts too bad!" She cried and moaned again loudly.

"Mommy!" Elsie was crying then too, scared from the commotion. Micah looked scared also. I moved Elsie and Micah out of the way to the corner and gave them my tablet from my bag. "It's ok, there's going to be a baby soon!" I told them, hoping that it would calm them down.

Weenie's tongue was hanging out and he was shaking even harder.

"I have 911 on the phone. They said you should lie down on your side," Leanne told her. I helped Ashley to the floor. She was sweating profusely and trembling.

"Call Antonio again!" Ashley cried. I wanted to tell her that we wouldn't be in this predicament if she had just gone to the hospital when we told her to, but I kept my mouth shut.

I tried him again; this time he answered. He's just gotten back from a call. "Antonio, we are in the basement, but Ashley is in labor, and I don't know if she's going to make it to the hospital before the baby gets here. Leanne has 911 on the phone."

"I'm on my way!" Antonio said, and hung up before I could say anything else.

I remembered the breathing method from when I had my kids, and I tried to help Ashley with that. I remember when the nurse in the hospital explained that the breathing techniques helped to distract from pain, relaxing the muscles and the mind, as well as helping with oxygen flow. It seemed to help her a little bit once she got the rhythm going. At this point, everyone in the basement should have been doing breathing exercises because we all needed to calm down a little.

The storm was still going strong, and the tornado warning was still in effect. I still hadn't heard from Will. I tried him again. **Are**

**you ok?  We are in the basement.  Please let me know if you're ok!**

Even from down in the basement, we could hear thunder cracking, and it sounded like the wind was still going strong.  In the backyard, something crashed against the door.

Ashley was screaming.  "I don't think Luca is going to wait!" she said, panicking while I tried to comfort her.  Leanne still had 911 on the phone.  Finally, we heard the sirens coming down the street.

"Babe!  I'm here!"  Antonio came barreling down the stairs, followed by paramedics.

Antonio scooped Ashley off the floor and somehow carried her upstairs and helped her onto the stretcher.  "If a tornado does touch down, I don't think it will be on this side of town.  The storm is starting to move north.  We'll be ok."  He picked up the hospital bag Ashley had waiting by the door and carried it with him.

"Call us when Luca comes!  We can't wait to meet him!"  Leanne called after them, waving.

The weather report returned a few minutes later, stated that the tornado warning for Willow Creek had been discontinued as the storm was beginning to dissipate.  I went back down to the basement to get the kids and Weenie.  He was still in full panic attack mode.

"Sydney, I cannot believe that just happened. We should have dragged her to the hospital when we had the chance before the storm came. We almost had to deliver a baby in the basement!"

When the rain stopped, we went outside to assess the damage. Tree limbs were down all over the yard, a section of fence was on the ground, and the back door window was cracked. The loud crash we heard must have been one of the lawn chairs hitting the door. Shingles were scattered in the yard, and I had a feeling she was going to need a new roof. I dreaded thinking about what our own houses looked like.

I called Mimi and Pop to make sure they were ok. Mimi answered and said everything seemed to be ok, except their porch swing was upside down and of course their flowers were all beat down.

My mom texted me to check on us. They were ok with no major damage.

I tried Will again. Still no answer. I was totally panicking now. What if his house blew down with him in it? He could be impaled by flying fence pickets or sucked up into the tornado and flown for miles through the air! The possibilities of terrible things that could happen to him are endless and the longer I waited, the more I started to worry that something horrible could have happened to him. And just when we were starting to get to know each other.

Finally, my phone rang. "Will! I've been worried sick about you!" I finally breathed out a huge sigh of relief and sat down, realizing I'd been pacing.

"I'm sorry. I took my neighbor, Mrs. Beasley, to the storm cellar, and I left my phone in my house. Then it was hailing too much to go back and get it. Are you all ok?"

"Yea, Ashley has a section of fence down, though. You missed quite a show here. Ashley went into labor, and we almost had to deliver her baby ourselves right in her basement! Antonio and the paramedics got here just in time. Is your house ok?"

"Oh wow! I hope everything is ok with Ashley and the baby! I probably need a new roof but everything else seems to be ok. Mrs. Beasley's greenhouse has quite a bit of damage and the roof came completely off one of the houses on the other side of the park."

"That's awful! On a side note, I have about 30 turkey balls. I'll let you have some. They are actually good."

"Turkey balls, huh? I hope that tastes better than it sounds." He laughed. "I'd be happy to fix Ashley's fence tomorrow. They should be focusing on their new baby, not worrying about their fence."

"Did you used to be in boy scouts or something when you were a kid? I totally see you in your little outfit doing good deeds for people, maybe helping a few old ladies cross streets." He seemed to be always helping others, and I found that to be an incredibly attractive trait.

"Yes, as a matter of fact I was," he said and chuckled.

After we hung up, Leanne and I worked on cleaning up the turkey ball mess and taped up the crack in the back door window.

About an hour later, Antonio called with an update. Ashley made it to the hospital, but Luca made his grand appearance in the hallway on the stretcher before they could make it to labor and delivery. 7 pounds and 9 ounces. Mom and baby were both fine.

# Chapter 9

## *Will*

I'd be spending the next few days helping with the storm damage cleanup and repairs. I put Ashley's fence panel back up before I went to work this morning. This weekend I'd be working on repairing Mrs. Beasley's greenhouse. Sydney told me a couple of her fence sections were down, including the one with the bungee cords. She finally agreed to let me fix it.

After work, I drove to Sydney's to take care of the fence. A green two-door car was parked in the driveway. I knew it was the car her dad gave her; she told me about it Wednesday night during our all-night phone marathon. She said she was frustrated because it was a free car, which she desperately needed, but she didn't know how to drive a standard. She'd only ever driven cars with automatic transmissions.

Today was her lucky day. I texted Brayden to get Leanne's number. Then I asked Leanne to come over to Sydney's for a little while to watch the kids.

Sydney hollered for me to come in when I knocked on the front door. She was watering her houseplants while Micah, standing on a chair in front of the sink, filled a smaller watering can. His shirt and front of his pants were soaked, and water was spilling onto the counter and floor.

"Hey there, Micah! Helping your mom water?" I said and turned off the water.

"Yea," he said, climbing down off the chair while water sloshed out of the can.

"He loves watering the plants!" Sydney said, grabbing a towel to clean up the mess that she was obviously used to when Micah assisted.

"I see you have the car!"

"Yea, my dad drove it over here today. It was my stepmom, Emma's, but she has a new car and doesn't need this one anymore." Sydney didn't seem happy about it.

"That's great that she was willing to let you have it instead of trading it in on her new one."

"Yea, but I don't know what to do with it because I can't drive it. I mean, who has a stick-shift anymore?" Sydney didn't just look frustrated; she actually looked a little terrified. "I told my dad I was going to learn, but I've tried before, and it was a catastrophe. I didn't want to look stupid telling him the truth, but I don't want to hurt his feelings either. I mean, he gave me an entire free car and I seriously do appreciate it." She looked like she could burst out in tears at any moment.

"Sydney, I don't mean to sound like I'm judging, but you can't just let it sit there. Plus, how long can you keep driving your granddad's Cadillac? I'm sure he didn't mean for you to drive it forever." I hoped she wouldn't think I was trying to tell her what to do, but a free car wasn't something she should ignore.

I looked behind Sydney where Elsie was leaning over a plant, piling wet potting soil onto one of her plastic toy plates. "Elsie, do not dig in my plants," Sydney said firmly, dumping the soil back in the plant and brushing off Elsie's hands.

In an act of sheer defiance that I hadn't witnessed before, Elsie looked right at Sydney and immediately put her hand back in the pot, plopping another mound of soil onto the plate. Sydney took the plate away and put it on the shelf out of Elsie's reach. It was hard for me not to smile. Despite her mischief, Elsie was still the cutest thing I'd ever seen. She finally gave up and walked away, sulking.

"Jeff had a manual car, and he attempted to teach me how to drive it once when my car broke down. However, I struggled with it, and he got mad and quit trying to teach me. He said I was going to cause a car accident." Sydney literally looked scared. This situation with the car was affecting her more significantly than I thought it was.

"Well, maybe Jeff just sucked as a teacher," I said as the doorbell rang.

There was a knock on the door. "Hi! Babysitter reporting for duty!" Leanne said as she let herself in. Sydney looked at both of us confused.

"I kind of asked Leanne to come over for a little while because we have a driving lesson to complete. Go get the keys and come on."

"Thanks, but I can't. Maybe I just need to sell the car or give it back to my dad. I just had a bad accident not that long ago; I don't want another one." She truly looked panicked, and I couldn't understand where this was coming from.

"I understand that you are scared, especially after what you went through with your wreck. You're not going to have an accident. We're out in the country, there's no traffic, and I'm going to be there with you. I promise, I will not let anything happen. Let's just give it a try." I was trying to be understanding, but I also didn't want her to not even try.

"Sydney, maybe the reason you didn't learn before is because Jeff was the one teaching you and he made you too nervous. This time it's different. You can do it, I know you can," Leanne told her.

Sydney sighed and said, "Fine." She looked disapprovingly at both Leanne and me and finally got the keys. Leanne mouthed "good luck" to me as we walked out the door.

"I'll drive first so I can explain everything. Then you can try," I said, getting into the driver's seat. "My uncle taught me how to drive on a standard jeep, it was the first car I ever drove. It takes a little getting used to, but then it's not too bad."

Sydney's street was still muddy in places, so I drove us to the next street, which was paved. I showed Sydney how to shift, reverse, put into first and second gear, ease off the clutch, and slowly press the gas pedal. "You can tell when you are up to the right RPM by the sound," I told her when it was time to push the clutch and shift to the next gear.

"Ok," she said, concentrating on everything I did. I drove around for a while, demonstrating several times until I felt she understood the steps.

"When you stop, make sure to put it back in first gear," I said, stopping the car on the side of the road so we could trade seats.

Sydney adjusted the seat, the headrest, the mirrors, the visor, looked in the mirror, put on glasses, and basically took as long as she possibly could before finally putting her hands on the wheel. Just when I thought she was going to get started driving, she made more unnecessary adjustments.

I cleared my throat and looked at my watch. She'd procrastinated long enough.

She sighed. "Ok, fine. I'm ready," finally putting her hands back on the wheel.

As soon as she tried to go, the car immediately stalled.

"It's ok, just ease off the clutch and onto the gas at the same time," I explained gently. I didn't want her to give up too soon.

She tried again. Stalled. Over and over, she tried and kept stalling. She was getting more and more anxious, and I could tell she was about to give up. As hard as I was trying to be patient, I wasn't sure how much longer I could endure this either.

Finally, she got it going and we made it all the way down the street. But we were back to the beginning after she had to stop at the stop sign. She hit the gas too hard, and the car jerked and stalled immediately.

"Dammit!" She hit the steering wheel and yelled; her eyes started to water. "I can't do this. I don't know why this is too hard for me, but I can't do it! Jeff was right." She got out of the car and walked around to the passenger side.

"Look, you're not ever going to learn if you give up this fast." I wasn't about to let her give up.

"I'm done trying. You can drive us home. I'll just have to tell my dad that I can't drive it. He's going to be pissed, but whatever."

I opened my window but didn't get out. "*I'm* not driving us home. The only way this car is getting back to your house is by you driving it there." I didn't want to come off as a jerk, but I'd committed to teaching her to drive this car and I was not letting her give up. I realized there was a lot of undoing that needed to be done from the way she had been treated by her dumbass ex.

This made Sydney mad. "What is it that you don't understand? I cannot do this! I'm not going to sit here and look stupid in front of you any longer. It's embarrassing and I'm not doing it."

A car was coming up behind us, so I got out and motioned for them to go around.

"Sydney, get in the car. You got us down the street once, you can do it again," I said calmly. I didn't want to upset her further, but I also wasn't about to let her give up because if she did, she'd never learn, and she needed this car.

"No, just drive us back home and we can fix the fence," she said, crossing her arms in front of her chest, tears streaming down her red face.

This was getting ridiculous, what did that asshole do that put so much fear and lack of confidence in this woman? It was obvious that a lot of this fear did stem from the trauma of her accident, but I didn't believe all of it was because of that. I put my hands on her shoulders. I wished I could shake some sense into her, but I also knew this was not her fault. I looked her in the eye and said firmly, "If I were you, I'd probably be just as terrified as you are, but I have confidence in you. Sometimes the only way to get through something is to face your fears, even though it's hard to do. I'll fix the fence after you drive us home. You can do this."

She finally got in the driver's seat and put her seatbelt on, but she started crying again. "I'm sorry. This is embarrassing. I understand if you want to back out of our plans tomorrow. I've made a fool of myself. I've been trying so hard to protect myself from feeling this way, but sometimes I can't help but feel like an idiot. Especially now, I already tried to learn how to do this, and I failed. Now here I am, failing at it again. What is wrong with me?" She dug around in the console until she found a pack of tissues.

Before I could answer, she started talking again.

"I just don't think anyone has ever had confidence in me or my abilities to do anything big. I think I ended up getting an identity of "dumb blonde" and anytime I'd make a mistake, I'd get made fun of. I've never had much self-confidence, and I'd protect myself by just laughing along with them, even though I wanted to cry. I'm sorry, I'm rambling, and this isn't anything you need to be hearing about," she said and wiped her face with a tissue.

She took a deep breath, blew her nose, and continued. "All I'm saying is nobody would ever be surprised if I never learned to drive this damn car, and they would all be fine with me giving up." She wasn't crying anymore. She just looked pissed now.

Well, this all spiraled quickly and took an unexpected turn. She wasn't just talking about driving a car anymore. It seemed Sydney had more issues she was dealing with than just her ex, and I was beginning to understand why she lacked confidence to keep trying something that she was sure she would fail at. But she was wrong, I wasn't going to cancel our plans for tomorrow. She just helped me understand her a little more and I appreciated that she trusted me enough to open up to me.

"Sydney, I'm sorry you were dealing with all that. And all I have to say is, you can do anything you set your mind to. That includes driving a vehicle with manual transmission. I have confidence in you. If you quit trying because of Jeff and anyone else that didn't believe in you, they win. Do not let them win."

That lit a fire inside her and she turned the car on. We went through the steps again and this time there was a determination I hadn't seen when we tried it before. The car stalled a few times, but this time she kept trying and finally got a rhythm going. She drove us down the streets in her neighborhood, went out on the highway, and even stopped at a drive through for a cherry limeade to reward herself. Finally, she pulled the car into her own driveway.

"Wooooo hoooo! You nailed it! I knew you could do it!" I picked her up and swung her around and she hugged me tightly around my neck while I still held her off the ground. I looked into her eyes and thought I saw something new there. There was a vulnerability in her gaze, no longer distant or guarded. Our faces were just inches apart, and I held her gaze for a moment too long before she looked away.

"I never could have done it without you! Thank you so much! I'm so excited! I can't wait to tell my dad!" She was just beaming as I set her back on the ground.

If Sydney gave me the chance, I was going to make it a mission to bring out more self-confidence than she ever knew she could have. I knew she had it in there, somewhere, deep inside her. She just needed to find it.

"Leanne! I did it! I can keep my dad's car now!" she yelled as she ran into the house.

"That's great! I told you that you could do it," Leanne said from the kitchen where she was busy making chocolate milk with the kids.

"I don't' know why I made it so hard! The next time you want me to go to the Iron Bar with you to see Brayden, I can drive us!" Sydney said to Leanne.

Leanne's smile faded. "Well, Brayden and I broke up today. I was about to call you when Will asked me about watching the kids."

Sydney and I glanced at each other. "I'm sorry, Leanne," I said. I noticed I hadn't seen her at the Iron Bar the last few nights that I'd worked.

"No, it's fine. We didn't have anything in common and it wasn't working out for either one of us. We wanted different things. I figured it was better to end it now since we didn't have a future together."

"I totally understand that. I'm sorry, though," Sydney said to her. "Well then, I can drive us to Ashley's this week to see little Luca! That sweet little thing will help get your mind off Brayden." The last part made Leanne smile.

"Ok, well, I still need to get your fence fixed," I said, picking up my toolbox.

"Thanks for watching the kids while Will taught me how to drive, Leanne," Sydney said to her. "See you later."

Sydney and I walked out to the fence where two sections were down. She made the kids go outside where we could see them.

"Thanks for coming to fix the fence. I don't like having it just open where people can walk through. I'm always afraid of burglars getting in. We've had a few houses robbed in my neighborhood lately and it just scares me."

This thought had already crossed my mind immediately when I found out it was down, which is why I was in a hurry to fix it.

"Oh, I understand. I don't mind at all. The bungee cords lasted longer than I thought they would! But that was remarkably resourceful," I said to her, picking up one of the cords off the ground and inspecting the floral wire wrapped around it.

"You aren't poking fun, are you? I live by the moto of fixing what you can with the things you already have. You wouldn't believe how much you can do with an L bracket, duct tape, and hot glue!"

"Oh, I'd never dream of making fun of your maintenance skills," I said, getting my drill and screws out of the toolbox. I could just imagine what kinds of things Sydney was able to come up with after looking at this fence repair.

Sydney helped pick up the fence panels and held them still while I reinforced them with some more 2x4s to make sure they didn't fall down again. Once everything was re-attached, we stood back and looked at the result.

"Perfect! Thanks so much for fixing that for me. You seem to be an all-purpose kind of guy. You help old ladies, volunteer at non-profits, fix fences, teach driving lessons, invent potato salad recipes, what else do specialize in?" she asked, looking much more relaxed than she had earlier when she was driving. She was so pretty when she was relaxed and happy. Her face had a healthy pink glow, and her eyes were lit up. Quite a difference from how she was when she was having her meltdown in the car earlier.

"I dabble a little in event planning," I said. Actually, I didn't dabble in event planning at all, except I'd been working on some plans for our date tomorrow night and I had something in mind that I thought Sydney might enjoy based on some things I'd learned about her.

"As payment for your fence repair services, would you like for me to heat up some turkey balls? You can eat dinner with us," she asked.

"Turkeys have balls?" I'd never heard of a turkey ball until Sydney told me about them yesterday. Am I about to eat turkey testicles to impress a girl? Because I'd eat a whole plate of them if it impresses Sydney.

Sydney laughed and playfully punched me in the arm. "Don't worry, it's not like it sounds. They are literally one of my favorite things in the entire world to eat."

"Ok, I'm curious about these turkey balls." What the heck was I about to eat? All I'd heard about Sydney's cooking was that it was questionable, though her mac and cheese had been perfect.

Thirty minutes later I sat at Sydney's table feasting on her famous turkey balls with her and her kids. They actually tasted amazing, and no testicles were included in the recipe.

"I'm sorry I was an asshole earlier with the driving lesson. I was just freaked out. I'm not a good driver, and I'm just not excited about having to drive a standard, it's so much more difficult than an automatic."

"No, you weren't an asshole. You were just nervous." I wasn't going to tell her this, but she wasn't the only one that was nervous. She was going to be driving that car to work and the thought of it did scare me to death, but she'd never gain any confidence any other way.

"Is the offer still on the table for dinner tomorrow?" she asked.

"Sure is. And take some shoes that can get dirty."

# Chapter 10

## *Sydney*

### Date night…

Will told me to wear jeans and bring some old tennis shoes or boots that I wouldn't mind getting dirty.  He said he had a surprise for dessert, but we might get dirty getting there.   That piqued my curiosity; however, no matter how many times I asked, he would not give any hints.

Was he going to take me hiking, or fishing, or gardening?  I'd never had anyone tell me I needed to bring old shoes on a date before.  I wasn't much of an outdoorsy kind of girl, so hopefully it was going to be something fun.

Nervous because I hadn't been on a date since high school, it took me forever to get ready.  I debated on my hair for way too long.  I tried it up, down, and straight.  I made such a mess of it that I had to re-wash it and start all over again.  I finally settled on wearing it down with the ends curled.

I had no idea what to wear on a date anymore. My bathroom floor was carpeted in all the clothes I tried on, decided against, then tried on again. The winning outfit was a black shirt and sandals along some wide leg jeans that made my butt look better than normal.

I put my old tennis shoes and socks in a bag for later, checked myself in the mirror for the 3,466[th] time, and looked at the clock. He'd be here any minute.

As usual, I'd made sure to pick up the living room and kitchen so he wouldn't think I was a slob. Basically, I just threw everything into my bedroom and closed the door, so I didn't have to deal with actually putting things away. No need to let him know the truth about me just yet, that I didn't have it all together like he probably thought I did.

Hopefully, he had already erased the events of the driving lesson from his memory. I'd made a huge fool of myself, and I was surprised he didn't come up with a reason to cancel our plans. By the way I'd behaved, I didn't even blame Jeff for saying I couldn't be taught. Will just had way more patience than Jeff did.

When I heard his truck pull into the driveway, I went into the kitchen to pretend like I was busy doing something else. I didn't want him to know that I was waiting as anxiously as I was. Then, I paused a few seconds before going to open the door after he knocked. Will stood on the porch, holding at least a dozen bright pink tulips that were tied with a white ribbon. In the other hand, he held a playdough factory.

"I hope you like tulips, I picked these out of Mrs. Beasley's greenhouse." He was wearing a brilliant blue, long-sleeved shirt that made his eyes pop.

"I love tulips! She didn't mind that you picked her flowers?" I pictured Will sneaking over, coming out of the greenhouse loaded with tulips, while his unsuspecting neighbor wasn't home.

"Mrs. Beasley knows everything the neighbors do. She caught me leaving the house. When she found out I had a date, she told me to pick some flowers for you. I was planning to get some at the flower shop, but she said store bought flowers are a scam," he said and laughed.

"I like Mrs. Beasley already. Tell her the flowers are beautiful!" I looked at the box he was holding. "Did you also know I love playdough?"

"I brought this for the kids as a thank you for sharing their mom with me tonight. I thought they might like it." OMG, he was too much.

"Wow! They will love it! They are spending the night at the neighbor's house, but I'll give it to them in the morning." I was shocked at how sweet he was, even thinking of the kids! I put the tulips in a vase on the kitchen table with the playdough factory next to them.

.....

We ate at La Pimienta for dinner, A Mexican food restaurant chosen and reserved by Will. While we ate, we learned more about each other and played a game where we took turns asking questions.

"Are you a convicted felon?" I asked him, already knowing that there was no way this man was a hardened criminal. He probably wasn't even the kind of guy that would put a can of green beans in the tomato sauce section after changing his mind on them.

"No. I can proudly say that I have a clean criminal history. Are you a convicted felon though because you seem a little sketchy." He narrowed his eyes, jokingly.

"I've never even had a ticket; much less been arrested. I'd never make it on the inside because I'm way too much of a weenie for all that. I'd probably get shanked with a sharpened toothbrush on the first day. My turn, what's your favorite food?"

"Chicken fried steak. My turn. Do you like parasailing?"

"Heck no. That's, way too dangerous. My turn. Have you ever wanted to sing professionally? Because your voice is amazing." I don't think I complimented him on his voice yet.

"Thank you! Yes, and I won a singing competition on TV a few years ago. The prize was a recording contract, but I had to pay for the band, and I couldn't afford that. It was exciting to win and get to be on TV, but I felt defeated when I couldn't come up with the money that I needed." That sucks. He could have been famous by now. But on the other hand, I wouldn't have met him if that had happened.

I made a mental note to learn to make chicken fried steak since it is his favorite, then came to my senses and scratched that because it is probably too far outside of my limited cooking abilities.

After we finished our food, I tried to get him to tell me what he had in store for dessert.

"I just don't understand why we need to take shoes that can get dirty," I said, stirring my margarita. "Are we going hiking? Digging trenches? Planting a tree?"

"No, we aren't doing any of that. But we are going to see my friend, Mark. You don't want to wear your good shoes at his place, trust me on this."

Wait. What? We were on our first date, which had been wonderful so far, but now we were going to spend it with his friend? My disappointment must have been obvious because he immediately looked worried.

"Don't be upset. I guarantee you are going to like Mark. He isn't what you'd expect. You'll understand once we get there."

I don't know who this Mark character is, but I don't think I like the idea of him taking part in our date.

After we left the restaurant, we drove out to Mark's house. I was still not particularly happy about having to go to his friend's house when I'd been looking forward to the whole night with just the two of us.

We drove to the outside of town, and he finally announced, "Here we are!" pulling up to a beautiful, white, ranch style house with an arena next to it. Mark must be some kind of farmer or something. "You should go ahead and put on your tennis shoes. Mark is probably around the back," he said, pointing to a large metal building.

I put my tennis shoes on and walked with him. Will opened the gate and we walked through.

"We are breaking and entering, I see."

Will laughed. Then he smiled when we got to the front of the building, which turned out to be a barn. "There he is!" he said, pointing toward the fence near the barn.

I didn't see anyone there. The only thing there was one of the most gorgeous Brahma bulls I'd ever seen. His coat was shiny black.

"Sydney, meet Mark. Mark, this is Sydney," Will said, making the introductions.

I stood there, staring at him confused. "Mark is a bull?"

"Not only is Mark a bull, but Mark is also a surprisingly tame bull. He loves attention. He even loves to be hugged."

What the heck, was he too good to be true? Will listened to me. He was thoughtful. The tulips, the playdough, and now a freaking bull? Who ever heard of a huggable bull anyway?

"You said you loved bulls so I couldn't just not bring you out here to see Mark. He was a rescue bull. His owner died and Mark was found severely dehydrated and malnourished. My friend, Kip, heard about him and brought him here to nurse back to health. He has him spoiled rotten. Kip is out of town, but he said we could come over."

Looking at this bull now, it was hard to imagine that he had ever been malnourished. He was thick and muscular and obviously well cared for.

"He's tamed? He isn't going to charge at me?" Even though I loved bulls, I also knew enough to know to be cautious with them.

"He's fine! Come on." We walked up to the bull and Will started petting the hump on his back. "Kip has people over all the time and Mark loves the attention."

"Hey there, Mark. You *are* a sweetie, aren't you?" I talked to him as I pet his floppy ears.

As if on cue, the bull laid down on the dirt. I looked at Will, surprised.

"I think Kip may have taught him that somehow because he does that all the time. Kip likes to get on the ground with him and just hangs out with him a lot."

I had always dreamed of cow cuddling, but bull cuddling was so much better! Leanne and Ashley weren't going to believe this. None of the bulls we'd been around were this tame.

"Kip seems to have a knack for naming animals," I said, I'd always loved people names for animals.

"Yea, it was a toss-up between Mark and Albert."

I plopped down in the dirt next to Mark's beastly head. He was unlike any bull I'd ever been around, usually I had to pet them from the fence because they couldn't be trusted up close. Mark nudged his head against me. As enormous and intimidating as bulls are, I always found something so peaceful about them. I could see why Kip spent so much time with him.

We sat with Mark for a while and took a few selfies. I was definitely going to pick one as my profile picture and proof that I'd made a friend with this sweet bull.

The sun started to set, reminding me that we still hadn't had dessert.

"So, what's for dessert?"

"I almost forgot! Let me go get it," he said and walked off to the truck.

Once he was out of sight, I pulled my inhaler out of my pocket and took a couple of puffs of it. The hay was starting to get my asthma going, but I didn't want Will to know. It was embarrassing always having to get my inhaler out.

He returned with a red and white cooler. "I'll go set this up on the patio. I'll holler at you when I get it ready." By then, Mark decided he had had enough cuddling and walked off for a drink. I looked around at the barn and the arena. Kip kept everything so neat and clean. Most people found barn aromas repulsive, but I always loved the smells in a barn, even though I was allergic to everything in it. It was nostalgic for me.

I spent so much of my childhood running around our own arena and barn, helping to feed the cattle, horses, and other animals. Even as a young child, I fed enormous bulls right out of my hand, not afraid of them at all. My siblings, cousins, and I were all tough when we were kids, and we weren't afraid of anything back then.

"It's ready!" Will shouted. I opened the gate and found Will on the patio.

I walked out to the patio and stopped to take in everything that Will had prepared. He went above and beyond the call of duty on this night, which was a every bit a date and not at all an unlabeled "let's see where this goes" kind of thing. The patio was already beautiful with Kip's potted plants and flowers, but Will added a few more thoughtful touches. String lights along the roof of the patio were turned on. The patio table had a white tablecloth and a single lit candle, and there was a piece of cheesecake with strawberry topping on both plates. To drink, there was a bottle of wine and one large can of beer. He had 80s music playing on the outdoor speakers.

He must have remembered that 80s was my favorite. The scene in front of me was literally breathtaking. He did this for me? The playdough, the flowers, the bull, and now this? Was this real life?

Will stood on the patio near the table, appearing a little nervous but so damn good looking at the same time. Every time he did something meaningful; he became even more attractive. "How's this for dessert?" he asked.

I walked up to where he was standing, and with a bit of unexpected confidence ran my fingers up and down the buttons on the front of his shirt and tilted my face up to his as if I were going to kiss him. I wanted to devour him but instead I smiled sheepishly and stepped back a little, wanting to see how long this could play out.

"This is amazing, Will. You completely outdid yourself. I don't even know what to say. I'm not sure I deserve everything you've done tonight," I breathed.

Will looked down into my face which was still just a few inches away. "When we talked last week, you said your favorite dessert was cheesecake." Then he lowered his voice and added, "I hope you like strawberry topping." We locked our eyes for a moment, and I couldn't breathe while I anticipated him kissing me. But he smiled flirtatiously, stepped aside, and pulled out my chair for me to sit down.

I sat down and breathed again, flushed, and tried to compose myself. Will had all kinds of tricks up his sleeve apparently. I couldn't believe it. He literally listened to everything I had ever said. He began pouring wine into my glass. "Peach wine. I hope you like it." I'd never had peach wine, but peach is one of my favorite flavors. I'd have to not overdo it, or I'd ruin this romantic night with my rhyming and talking nonsense.

"Let me do the cheesecake test." I picked up my fork.

"Cheesecake test?" he asked.

"Yes, the cheesecake test. First, you have to inspect the texture. The texture looks perfect on this one. Then you have to put the bite in your mouth and let it sit there for a few seconds. Then, you pull the fork out extremely slowly. If the cheesecake sticks to the fork, then it's perfect." I slowly demonstrated, just slightly seductively but enough to get a response out of him.

Will raised his eyebrows, obviously enjoying my demonstration. "Well? Does it pass inspection?" Our cheesecake conversation had somehow become a turn-on.

"Sure does, perfect," I said, pleased with Will's reaction. Will and I had chemistry for sure, and I was comfortable with the back-and-forth teasing.

I tasted the wine. I'd never been a wine drinker, but I could see myself getting started on a wine drinking journey with this peach wine.

"Will, I don't know what to say. Everything you have done tonight has been perfect. I don't think you can top this next time."

"So, there's going to be a next time?" he asked, with a playfully hopeful look in his eyes.

"Oh, I don't know. It's a possibility." I shrugged, smiling innocently. I was certain that I wanted there to be a next time and probably a bunch of times after that if things kept going as well as they were between us.

We ate the rest of our cheesecake and talked about our jobs, our families, my kids, our hobbies, and our preferences in cups.

"Styrofoam or metal cup with a lid, the good kind of ice, and a decent straw. A plastic or paper cup will ruin your drink faster than anything," I said. I was one of the biggest cup snobs there was. I stood behind my theory that a cup would make or break a good drink.

"You're just a little particular about your drinks, huh? I just drink a bottle of water, doesn't even have to be cold," he said, as I pretended to be appalled. I would have to get him the gift that keeps on giving, a good cup. He needs to know what he has been missing out on.

The more I learned about Will, the more I liked him. We seemed to just click. Talking to him was easy and I didn't feel self-conscious with him, even after the driving lesson fiasco.

"So, when you aren't working, what kinds of things do you do for fun?" I asked him.

"I love watching football and playing golf, but I haven't done either of those in a while. After I found out about Shell's Place, I've been doing some things with them quite a bit. It's just down the street from my house and I've been volunteering there a few times a month. I've done their yard work, grilled burgers for their picnic, and I've taught some of the guys to play basketball. That's kind of what has kept me going lately. I kind of feel like it gives me a purpose, you know?"

"I love that you are doing that. They are so lucky to have somebody like you to help them out. I'm sure they all appreciate it more than you even know." The thought of Will volunteering at a non-profit was literally the icing on the cake for me, especially having a sister with a disability that could be living in a group home if she wasn't living with my mom.

A slow song came on and Will stood up and formally held out his hand. "May I have this dance, ma'am?"

"Why yes, you may, sir," I said and laughed as I got up and took his hand.

We danced on Kip's patio, by the light from the moon, the string lights, and the candle. Mark grazed in the arena next to us. I loved the combined smells of the barn, the freshly mowed grass, and

Will's cologne. It was the most amazing night that I could even remember.

Will was taller than I was, so I stood on my tiptoes to dance with him. I could feel his breath in my hair and the warmth of his hand on my back. It felt good, too good to be true almost.

How could this man that just met me, already know me so well? I wondered why he liked me and what made me special, enough so that he went through all this trouble for me tonight. The best part was that he tried to get to know me, he listened to what I said and acted on it. These things may not have seemed significant to anyone else, but this was huge for me. Nobody had ever done that for me before. It's funny how I already felt more comfortable with Will than I ever did with Jeff or anyone else I had ever dated before him. But I still didn't want to rush into anything super serious just yet, I just wanted to get to know him, see where things went.

When we left, I stopped to say bye to Mark, who was busy shaking flies off his face.

"I'll have to make regular visits to see Mark, if Kip doesn't mind. I already love him."

"Kip won't mind. I'll bring you out here anytime you want. Mark is an attention whore anyway," he said, giving the bull one last pat on the side.

When we got back to my house, Will started to say goodbye, but I didn't want him to leave yet. Besides, I didn't like coming home to an empty house at night. It always made me worry that somebody was hiding inside the house.

"There is still more peach wine that I need to finish, and I don't like to drink alone."

Will and I watched TV, I drank the rest of the wine, and we talked. I was a little more than just buzzed from the wine though.

"Have you told anyone my lawyer joke yet?"

"Well, no... I mean, it's a great joke... but I'll let that be all yours."

"I'm going to change clothes. I'll be right back," I said as I walked off to my bedroom.

I came back wearing pajama pants with a pink elephant print and an oversized T-shirt that read 'I'm nicer than my face looks.'

"Just because I'm wearing something sexy doesn't mean you can take advantage of me," I said, even though I could think of worse things that could happen.

"Of course. I wouldn't dream of it," he responded seriously but with a look at his face that indicated he would definitely dream of it.

I appreciated that Will didn't make me feel like I had to dress in a certain way. I felt silly for stressing so much about what to wear tonight. I had a feeling that I could wear anything I wanted to, and he would be ok with it. I already knew without a doubt he would never insult my appearance or make me feel insecure. It was a comfortable feeling, being allowed to be myself. I'd only ever felt this way with my family or my best friends, but never men.

I scooted closer to Will, and he took my hand and rubbed his thumb over the back of it. That little bit of touch made me feel safe and protected.

I'd never felt like this with Jeff. He had never made me feel desirable, secure, or valued. I always felt on edge for most of our marriage and if he had been nice to me, then there was always an ulterior motive. Any intimacy was one sided and there were no feelings behind it. Plus, there was always an ultimatum, making me feel that I had no choice. He had control over me by the threats he would make, and now that I look back, I wonder if he even meant any of it or if I just played right into his hands being gullible and too easy to manipulate.

"You know you're the first person I have felt this safe with. You don't judge me, you listen to me, I just feel like I can be myself around you. I just wanted to thank you for that."

Just saying that made my eyes water because this was a new feeling, and it scared me a little because I wasn't sure what to do with those feelings. I was in all new territory that I hadn't experienced before. I had to remind myself this was our first date, but we had such a connection that it didn't feel like a first date anymore.

Will pulled me closer to him where my face was against his chest and started playing with my hair. I melted into him; nobody had played with my hair since I was a little girl. "You are always safe with me. And you couldn't look anything less than beautiful even if you tried. I mean, you are gorgeous in pink elephant pajamas."

I must have fallen asleep on the couch, but I woke up in the middle of the night in my bed. Will was gone but there was a note on my end table that read "*I tucked you into bed, but don't worry, I didn't take advantage of you even though those pajamas are SEXY.*"

I smiled to myself and went back to sleep feeling happier than I had been in years.

# Chapter 11

## *Will*

### The Next Monday...

I'd been awake for a few minutes when I heard my phone chirp. **Good morning! Have a good day and observe ladder safety protocol!** It was from Sydney, and it made me smile.

I lay there thinking about our date and how I carried her to her bed after she fell asleep on the couch. She had a little twin sized bed. During one of our phone conversations, she told me her ex-husband took the bed when he moved out. That irritated me because he could afford to buy a new bed. She couldn't. She was using her childhood bed from her parents' storage until she could get something bigger.

Before I left, I wrote her a note and left it on her nightstand so she would see it when she woke up.

In just a short time, my life changed for the better because of Sydney. I was happier than I had been in a long time, even though we hadn't known each other for long and had only been on one date.

For the past few years, I'd been in a hopeless slump. I couldn't find any reason to be proud of myself. I never felt that I was good enough for my family, like I was a constant disappointment to everyone. Sydney accepted me for who I was. Sydney had already learned more about me than anyone else knew. Nobody else had ever seemed to care to know that much, and I told her things I could never tell anyone else.

My phone chirped again. **Also, stay away from wasp nests!**

I laughed. A few days ago, I told her I was allergic to wasps, and she immediately started lecturing me on getting an epi pen. It was nice having somebody that worried about me and wanted me to be safe.

I got ready, stopped for a gas station breakfast burrito, and went to work. We were removing a few large oak trees from an older couple's property that day.

We'd been working for about an hour. As we unloaded the stump grinder, Gerald, my supervisor, said, "I heard you had a date. You didn't tell me you had a girlfriend." Gerald was my supervisor but wasn't exactly the poster child for professionalism.

"How would you know that?" I asked. I hadn't told anyone at work about Sydney and I couldn't exactly call her my girlfriend yet.

"Lisa was at La Pimienta with some of her friends and she saw you." Lisa was his wife. I hadn't seen her there. "One of the ladies she was with works at Greenridge Townhomes and knew your date from work," Gerald said as he opened a can of snuff and packed some into his bottom lip.

Oh, great. All I needed was Gerald and his wife butting into my personal life. I got a chainsaw and ladder out of the truck, not wanting to continue this discussion.

"Did you know she just got divorced?" he asked, as if this was news she was keeping from me.

"Of course, I know that. So? Fifty percent of all marriages end in divorce, it isn't exactly unheard of."

"And do you also know she has two little kids?" he asked as he climbed the ladder to start cutting branches.

"Yes, I've already met them. They're great kids. Why are you so concerned about this?" I asked him annoyed. He had crossed a line. This had nothing to do with my job and it was none of his business.

"Will, use your head. You're probably the first guy she has been out with since she split up with her ex-husband and she has two little kids."

"And?" I said, throwing a large branch into the trailer.

"And you need to get your head out of your ass. This is just a rebound and it isn't going anywhere."

"What the hell? You don't even know her, and you don't have any business worrying about my personal life. Worry about what I do at work, but my life outside of that is my own damn business." This was bullshit. I could feel my face getting red.

"I've seen this before. And if I were you, I'd break it off with her now before things get carried away. I know how you are. You're going to get attached to her, you're going to fall in love with her kids, and then you're going to get hurt. I don't want you here all sad and forlorn like some pitiful little puppy and end up doing a sucky job at work."

"Puppy? What the f..." I hit the trailer with the side of my fist and went to my truck to calm down. As mad as I was, I wasn't in any position to get myself fired. What was Gerald thinking interfering in my private life? It pissed me off that everyone was talking about me and Sydney.

I drank a bottle of water and took a few minutes to get my head straight, then went back and took my frustrations out on the trees.

About an hour later, Gerald was the first to speak, "Look, I'm sorry. I'm just looking out for you," he said, then spit his snuff out on the grass.

"I know, Gerald. I get that you're trying to help, but my personal life has nothing to do with work, and honestly, I'd prefer to keep that private. I'm a grown man and I know what I'm doing."

"Understood," Gerald said, sounding irritated.

I took out my phone and texted Sydney. **What are you doing tonight?**

She replied: **Nothing. Do you want to come over? I'm making spaghetti. And beans…**

**Perfect. I'll be there at 6:30**. I texted back.

I took a shower after work and headed over to Sydney's. What Gerald said couldn't be true. This wasn't a rebound. I mean, yes, I was technically the first person that Sydney went out with since her divorce, but did that mean we couldn't work? It's not like there's a specific number of people a person has to date after a bad relationship that increases the likelihood of it working out. That's what I tried to tell myself. But seriously, what if Gerald had a point. This could seriously just be a rebound for Sydney as much as I didn't want to admit it. With everything that she has been through, would she even be able to fall in love with me if we continue to see each other? I could just be a comfort tool, a security blanket for her right now. I couldn't help but worry that once Sydney regains some confidence, she may not need me anymore. As much as I want to be close to Sydney, I also don't want to be a practice test to get her back into the dating scene.

. . . . . . . . . . . . .

The air was smokey and I could smell a combination of something burned mixed with the smell of spaghetti cooking when she opened the door. "Smells great!" I said, looking around for the source of the offending odor as I walked in. Sydney greeted me with a big, beautiful smile, and I immediately felt guilty for entertaining Gerald's comment about her. I hugged her and she didn't stiffen up anymore, instead she hugged me back tightly. She was in shorts and an oversized T-shirt with her hair piled on top of her head. I loved the way she looked when she was natural and effortless. I'd always found women more attractive when they were comfortable and relaxed rather than all dressed up with a lot of makeup and perfect hair. I wanted to see the real person, not a decorated version of the real person. I also loved that she didn't feel the need to impress me, and she didn't make me feel like I needed to impress her. We were both perfectly comfortable just being ourselves, no matter how we looked in the moment, without worrying about what the other might think.

"Excuse the smell, I had a little mishap."

"I didn't notice anything," I lied, wondering what she burned.

"Spaghetti is my specialty. But don't get too excited, it is the basic three ingredient kind. Sometimes I'm fancy and even have garlic bread, but not tonight. We do, however, have pork n' beans as a side dish. Elsie wants beans with every meal." She laughed.

Elsie walked in wearing a pink swimming suit and fuzzy red Elmo house shoes. As soon as she saw me, she went to get a book out of a basket in the living room and handed a book to me.

Sydney didn't like clutter. Most of the kids' things were kept in their bedrooms. Anything that wasn't, like some of their books and games, were stored neatly in baskets or in the ottoman. Sydney had put a lot of thought into making their rooms functional but not too overwhelming for the kids.

"Will, will you read this to me?" Elsie asked in her high-pitched little voice.

It was completely impossible to say no to that cute little face. "Do we have time to read a book?" I asked Sydney.

"Yes. One book, Elsie. Then it's time to eat," she said to Elsie as we sat down on the couch. Elsie climbed into my lap as I started reading.

We'd read a few pages when I looked up and caught Sydney leaning against the kitchen doorway, watching us with a tear in her eye. My guess is that Jeff never read to the kids. He probably didn't do much of anything with them and it made me sick. These kids were so young and innocent and even though they had lived in the same home with Jeff until he moved out, they never had a real father figure.

"Ok! Come eat, everybody!" Sydney yelled from the kitchen a few minutes later. Elsie threw the book on the floor and ran to the table. Micah walked out of his bedroom, already in pajamas.

Passing by the trash can, I spotted black brick-like objects near the top that looked suspiciously like burned garlic bread.

After I sat down at the table, Sydney jumped back up. "Oh, I almost forgot!" She hurried over to the counter and opened up a bag, pulling out a large red and black cup. "I got you your own good cup! You'll feel like a whole new man when you find out how much better your drink is with a good cup. You'll never go back to a plastic water bottle again. Trust me on this one." She put ice and water in it and handed it to me proudly.

It lightly rained while we ate, and we took the kids outside to play when they finished eating. It was still sprinkling and there were tiny baby frogs jumping all over the yard. We'd never seen so many frogs; there had to be hundreds of them. Elsie ran into the house and came back with a little purse that had her name painted on it. We watched, laughing, while she chased after the baby frogs, putting them into her purse and trying to close the flap before they jumped out. Micah helped, and before long, the purse was almost full of baby frogs.

After a while, Sydney said, "They aren't going to like it when they find out they have to let them go."

"Let me tell them," I said and walked over to the kids who were crouched down looking for more unsuspecting frogs to hold hostage in Elsie's purse.

"Now, you know these are just baby frogs and they still have to grow up to be big frogs. I think they're hungry. Let's let them go here in the flower bed so they can eat. Then we can try to catch them again when they grow up!"

Micah thought about it a few seconds and said, "OK," then tried to take the purse from Elsie but she held onto it tightly. Elsie's bottom lip stuck out like she was going to cry but gave up and let Micah help shake the frogs out of her purse. I inspected the purse to make sure no frog was left behind.

"Good job! See how happy they are now!" I said as the kids watched the frogs jump around on the ground.

Sydney's phone rang and she walked across the yard where she could hear better. She came back looking worried.

"That was Mimi. Pop tripped and fell. She doesn't think he's hurt, but she needs help getting him up. Can you stay with the kids while I go help?"

"Why don't I go help instead? It might be easier for me to get him up anyway. Do you think they would mind?"

"OK, thank you. I don't think they'll mind at all. It's just on the next block, the yellow house with the tractor mailbox. I'll let them know you're coming."

When I got to the house, Mrs. Richardson answered wearing a long blue robe and matching house shoes. "Thank you for coming to quickly! I don't know what I'm going to do with him if he keeps falling."

Mr. Richardson was lying across the living room floor on his side.

"I tripped on something, and I can't get myself up. Can you help me back to my chair?"

I helped him up and got him back in his chair. He seemed to be ok. I noticed there was a piece of loose carpet that had come up from the tackboard. I pointed it out. "Here's the problem, the carpet is loose, Mr. Richardson. Let me fix that for you right now so you don't trip on it again."

After Mrs. Richardson showed me the tools, I stretched the carpet out the best I could and rehammered it down to the tackboard.

"This should hold for now, but I'm coming back tomorrow after work to do a permanent fix on it."

"Oh, Will, that would be wonderful. We'll pay you," Mrs. Richardson said.

"Absolutely not, ma'am. I just want to help."

"Will, go get us both a beer out of the icebox," Mr. Richardson said, pointing to the refrigerator. "And stop calling me Mr. Richardson. I already told you to call me Pop," he said in a gruff voice. If felt odd calling people Mimi and Pop when they weren't my grandparents, but that's what they insisted on.

I texted Sydney to let her know I'd be gone for a few more minutes. **I'm having a beer with Pop. I'll be here a little bit longer.**

**Um… What??** she texted back.

I replied with a smiley face emoji.

Thirty minutes later, Mimi, Pop, and I said goodbye. They also instructed me to bring Sydney and the kids with me when I fixed the floor, and Mimi would have dinner ready by 6:30.

"What did you do over there!?" Sydney asked wide eyed. "You just went over to help Pop up, and you came back their adopted grandchild."

"Nothing. I just helped him up, fixed the floor, and promised to come back tomorrow to fix it permanently. Next thing I know, we are drinking beer, and he's telling me jokes about your grandmother and showing plans for a deck in his backyard. Your grandmother had me change the batteries in the smoke detectors too. They're great people. You're one lucky girl."

"Yes, Mimi and Pop are the best. They've always been a huge part of my life. I've just been worried about Pop lately. He's going downhill and I'm afraid we won't have him much longer."

"You never know. Maybe he'll surprise you. I'm glad I came over tonight. I had a terrible day at work, and this was exactly what I needed." Being around Sydney was all it took to turn my day around and make it better.

"I'm sorry you had a bad day. Do you want to talk about it?"

"Nah, it's ok. My boss just pissed me off. I'm over it now." I didn't want Sydney to know what Gerald said to me about her.

I helped Sydney get the kids to bed. The routine consisted of a story for both, two rounds of Twinkle Twinkle Little Star for Elsie, and checking Micah's closet for aliens.

"I'm glad you came over, too. The kids adore you. That's a big deal for Micah; he won't even speak to most people."

"They're great kids! I'll see you tomorrow for dinner at your grandparents' house at 6:30 sharp. They let me know in no uncertain terms that attendance isn't optional."

Sydney didn't say anything and stared at me for a few seconds. "Will, you know you don't have to leave yet, right?"

"I don't?" I asked, curious what her intentions were, as she shook her head no.

Five minutes later, I ran up to the convenient store and got two pints of ice cream and two fountain drinks. We shared a blanket and ate our ice cream as we binge watched our favorite show on Netflix. I'd gotten us both hooked on this survival reality show where people are dropped off in the middle of nowhere to fend for themselves.

It got late. I got up again to leave, but Sydney said I might as well spend the night. She'd been afraid at night the last few weeks because several of the houses in her neighborhood had been broken into and she didn't like being there alone at night with the kids.

We both slept in her twin bed. Nothing happened, unfortunately. I was a perfect gentleman, and I slept in my clothes. I was pinned up against the wall, but it was ok with me. I'd rather be sleeping uncomfortably in Sydney's twin bed than sleeping alone in my own king-sized bed.  I got up early to leave before the kids woke up.

# Chapter 12

## *Sydney*

Elsie and Micah had named the green car The Greenie Weenie. I was making it my own and added a few personal touches including a fake succulent in a macrame hanger hanging from the rearview mirror. I had an awful habit of going to the wrong car, and I mean this happened all the time. I was lucky that there weren't as many green cars, but to be on the safe side, I could look for the succulent in the window as my clue that it was the correct car. I'd been to so many wrong cars, it was a miracle I hadn't been accused of trying to break into a vehicle yet.

Will checked the tires, the oil, the fluids, and detail cleaned it for me. He also bought an emergency kit and put it in the trunk. He even bought an "S" sticker to put on my back window in case the plant wasn't enough of an indicator that it was my car.

"You can't possibly get in the wrong car. Look for the clean, green car with a plant in the window and an S on the back," he'd said, sure that this was fool proof. I wasn't going to tell him that the very next day I tried the handle on a completely different green car.

Driving the Greenie Weenie was going well as long as I didn't have to stop on any slopes. There was an unfortunate mishap at the donut shop drive through window a couple of days ago. The shop sits on a small hill and there is a slope where the drive through window is. Every time I let off the clutch I would roll backward before I could get the car going forward. I completely panicked because I couldn't get the car to go forward, and I kept going backwards until I thought I was going to hit the car behind me. There were at least five cars in line behind me. The lady in the car behind me realized what was happening and backed up as much as she could. This wasn't enough because I rolled backwards more. At the drive through window, the worker's head was sticking out trying to see what was going on. One of the donut shop employees actually went outside to direct traffic and made everyone back up. Eventually, I had room to get the car going forward. Then, I sped right past the window and kept going, too embarrassed to spend another second there. I used to love that donut shop, but I didn't think I could show my face there ever again. I'd have to find a new donut shop on a level surface.

Will and I spent most of our free time together. Since our first date, we had only been out alone a couple times. Our alone time was mostly after the kids went to bed. We'd developed a strange love of playing board games. One night, I even surprised him with *romantic* board games. I'd spread a blanket on the floor in front of the fireplace and set out candles, wine, cheese, and grapes by the game board.

Usually, we take the kids with us if we go anywhere. I loved that Will respected the fact that I was a mom first before anything else. The kids were my first priority, and I didn't like to leave them with a babysitter often. Will truly loves the kids, and the relationship that he and the kids were forming seemed so natural.

We'd taken them out to see Mark, whom both kids thought was amazing. I was proud of how well they did in public. I'd always been able to take them anywhere with me and they never caused any problems. I'm not sure how I lucked out with that. I knew a lot of parents who couldn't take their kids anywhere because they couldn't control them.

We had dinner twice at Mimi and Pop's house. They certainly liked Will, which was surprising because they were extremely protective and particular about who their daughters and granddaughters dated or married.

Pop and Will even worked together on some plans for a new deck in the backyard. Pop's health wasn't good, and he was on oxygen most of the time now. Designing the deck gave him a little spark that I hadn't seen in a while.

Mimi had him doing little tasks like spraying the weeds along the driveway and checking the air in her tires. He didn't even mind, he liked helping them and he loved being needed. They had never even bothered to ask Jeff to help them with anything, probably because they knew it would be a waste of time to even ask. The fact that Mimi and Pop liked Will so much was a sign for me.

I wanted this kind of life all the time. Other than my kids, Will was the best thing that ever happened to me. When he wasn't here, I missed him. I liked to hold the throw pillows on the couch because they smelled like his cologne. It seemed silly, but it made me feel closer to him. He made me feel safe, but he also made me have courage that I never had before. He was the only man that I'd ever worried about so much. I worried about him getting hurt at work, getting stung by a wasp and going into anaphylactic shock, being struck by lightning walking through the parking lot in the rain. I couldn't imagine not having him in my life.

Leanne texted me and asked if I saw the news. Another one of our neighbor's houses got broken into. This was getting ridiculous. It almost seemed like it was every night now.

I found a video doorbell camera on sale and planned to get one and install it on the front door.

I texted Will: **Another one of the neighbors' houses was broken into...**

Will: **Do you and the kids want to stay at my house for a little while until they catch the guy?**

Me: **Thanks, but that would be hard with the kids.**

Will: **I'll call you during lunch.**

As promised, the phone rang about five minutes into the lunch hour.

"So, I've been thinking. And you can say no, and I won't have my feelings hurt," Will said.

"OK, you've got my attention," I said, anxious to hear what this was all about.

"I don't like you being home alone with the kids with all these break ins going on. I could stay at your house if you want. I mean, until you feel like things are safe again."

"Really?"

"I could sleep on the couch. Then, when things go back to normal and the break ins stop, I'll just go back to my house," he said.

"Okay, I think this is actually a great idea. I would feel much safer with you here," I said, which was true. He always made me feel safe and I had no doubt that he would never let anything happen to me or the kids.

Did it have to be temporary, though? By anyone else's standards, it probably seems a little soon, actually way too soon...

But it wouldn't be much different than what we were doing right now. Not just to protect us from burglars, either.

My mind was racing. Will was at my house most days after work except for a couple nights a week when he had to DJ. We were together a lot during the weekends. What difference would it be if he just moved in for real? He wouldn't be driving back and forth to his house. It would be a win-win situation for both of us.

"You know, you're at my house pretty much every day and we spend most of the weekends together, and…"

"Wait," Will interrupted. "Are you thinking we need to slow down? I'm sorry if I'm crowding you, I just thought…"

Oh gosh. "No, no. Hold on, that's not it at all. I was actually going to ask if you might want to officially move in with me? Not just as my bodyguard, but really move in?" I held my breath waiting for his response.

Silence.

"Will?" Oh great. He probably thinks I'm a psychopath. I was still holding my breath.

Finally, he spoke, "Seriously? You want me to move in with you for real?"

"I mean, yes? It all makes perfect sense. You would already have been staying over to protect us from evil. And you've been paying rent for a house that you are literally never at. The only thing you do at your own house is go over there to occasionally sleep, take a shower, and check in on Mrs. Beasley. We can still go check on Mrs. Beasley even if you don't live there. And this way you could save the money on rent, save the gas from driving 30 minutes back and forth. You practically live at my house anyway."

More silence. Ok, this was a mistake. It was too soon, he didn't want to move in. He was probably trying to find a nice way to let me down easy.

"Will, I love you. I love everything about you, like the way you sing when you drive, the way you bring me a drink when I don't ask for it, the way you play with the kids, and how the three of us are happier when you are there. I'm sorry if this is too soon. You can say no, and I totally understand." Please don't say no, I thought.

More Silence. He was killing me with all this silence.

"Hello?" I was panicking. I'd blown it. What the heck was I thinking?

"Honestly, I would absolutely love to move in with you. I'd love that more than anything. I kind of feel like that's where I belong," he finally said.

I finally breathed. "Oh my gosh, Will! You scared me! I thought you were going to say no." I laughed, so relieved.

He laughed. "Oh no, I'm sorry, you just surprised me, a good surprise, though. Are the kids going to be ok with it?"

"I think so, they both think you're wonderful. They look forward to seeing you and they have literally been happier since you've been in the picture than they have been in a while. They love the extra attention too."

"Oh, good. That makes me feel good. I love being around them too."

"One thing is for sure; we cannot tell anyone in my family other than Ashley and Leanne. My family's ridiculously old fashioned." I don't know why I worried so much about what everyone else thought, but I did.

"Yea, my family would all go into cardiac arrest if they knew I was living such a scandalous lifestyle. Speaking of my family, you still haven't met them. Maybe this weekend we can go over there for dinner or something. They'll love you."

"Of course! We can talk more about everything tonight." I couldn't wait to get his things moved in, especially his bed. My twin bed wasn't going to cut it.

"I'm going to be late tonight though because I promised Mrs. Beasley that I would mow her yard and put together her new curio cabinet. One can never have enough piano shaped music boxes, it seems." He scoffed.

"I'll be fine if you want to just stay at your house tonight. I don't want you to have to come late. Can I bring something to eat for you and Mrs. Beasley? I 'd love to meet her." One of the things I loved most about Will was how he loved helping others. It was so sweet the way he talked about Mrs. Beasley.

"That's sweet, but I don't want you to have to drive all the way out there for that. You can meet her when we move my stuff over."

"Ok, well, just call me tonight when you get finished and we can work out the details. I'm so excited!" One thing about Will was he wasn't as dramatic with his emotions as I was and sometimes it was hard to tell what his feelings were unless I could see his facial expressions. It was a little fast, I'll admit, but I hoped he was as excited about moving in with me as I was.

........

When I got home from work, I didn't want to cook dinner. "How does The Crunchy Chicken sound for dinner?" I asked the kids.

"Yea!" Micah said excited. They were always excited when they didn't have to eat whatever I was cooking.

The kids and I ate near the play area and then I let them play on the playground for a while. I decided to surprise Will and Mrs. Beasley and take some food out even though Will said not to. He didn't want me to drive all the way out there to take them food, but I honestly didn't mind, and I'd love to see where he lived. I'd never been to Will's house before since we were always at my house, but he told me where it was, and I knew Mrs. Beasley lived right next to him. I was excited to meet Mrs. Beasley, too. Will told me so much about her.

GPS showed me how to get there. I pulled into the trailer park and spotted Will's truck in front of a brown house. I started to drive over to his house when his front door opened. A blonde woman walked out onto his front porch followed by Will. From what I could tell, she was very pretty with a good figure. Shocked, I stopped the car immediately hoping he didn't see me. The woman turned around and hugged Will, then walked out to her car and came back with what appeared to be an overnight bag. Then they went back into his house and closed the door. *This* is why he went home tonight, not to help Mrs. Beasley. Will was cheating on me. This is why he didn't want me to come over tonight? Tears streaming down my face, I turned the car around and drove away before he noticed me.

"What about Will, Mom?" Micah asked.

"I want Will, Mommy!" Elsie chimed in.

"Not now. We're going home." I couldn't explain to them what the problem was, and I wasn't thinking clearly enough to figure out something to say about it.

I cried all the way home. How stupid could I be, asking him to move in with me already? And the whole time he was cheating on me! Or was he cheating on her with me? What difference did it make? Either way, he had another girlfriend, and he was damn sure not going to be moving in. I let myself fall in love with him. I trusted him with my kids! I was furious now.

When we got home, I threw the stupid board games into the trash. I threw away his jacket that was lying on the couch. I went through the house looking for anything that was his. I didn't want any reminders of him. Why would he agree to move in with me if he had a whole other girlfriend on the side?

"I'm sorry, Mommy," Elsie said and handed me a tissue. She could be so sweet sometimes.

"Thank you, Peanut. Mommy is ok. Can you go play with Micah?" Elsie nodded and went into Micah's room.

I ran out of tissues and took a roll of toilet paper to the couch and cried until my eyes were swollen. I'd been cheated on before and I couldn't believe it was happening again. There was nothing worse than thinking somebody is devoted to you and then find out they aren't and that they have been lying to you.

Will called but I didn't answer. He had no idea that I knew the truth or that I didn't want to talk to him right now.

He texted: **Just finished with Mrs. Beasley's things. Call me when you can!**

That freaking liar. I didn't respond.

He called again. I still didn't answer.

**You can get rid of your little bed now. I have a king size!** He texted. That damn freaking asshole. He was probably just in that stupid bed with his girlfriend!!

**Just checking to see if you're ok.** He texted again.

Then, the phone rang.

A few minutes later. **Syd, I'm getting worried. I'm coming over if I don't hear back from you.**

I finally responded. **I'm fine. Stop calling me. Stop texting me. I don't want to talk to you.**

The phone rang immediately. I still didn't answer.

**Syd? What's wrong? Did I do something to upset you? Stop or I'll block you.**

He didn't call or text again.

I put the kids to bed and then I did what I do best when I am mad. I cleaned. I took everything out of the closet, organized it, and put it back. I cleaned out the refrigerator, re-organized the pantry, sorted the spices in alphabetical order, and arranged the cups and glasses according to size. I cleaned glass, dusted wood, and cleaned the tops of the ceiling fan blades. I dumped all the books off my bookshelf and arranged them in order according to the author. With all the manic cleaning, I gave myself an asthma attack and used my inhaler. Then I finally ran out of steam.

I got a text from Leanne. **Is everything ok? Will texted me. He's worried because you're mad at him, and he has no idea what he did.**

I called her. "Will is an asshole and I am not speaking to him. Not now, not tomorrow, maybe not ever. We are so freaking done!"

"Sydney, what happened?"

"I'll tell you what happened. I caught him cheating on me. That's what happened."

"What? I can't believe this!"

"Well, believe it, because I saw it with my own eyes. I went to his house to surprise him with dinner, and I saw him coming out of his house with some blonde girl and hugging her on the porch. He told me he was going to be late coming over because he was going to be mowing his neighbor's yard! And just a few hours ago I asked him to move in with me! What kind of idiot am I anyway!" I was crying again. My face was raw from using toilet paper instead of a proper tissue.

"Wait. You asked him to move in with you?" Leanne asked, sounding shocked.

"Yes. I already know what you're going to say. Too early. I know."

"Okaaaaay," she said, and I could tell she agreed. "Well then, the good thing is he hadn't already moved in before you found out what a lying, cheating, asshole he is."

"The worst part of it is that I literally fell in love with him. Like so fast. I thought we had this connection. The kids love him. And the strangest thing is that *Pop* even loves him! I mean what the hell?"

Elsie and Micah don't deserve to suffer for my mistakes. I brought Will into their lives, they love him, he has been more of a father figure than they have ever had. Now, it looks like that isn't going to work out anymore either. Not only is everything bad that happens to me my own fault, but everything bad that happens to my kids is also my fault. I hate that, knowing I am responsible for something that will end up hurting them. I'm so stupid. How could I put my own kids in a situation where they will lose somebody who they were already so close to? I trusted him with them. I didn't think he was the type to cheat on me. You would think I'd have a sixth sense for that since I've already been through it before.

"Do you think maybe there is an explanation to this, and you misinterpreted what you saw? I mean, I just can't imagine Will cheating on you. He just doesn't seem the type to do that."

"Leanne, I saw Will and the girl come out of his house together. Then they stood on his porch, hugged, and she got an overnight bag out of her car and took it in! I'm not sure how I could be misunderstanding this."

"I'm sorry, Sydney."

"And he was obviously already planning on her coming over tonight because he told me at lunch that he was going to be late because he had to help his neighbor. What the flapjack!! He never even planned on helping his neighbor. He was going home to be with his cute little blonde girlfriend! What is it with me and cheaters?"

"Yea, that does sound suspicious."

"And to top it off, I offered to bring him and Mrs. Beasley dinner tonight and he told me not to come! He acted like he didn't want me to have to drive so far for just that, but now I know it was because he didn't want me to find out about him and his hot little girlfriend!" I was not even crying anymore. I was just pissed off.

"Will just texted me asking if I found out what you're mad about," Leanne said.

"Tell him yes, you found out he is an asshole."

"Ok. Texting him now. I'm saying 'yes, we found out you're an asshole.' Sent," she said.

"Perfect. Thanks, Leanne. I'll talk to you tomorrow."

"Ok, call me if you need anything. I'm sorry this happened to you. Again."

I think back to when I was told "everything bad that has ever happened to you has been your own fault." It's true this time. I wasn't careful. I rushed into things against my better judgement. I won't make that mistake again.

# Chapter 13

# Will

### The next day...

I'd been awake all night holding my phone, hoping to hear from Sydney or at least Leanne. No calls all night. The only text was from my sister, Lilly. She was excited because Beatrice, her Chinese Crested/ Pug mix, won the ugly dog contest that I signed her up for as a joke. I was surprised she actually showed up for the contest. Lilly even ordered matching T-shirts for both her and Beatrice. They had Beatrice's homely face on them that read "Vote for Beatrice."

Lilly had called at the last-minute last night and came over to bring me some clothes that didn't fit her anymore and she thought Sydney might be able to wear them since I'd told her she probably wore a small.

Everything was wonderful during lunch yesterday. Sydney asked me to move in with her. That caught me off guard for sure, I mean, I never dreamed Sydney would even be thinking of that right now, but I was all for it. I'd been excited and couldn't wait to start moving my things in, especially the bed.

I'd planned to take her to my house this weekend so we could start sorting through my things and deciding what we could use at her house. I wanted to clean first, though. I hadn't shown her my place yet because it was such a wreck. I'd spent all my time either at work or at Sydney's house and the mess was just piling up. I'd also wanted to take her next door to meet Mrs. Beasley. Sydney had been wanting to meet her, and I knew Mrs. Beasley would love her.

Then, everything changed drastically last night. Confused and hurt, I still didn't know what happened, but it had to be a horrible misunderstanding. It felt like I was in the middle of a bad dream. I hadn't spoken to her since lunch and somehow since then, Sydney had an abrupt change of heart. At lunch she loved me, by dinner time Sydney and Leanne both decided I was an asshole. I was afraid to make any more attempts to call or text either one because they threatened to block me if I tried again.

I'd driven out to Sydney's house last night after Leanne's text. I sat in her driveway trying to figure out what to do. Then I stood on her porch for what seemed an eternity. I'd started to knock several times but each time I stopped myself. I went back to the truck to find something to write on. I found a receipt and wrote a note on the back of it. *Please talk to me. I don't know what*

*I did wrong. I love you, Will.* I slipped the receipt under her front door and waited a few minutes hoping she would see the note and open the door. Finally, I just went back home for fear that showing up would make things worse. I just wanted to talk to her so badly and it was driving me crazy not knowing what was going on.

I drank an extra cup of coffee on the way to work, but I didn't feel like eating anything.

"You look like shit," Gerald said. Nice. I knew I should have just taken the day off.

"Thank you. You're too kind," I said.

"The work truck has a leaky front tire. We've got to take it in and get it fixed before we can get started," Gerald informed me.

We took the truck in and sat in the waiting area while they put on a new tire. I kept checking my phone, hoping Sydney would eventually text me.

"So, what's going on with you this morning? You look terrible and you've barely said a word so far," Gerald asked, looking at me.

"I'm fine. Just not feeling talkative today." The last person in the world that I wanted to talk to about this with was Gerald, especially after he already told me I should break up with her. I could almost hear the "I told you so's" coming.

"Fight with Sydney?" he asked. There was something almost sarcastic in his voice.

"No, we did not have a fight." This was true. There was no fight. Sydney decided I was a jerk somewhere between lunch and dinner.

Finally, the truck was ready. We drove it back and hooked the trailer up to it. The trailer was still loaded with the tree brush from the day before, so I was going to have to drive it to the city dump. Gerald took his own truck. I was glad he didn't ride with me because I didn't feel like talking to him.

On the way to the dump, I contemplated some strategies to talk to Sydney. Most of the time she took her lunch to work and ate at her desk. I could try calling her on the office phone during her lunch. I knew I was risking it, but I couldn't stand it. I had to know what was going on. If that didn't work, I would write a letter and mail it the old-fashioned way. I didn't know her email address. I had a feeling she would block me on social media if I tried to send her a message that way.

About ten minutes away from the dump, I was driving on the highway headed up the overpass when suddenly the steering wheel began to shake, and the truck started wobbling. I started to slow down, but the front right wheel came off, causing the truck to jerk hard to the right. I tried to regain control of the truck, but it was too late. I crashed right through the metal guardrail and came to an abrupt stop in just enough time to keep me from completely going off the side. The entire font end of the truck was hanging over the overpass. Fortunately for me and everyone underneath, the weight of the trailer was just enough to keep the truck from going over. I sat there, frozen, not sure what to do, and afraid that any movement could send the truck completely over.

"Shit." What do I do now? Looking out my windshield it was as if I was in the air with nothing underneath me.

Was this it? Was this how I was going to die? I wasn't dying without saying bye to Sydney. I tried to call her, no answer. I texted her telling her how much I loved her. **Sydney, I don't know what I did to make you suddenly hate me. I love you and I'll always love you. You are my reason for everything. You saved my life when I was so depressed it was a struggle to stay on this side of the ground. I've had an accident. If I don't make it, please know that I love you and I will never do anything to hurt you. Love, Will.** I always thought I would die of old age, a heart attack during the night. Never thought about it happening in my 20s before I'd had a chance to achieve anything and with so many unresolved issues that I'd never had a chance to take care of. Would dying feel like it was in slow motion where my short life flashed before my eyes all the way down? Or would it be just a matter of two seconds and I'd die instantly as my truck plummeted into the ground and the vehicles beneath me?

A couple of cars pulled over and stopped on the shoulder to assist, or more like watch. "We called 911!" one of them yelled at me. They damn sure better hurry. I didn't know how long the truck could stay there without going over, and I decided I wasn't willing to sit in it long enough to find out.

The adrenaline spiked and I set into action. If I was going to die, I was going to do it trying to save myself, not just sitting here waiting for it. I couldn't open my door because part of the guardrail was bent up against it, so I opened the window. When I looked down from the window, I realized that the front tire was hanging off the side and there wasn't enough ground for me to jump out onto. The only thing I could do was climb through the window and try to get to the truck bed. I could get on the ground from there.

As I started climbing through the window, a few elderly onlookers yelled at me to stop. "Stay where you are! You're gonna get yourself killed!" Well, I could also get myself killed staying where I am.

I just wanted to get out of there. The trailer was sticking too far into the highway and if anyone hit it, even just a little, it would send me right over. I climbed through the window and pulled myself into a standing position in the opening. I didn't have much to grab hold of, but I was able to climb on top of the truck and slide over to the bed. I was so focused on just getting off the truck that I jumped off the back of the bed instead of climbing over. I felt my left ankle roll when I hit the ground.

Two men scurried over to help me stand up, but I couldn't put any weight on my foot, there was sharp pain, and it seemed to already be swelling. I could hear the sirens coming and sat on the side of the street waiting for them.

I called Gerald. He wouldn't be far from here. "Hey, I just had a wreck on the overpass. The truck's hanging off. They must not have tightened the lug nuts when they put on the tire because the wheel came off. Also, I think my ankle might be broken."

"Aww well crap. Dammit, I'll be right there."

I kept checking my phone, hoping to get a response from Sydney, but there was nothing.

About half an hour later, I arrived at the hospital by ambulance. Gerald handled everything concerning the truck.

Having my shoe removed was excruciating, and the pain increased significantly after that. There was no way I was going to be able to work for a while. I hadn't had an X-ray yet, but my foot, ankle, and lower leg were swollen and purple. There was no way something wasn't broken.

Sure enough, about half an hour later, X-rays showed a broken fibula.

"You're going to need surgery. When the bone fragments are misaligned like yours are, we have to go in and realign them with screws and plates. I'd like to do this as soon as possible, but let's try to get some of this swelling down first," Dr. Ramos said while she entered notes on the computer.

"How long until I can work?" I didn't have sick time or any type of benefits at work to cover this type of thing. I only got paid for the time I worked.

"Judging by your uniform, I'm guessing you do manual labor. You need to plan on about six weeks out to be safe." Dammit, I couldn't afford to be out of work for six weeks.

I wanted to call Sydney again more than anything. If there was anyone that could make this situation even a little better, it was her. But instead, I called my mom.

"Don't panic, but I've had a wreck and I'm at the hospital. It's just a broken ank—"

She cut me off before I could say anything else. "I'm coming up there," she said, then yelled for my dad, "Leonard! William is in the hospital."

I could hear my dad in the background say, "What?!"

"No, Mom, it's fine. You don't need to come; it's just a broken ankle."

"William Steven Scott, I'm not going to have you sitting there all alone. Your father and I are on our way. Don't worry, everything is going to be ok."

"You don't need to come..." But she had already hung up. I already knew she was yelling at my dad telling him to hurry up as if I was at death's door.

About half an hour later, my parents made their grand entrance into the emergency room. I could hear them coming from all the way down the hallway before bursting into my room. Most people were quiet in a hospital, not my parents, and they had no filters either. Soon, everyone in the nearby rooms would know all our personal business.

"We brought things to keep you busy." My dad started unloading a paper bag and soon, there were games, cards, and wordsearch books piled up on my bed. My parents owned a vintage toy store called Back in Time.

"Thank you, but it isn't necessary. I'm fine watching TV and playing on my phone."

My mom started unloading her bag. "I brought my crochet. I've been working on Christmas presents." Every year, we all got something from the toy store, and something crocheted. Last year I ended up with a tabletop arcade game and a crocheted blanket in my old high school colors.

My ankle was throbbing. The nurse elevated it on some pillows and put an icepack on it. I wasn't sure yet when my surgery was going to be. I'd never had surgery or anesthesia before, and I was nervous. I'd heard stories of people waking up in the middle of surgery and feeling the whole thing but not being able to talk or move.

"William, is your girlfriend coming up? We'd love to meet her," my mom asked. I told her about Sydney a couple of weeks ago.

"No, she can't make it." I didn't want to get into the details right now. Fortunately, Dr. Ramos came in at just the right time.

"We can get you into surgery soon, we've got one ahead of you and then we should be able to get to you, I'd say probably in about two hours. Then, I'd like to keep you in the hospital overnight. If everything looks good tomorrow, you should be able to go home."

"I've heard about Dr. Ramos. She's done surgery on a few of our friends, and she is supposed to be one of the best. You'll do great," my dad said after the doctor left.

My mom was already on the phone, calling Lilly and my brother, Toby. Lilly said she was headed to the hospital. Toby lived in New Mexico but asked for them to keep him updated.

When my mom got off the phone, she said, "William, why don't you call Sydney and let her know your surgery is coming up soon. I'm sure she would come if she knew that."

There is no doubt Sydney would have been here the second she found out that I was hurt if she didn't hate me all the sudden.

I finally just told her, "I tried to call her from the truck, Mom, and I texted her. I don't know what happened, but she doesn't want to talk to me. I haven't talked to her since lunch yesterday. It must be a misunderstanding, but she won't talk to me, so I can't find out what I did."

"Do you want me to call her?" she asked. I had a feeling that having my mom call her wasn't going to solve any problems.

"No, I don't want her to feel pressured to see me just because I'm having surgery."

My mom looked at me a minute and said, "William, I know you better than anyone. You really do love this girl, don't you?"

I never talk much to my parents about my relationships, but I let it all out anyway. "I do, Mom. I love her. She's everything to me, and I thought she was the one that I'd be with forever. I've never felt this way about anyone in my life." I wiped a tear off my cheek.

"Then don't give up. Fight for her, get on the phone and call her again."

I picked up my phone and thought about what Mom said. I'd psyched myself into calling her when Dr. Ramos came in.

"We're ready for you a little sooner than we expected. Since you've got your parents here, let me go ahead and give all of you the post-op instructions, because I have a feeling that you're the kind of guy that tries to get up and do things way too soon." She looked at me sternly. "No weight bearing for 4 to 6 weeks until the bone heals. You'll need to elevate your leg for the first couple of weeks. Sutures will be removed in about two weeks. We'll set you up a follow-up appointment for X-rays in six weeks. Mom and Dad, make sure he behaves."

"Thank you, Dr. Ramos, we'll take him to our house for a while," my mom said. That's where she was wrong. I would absolutely not be going home with them, but I wasn't going to say so in front of the doctor. I could get around with crutches just fine in my own house.

Lilly showed up just as the transporter arrived to take me to surgery. "Good luck, break a leg!" she said and laughed, and they started walking toward the waiting room.

"Lilly! It's a little too early for broken leg jokes, don't you think?" I heard my mom tell her.

"We'll be waiting in the waiting room for you! Don't worry, you'll do great!" my dad called after me even though I was halfway down the hall.

As they pushed me into the elevator, I saw her coming around the corner.

"Sydney!" I called. We made eye contact just before the double doors closed behind me. She came! How did she know I was here?

# Chapter 14

## *Sydney*

I didn't sleep much last night. Before heading to bed, I heard Will's truck rumble into my driveway—he must have no idea just how loud that thing is. Peeking through the peephole, I watched as he stood on my porch, motionless. He didn't ring the bell or knock, just stood there. It took everything in me not to open the door and let him explain, but I'd been down this road before. I already knew exactly how it would end. There would be a "misunderstanding" and he'd say I didn't see what I thought I saw. He'd slipped a note under the door, too, but I just couldn't allow myself to give in when I'd heard it over and over from Jeff and I wasn't going to fall into that trap again. I went ahead and turned off notifications for his texts. He wasn't blocked, but I didn't want to see his texts coming through.

As unmotivated as I was to start my day, I'd managed to get everyone ready. Micah was in kindergarten, and ever since my wreck, I'd started letting him ride the bus instead of dropping him off at school. The bus stopped right in front of our house, which was perfect for all of us. It arrived on time, and after he got on, I dropped Elsie off at daycare on my way to work. The morning had gone surprisingly smoothly, with just one small battle: Elsie insisted on bringing her baby doll, but the daycare had a strict no-toys-from-home policy. Fights were guaranteed to break out at the daycare if somebody showed up with a toy.

Walking into the breakroom to fill my cup with ice water, I noticed a plate of banana bread and a container of orange juice were set out on the counter with a purple sticky note that read "Orange you glad there's banana bread?" It was obvious that my co-worker, Jamie, brought this.

The only other person that worked there was my supervisor, Mei. She wasn't known for bringing sweet surprises to us, or even being sweet at all for that matter. She also did not eat unhealthy carbs and often lectured Jamie and I on our carefree eating habits. To say Mei was physically fit was an understatement. She used to play college basketball. Now she is into tennis, running, biking, hot yoga, and mountain climbing. On top of that, she teaches a weight training class at the gym—a class Jamie and I had not signed up for.

After helping myself to a generous portion and thanking Jamie for breakfast, I went into my own office to eat instead of stopping in her office for our morning debrief. The first thirty minutes of our day were usually spent in each other's offices just wasting time, discussing whatever TV show we were watching, or complaining about Mei. After that, we were messaging each other on Teams off and on all day about topics that had nothing at all to do with work. If anyone was monitoring our Teams activity, we would probably lose our jobs.

A Teams notification popped up. **Are we not debriefing?** It was Jamie.

I went to her office, a bright and cheerful space that showcased her crafty side. She'd decoupaged office supplies, crocheted a purple ombré pen cup cover, sewn floral chair cushions, and even made a braided purple rug for the floor.

My office was nothing like Jamie's. Every time I tried adding color, it only stressed me out. I worked best with neutral tones. While some found my colorless decor boring, it was calming for me, and it helped me focus.

I was lucky to have a south facing window which was perfect for the fifteen plants I'd accumulated. Hoping to turn Jamie into a plant lover, I'd given her one of my plants for her desk, but she'd killed it almost immediately. Once, after overwatering, my plants developed a terrible gnat infestation, which extended into Mei and Jamie's offices. Mei said if one more gnat ended up in her coffee, she was banning plants altogether.

"OK, spill the beans. Something's off with you today," Jamie said, applying an adhesive nail polish strip to her thumb nail.

Not ready to dive into it, I went with the classic excuse, "I'm just tired. I didn't sleep much last night."

"Why not?" she asked, knowing there must be more to the story.

I exhaled deeply. "It was just an argument with Will," I lied. There hadn't exactly been an argument, but I didn't want to tell the truth because it was embarrassing that the first person that I dated since my cheating ex-husband turned out also to be a cheater.

My phone rang, it was a long-distance number. I'd been getting these a lot lately. They were bill collectors calling for Jeff. How could he make as much money as he does and still not pay his bills? I waited for the voicemail and sure enough, it was for him, so I blocked the number.

My phone rang again. This time it was Raymond, which was strange. He never called me during work hours unless it was urgent.

"Sorry to bother you at work, but your mother had a little accident with the welder and we're at the ER," he said, almost sounding like he knew this was going to happen.

My mother loved exploring different art mediums. Recently, she and her best friend, Diana, decided it would be fun to take up welding. They had welded just about everything they could get their hands on. Finally, my mom became good enough at it that she had been trying her hand at metal sculptures. She was working on a dolphin sculpture to display on the countertop in her guest bathroom.

"Oh no! How bad is it?" I asked, hoping it wasn't something that would require skin grafts.

"It's pretty ugly. She forgot to change into her welding shirt and the shirt she had on was flammable. Her left sleeve caught fire. We are waiting for the doctor to look at it."

"I'll be there in a minute." This was exactly the type of thing that Raymond and I had been afraid would happen when she decided to take up welding. My mom and I both loved a good project, but neither of us were great at the preparation work, including putting on appropriate clothing for the occasion. In this case, proper clothing was essential for safety, and Raymond and I knew that eventually something like this was bound to happen.

I told Mei and Jamie that I would be out the rest of the day and headed to the hospital. Although Mei was very strict as far as policies and procedures, she was generous when it came to taking time off work. She never gave us any grief when we wanted off. That was helpful during the time I had to take off after my wreck. She also was a firm believer in mental health days.

Hope Methodist Hospital was under a constant state of renovations. Due to the ongoing construction, parking was always an issue. I finally found a spot in the parking garage, which was as far from the emergency department as it could possibly be.

Finally, I spotted the arrow for the ER. As I turned the corner, I heard Will's voice call my name. I turned and saw him, just as the elevator doors closed. I stood there, confused, staring at the elevator trying to figure out what I just saw. Will was in a hospital bed, wearing a hospital gown. He seemed perfectly fine yesterday afternoon when I talked to him, and he also looked ok when I saw him enjoying his evening with the pretty blonde. As mad as I was at him, I didn't want anything to be wrong with him. But he was awake and alert, so hopefully, it was something minor. I found a nurse's station to get more information.

"Excuse me, can you tell me where William Scott is?" I asked the nurse.

"Are you family?" she asked.

"Yes, I'm his wife," I lied.

"And your name, ma'am?"

Crap. "Sydney," I said, realizing my lie wasn't going to work.

"Ma'am, his chart shows he is single and I'm not finding your name listed anywhere. I'm not able to give out any information at this time. I'm sorry."

"Thank you." I'd have to come up with a different strategy.

Still trying to put the pieces together on why Will was in the hospital, I found my mother's cubicle and walked in.

Kennedy was in rare form; it was her time to shine. Not only did she have her CPR and first aid manual, but she also had a clip board. It was serious when she had her clip board. She had a stern expression on her face and looked very official.

"The patient has a myocardial infarction with elevated white blood cells," Kennedy said to me. I tried not to smile at Kennedy's inaccurate diagnosis.

"Thank you for the information, Doctor Kennedy," I said to her.

"Sydney, you didn't need to come up here. I'm fine. I feel so stupid though, I was so excited to work on my project that I forgot to change into my welding shirt first," my mom said.

"Has the doctor been in?' I asked, I wanted to talk to the doctor myself because there was a ninety percent chance she wouldn't tell me the whole story.

"No, not yet. I'm sure it will be a while. Did you happen to see anywhere to get a drink when you came in?" she said, looking at me with puppy dog eyes. I was expecting that request at any moment. If there was one thing about my mom, it was that she wouldn't be caught without something to drink. That was something else we had in common.

I knew there had to be a vending machine somewhere, most likely in the waiting room. Fortunately, the waiting room not only had two vending machines, but there was also a coffee station. There were three people sitting in the waiting room. A woman crocheting, a man playing an obviously outdated handheld video game, and a young blonde lady chatting away on the phone.

Pouring my coffee, I listened to the lady talking about her loved one having surgery on his broken ankle. As I chose a diet soda and a granola bar for my mom, I heard her say, "Will's way too stubborn to listen to the doctor, I can stay at his house for a while to help him out."

She was talking about Will. This was the girl from the porch? I tried to process what was happening. In a matter of 24 hours, we had gone from planning for Will to move in, to me listening to his other girlfriend planning to stay with him after his ankle surgery. I felt a combination of hurt, regret, and rage build up inside me. Why didn't I figure this out before now? I should have been on high alert for something like this after what I went through with Jeff. I'd been so caught up in how Will seemed to be so different than Jeff, that I didn't see that he was still a lying cheater, just like him. My face felt hot, and I was sure it was bright red.

I'm not one for confrontation, but I couldn't hold back. As I walked to the door, I paused in front of her. "Will makes you think you're the best thing that's ever happened to him, doesn't he? He said that to me too. Yesterday," I said and rushed out of the waiting room, leaving the girl with a bewildered expression on her face.

"Wait!" she shouted after me, but I was already out of sight. Fortunately, the restrooms were just outside of the waiting room. I hurried in and sat in a stall trying to compose myself before going back to my mom's cubicle. The last thing I wanted to do was talk about this with my mom and Raymond, especially after I'd painted him out to be the most amazing man on Earth, which I truly did believe just yesterday.

After a few minutes and several deep cleansing breaths, I walked back to my mom's cubicle.

"Oh, thank you, dear!" she said as I handed her the drink and snack. Then she took another look at me and frowned. "Are you ok? You look mad," she said.

"I'm fine, just had something on my mind. Nothing big," I said and busied myself with finding something on TV.

"Wow, thanks for the drink and snack," Kennedy said sarcastically because I didn't get her anything. I pulled a couple of dollars out of my purse and handed them to her. "Here, go get something."

The doctor came in to assess her arm. It was a second-degree burn, nothing too severe. He applied ointment, dressed it, and gave instructions for taking care of it at home.

It was still early in the day, and I thought about going back to work; however, I did tell them that I'd be out all day, and I certainly didn't see myself getting any work done anyway.

Stress eating was my coping mechanism. I stopped at The Crunchy Chicken for my chicken sandwich meal but added a banana milkshake and two cookies. This was no time to be concerned with healthy eating.

Once I got home with my emotional support food, I ate it on the couch, still wondering about Will, how he broke his ankle, and how or when the blonde girl came into the picture. Something about this wasn't making sense.

With Jeff, I wasn't surprised when he had an affair. Jeff was already an asshole even without cheating on me. I got myself into that mess with Jeff because I never should have continued a relationship with a man that wasn't good to me. However, it was different with Will. Will had only been good to me. Even though we hadn't been together long, I thought it was both of our understanding that we were exclusively together, not dating anyone else, especially with the plan for him to move in. I never would have imagined that he wasn't being truthful to me, which is why this whole thing with the girl completely caught me off guard.

The phone surprised me when it rang. I didn't recognize the number on the caller ID.

"Sydney? My name is Lilly Scott. I'm Will's sister."

Confused as to why Will's sister was calling me, I could only say, "Hi."

"I'm sorry, I know this is weird. I got your number off Will's phone. Can you believe he still uses his school lunch number for his password?"

"Is there something wrong?" I asked her.

"Actually, yes. I think there has been a huge misunderstanding, and I think I can fix it. Will told our mom that you were angry with him, and he doesn't know why. He's just crushed and confused," she said.

"Yes, I am, but I'm not sure how you can fix it." Was he sending his sister in as his reinforcement?

"I was the girl in the waiting room," she said.

I felt the blood rush to my head and felt suddenly dizzy. "What? You are the lady with blonde hair that I talked to?" I couldn't believe this. It was starting to make sense.

"Yes, I was in the waiting room with my parents. When you heard me on the phone, I was talking to our brother, Toby, updating him on Will. I don't mean to sound rude, but I'm a little perplexed because you seemed to think maybe I was a girlfriend or something?"

I was the most terrible girlfriend ever if this was all adding up the way it looked. "Did you happen to be at Will's house last night?"

"Yea, I dropped by to give him a bag of clothes that I thought you might be able to wear. I cleaned out my closet and had some things that didn't fit me anymore. I need to lay off the ice cream."

I'd never felt so much remorse for anything in all my life. I treated Will like crap, and I even got Leanne to do it too. He must be so hurt and confused. I'd do anything to take back the last 24 hours.

"I don't know what to say. I tried to surprise him by bringing him dinner last night. When I drove up, I saw you there hugging him. Then I saw you with a bag going back into his house with what I thought was an overnight bag. When I asked him if I could bring him dinner, he told me not to come because it was too far out of the way. So, when I saw you, I thought he just didn't want me to come because he didn't want me to know he was going to have a girl there."

"Oh my gosh. I'm so sorry. I can see how you would have thought that."

"Then when I saw you in the waiting room and you were talking about staying at Will's house, it just confirmed the whole thing to me. I'm so sorry. I had it all wrong and I'm so ashamed! I was terrible to Will, and he didn't do anything wrong. I have to fix this."

"I tried to follow you out of the waiting room to explain, but I couldn't find you. Will is in surgery right now. I think it would be great if you were here when he woke up."

"I heard you say he had surgery on his ankle. What happened?"

"His wheel came off his work truck and he ended up crashing through the guardrail on the overpass by the dump. The truck was hanging off, but fortunately the trailer was heavy enough to keep it from going any further. He had to climb out his window and crawl to the bed. When he jumped out of the bed, he broke his ankle."

This kept getting worse. He went through all that after I was so hateful to him. I thought of him standing on my porch last night. I looked at him through the peep hole and let him just stand there. He didn't deserve anything that happened to him, and now he is having surgery, still not knowing.

"I was at the hospital because my mom was hurt, I saw him when I came in. He was in the elevator. I heard him call my name, but the doors closed before he could say anything else. I can't believe this. I'm so sorry. I apologize for everything. I jumped to conclusions, and I should have just asked him, but I didn't. He probably hates me."

And again, this was completely my fault. Will had nothing to do with this at all, he was only the victim of me jumping to the wrong conclusion without giving him a chance to set me straight.

"I understand, I'd probably have thought the same thing if it had been me. Can you come up to the hospital?"

"I'm on my way right now. I'll be there in 20 minutes," I said, already in my car. As soon as I hung up with Lilly, I called Mimi.

When I picked up my phone to call her, I noticed a missed call from Will. I didn't even notice he had called with all the commotion of the day. I looked at the texts, sure enough, there was a text from Will. I didn't hear the ding since I'd turned off his notifications.

The time stamp was 9:57 AM this morning. **Sydney, I don't know what I did to make you suddenly hate me. I love you and I'll always love you. You are my reason for everything. You saved my life when I was so depressed it was a struggle to stay on this side of the ground. I've had an accident. If I don't make it, please know that I love you and I will never do anything to hurt you. Love, Will.** I was horrible and I wouldn't blame him if he never forgave me for the way I treated him.

I called Mimi. "Hi, Mimi. Will has been in an accident, and he is having surgery on his broken ankle. I am going to the hospital, but I'm not sure if I'll make it back before the bus gets here with Micah. Do you think you could go to my house and wait for him at 4:00 if I'm not back?"

"Poor Will! Of course I will! Stay as long as you need. I'll pick up little Elsie at daycare too if you aren't back by then. I'll plan on them eating with us."

"Thank you so much, Mimi!" I don't know what I would do without Mimi and Pop. They were lifesavers sometimes.

I found Lilly in the waiting room, along with the two other people that I now knew were Will's parents.

"Hi, Sydney, it's nice to properly meet you in person. These are my parents, Barbara and Leonard," she said, gesturing toward the couple.

"Sydney, it's so nice to meet you!  William has told us all about you," Will's mom said to me.

Will's dad gave me an unexpected hug and said, "I'm so glad Lilly was able to help clear up the little mishap."  He looked just like Will, just an older version and a little taller.

"I'm so sorry.  I'm embarrassed that it turned into this.  It's not the best first impression that you are getting of me."  I was truly embarrassed and ashamed of myself.  It was a terrible feeling hurting Will this way and his whole family there to find out about it.

"Don't worry about us.  It will be ok.  Will should be out of surgery soon and he'll be so happy that you are here.  He was about to call you when they came to get him for surgery," Barbara said.

Dr. Ramos came into the waiting room.

"Doctor, did everything go ok?"  Barbara asked, rushing over to her.

"We were able to repair the ankle with no issues; however, Will had trouble coming out of anesthesia and had to be re-intubated.  He is stable now, and we will be taking him to ICU when he is out of recovery.  We'll let you know when you can see him."

# Chapter 15

## *Will*

### Two hours later...

I heard voices and struggled to open my eyes. Then I realized I was suffocating. Something was in my throat, and I couldn't breathe. I tried to pull it out, but my arms were tied down. Panicked, I tried to break free of whatever was holding my arms down.

"It's OK, Will." It was Sydney. She had her hand on my arm trying to comfort me, but her face looked worried. I wasn't ok, I couldn't breathe, but I couldn't tell anyone because I couldn't talk with that tube down my throat.

I'd never had so much anxiety in all my life. It was more than I could handle. I wanted to yell and tell them to get this thing out of me before I died, but I couldn't speak. All I could do was try to tell them with my eyes that I needed help.

"Ok, let's extubate him," I heard somebody say. Sydney stepped aside, out of the way.

"Will, I'm going to sit your bed up a little and we are going to get this out, OK? I know this is uncomfortable, but you are ok, and I just need you to hold still a second," the doctor said to me, trying to sound reassuring.

I tried to relax, but it wasn't possible to relax with something stuck down my throat. It was like trying to breathe through a coffee stir stick, and I didn't think I could go a few more seconds that way.

"Ok, Will. Take a deep breath and then cough." I did as I was instructed, and finally the tube came out and was replaced with an oxygen mask. They also took the restraints off my wrists.

"Why did I have that?" I tried to ask, but my throat hurt, and my voice sounded hoarse. I'd never had surgery before, but I didn't think something like this should be happening with just ankle surgery. My fear all along had been waking up during surgery, but I decided this had been just as terrifying.

"You had a complication with the anesthesia during recovery and had to be re-intubated, but you are going to be just fine now. You put up quite a fight, so they had to use the restraints. Also, your ankle surgery went well, and you should expect a full recovery from that," the nurse said as she took my vitals. It was an extremely good thing that I didn't have any memory of being intubated.

"How's your ankle pain?" the nurse asked.

I'd forgotten about my ankle until now and realized it was throbbing. "It hurts."

Sydney was there. After all the commotion and anxiety had calmed down a little, it sunk in that she was there, and she didn't look angry. She was worried about me. I could see it in her face. Even with everything else that was going on, there was nothing that compared to the relief and joy that I felt seeing Sydney standing next to me.

After I was given pain meds and deemed stable, I was finally left alone in the room with her. As happy as I was that she was there, I was also still particularly confused about how she knew I was there and if something had changed about how she felt about me last night.

"Oh, Will, I'm so glad you're OK. You scared us!" she said, standing next to me with her hand on my shoulder.

I started to talk, but my throat was hurting and dry. I took a sip of ice water. "How did you know I was here? I saw you from the elevator," I said to her. I'd been surprised when I saw her coming around the corner but confused about how she found out about me. Then the elevator had closed before I could say more than her name.

"Will," she said and then paused a moment. "When you saw me, I didn't know you were here. I was here to see my mom. She had a welding accident."

"Oh," I said, disappointed and embarrassed. "I hope your mom's ok."

"She's ok. Your sister called me and let me know about your accident. She got my number from your phone. I'm so glad you're ok. It's truly a miracle. You could have gone completely over the overpass," she said, a tear rolling down her face.

"Sydney, what happened?" I asked her. I absolutely had no idea what was happening.

"You had a wreck and then you had a reaction to the anesthesia during surgery."

"No, I mean what happened with us? I don't know what I did. Why were you so mad at me?" I needed an explanation. One minute she was asking me to move in, a few hours later she thinks I'm an asshole and won't speak to me. Then I wake up with a tube down my throat and Sydney sitting next to me as if nothing ever happened. None of this was making any sense to me at all.

"Will," she started. "You didn't do anything."

I looked at her confused. "Well, I must have done something. People don't freak out like that for no reason."

"It was me. I got it all wrong. I'm so sorry," she said, her blue eyes had turned turquoise which I'd noticed they always did when she was upset.

"What did you get wrong?" I asked her, needing the whole story. The pain meds were starting to kick in, and I was feeling groggy, but I needed to hear this now.

"Last night I went to your house to surprise you and Mrs. Beasley with dinner. And I saw you hugging Lilly on your porch. Only, I didn't know it was Lilly," she said.

"Who did you think it was?" I asked her, starting to understand.

"I'm sorry, Will. I misunderstood. I'd never met Lilly, I didn't know," she said, tears streaming down her face.

I took the oxygen mask off my face. "Oh, Sydney. You thought I was cheating on you." It was all making sense now.

"I didn't know she was your sister, I thought..."

I didn't let her finish. "It's ok. You've never met my sister; you didn't know it was her." Now it all made sense. She thought she saw something that she definitely did not see, but how was she supposed to know?

"Are you sure?" she asked, looking hopeful.

"I promise. I'm just glad we got it figured out. I'm sorry you were upset though, especially after what you have already been through with cheating." I could barely stay awake, but I wanted to keep talking to her.

"You do not have one single thing to apologize for. It isn't your fault I was upset. It was my fault entirely. I am truly sorry," she said, wiping her eyes with a tissue. "You've been through so much the last two days and half of that was because of my stupidity. You are such a good person, and I never should have jumped to such a ridiculous conclusion. You didn't deserve that, Will. Please, I hope you know that."

"Yes, I do. Really, it's ok." I said, taking her hand. I actually did understand. I could see what it looked like and why she would think that.

She wiped her face and looked at me for a moment. "I just hated seeing you with that tube. I can't imagine how scary that must have been for you."

"I would rather wake up in the middle of open-heart surgery than ever wake up intubated again," I said and put the oxygen mask back on, feeling so much better knowing that Sydney was there, we'd resolved the misunderstanding, and now I could allow myself to fall into the medication induced slumber knowing that everything was going to be ok.

I woke up to the sound of my parents talking to each other, loud enough that the people in the next room could surely hear them. My ankle was still throbbing.

"I thought she seemed like a nice girl. King me," my dad was saying. They were playing checkers?

"I know. She does seem nice, but she has two little kids and she's been *divorced*! I'm sure there is a lot going on between the ex-husband, the kids, you know how complicated everything might be. I wouldn't want William getting in over his head. You know how he is, Leonard. He's too young for all that."

They must have been concentrating on the game because there was silence for a few minutes followed by the sound of the checkers clicking loudly on the game board.

"King me, again," my dad said. "Barbara, William is a 26-year-old grown man, he's not a child. He is going to make his own choices no matter what we think he needs to do."

I rolled over and looked at them. "You know I can hear you, right?" They didn't seem to understand how loud they talk, even when people are trying to sleep. Not to mention, I didn't want to hear their thoughts on my relationship with Sydney.

"William, did we wake you?" my mom asked. "How are you feeling, dear? Do you need anything?"

"I'm ok, other than my ankle hurts." I wondered when it would be time for my next pain pill. I didn't like taking medication for anything, I usually just toughed it out, but this pain wasn't something I could handle on my own.

"Here's some things to keep your mind off that," my mom said, pointing to the games and activity books they had unpacked and set out on the tray next to my bed. The last thing I could imagine myself doing was playing checkers or doing a crossword puzzle on 80s sitcoms.

There was a knock on my door and Lilly stuck her head inside. "The sign says two visitors at a time, but I need to get back to work in a minute. I've still got three cakes left that are due tomorrow." Lilly owned a bakery that specialized in custom cakes. She was always busy this time of year as it was one of the busier wedding seasons.

"Your mother and I are leaving. Let us know if you need anything," my dad said, putting the checkers back in the box while my mom gathered her crochet.

"You make sure you call us if you need anything, William," my mom said sternly as they walked out the door.

"Hey, I thought you might need a break from them," Lilly said, sitting down in the chair next to the bed.

"Thanks, I did." Her timing was perfect.

We heard a knock on the door as Dr. Ramos walked in. "How's the ankle feeling?" she asked.

"Painful."

"Well, that's to be expected for a while. But the good news is that we got everything repaired as well as we could have hoped. Give it about six weeks and you'll be good as new. I'm going to move you to a regular room and keep an eye on you overnight, but you should be fine to go home tomorrow morning."

"Thank you, Doctor." I couldn't wait to get out of here. My first experience with surgery did not turn out the way I thought it would.

After the doctor left, Lilly looked at me seriously and said, "I hope you don't mind that I called Sydney. I got her number out of your phone."

"I'm glad you called her. She told me you cleared up the little misunderstanding we had." If Lilly hadn't called her, we could still be in the same mess we were in last night. The fact that things turned out the way they did was undoubtedly nothing short of a miracle.

Lilly laughed. "Yea, it was kind of awkward for a bit, but it's all good now. She's kind of a firecracker, isn't she? But I like that about her. She had to go home, but she said to tell you she would check on you later. And she showed me some videos of her kids. They are so cute! She said you are so good with them."

"They are great kids. I can't wait for you to meet them. I heard Mom talking and she seems to think I am not ready for a relationship with somebody that has kids," I said, rolling my eyes.

"Geez, of course she would say that. And how did you even get her to go out with you anyway? She's kind of out of your league," she said laughing.

I rolled my eyes. "I told her I was rich," I said and laughed. "But really, I have no idea. I guess I'm just lucky."

I heard my phone ding. It was Kip sending me a picture of Mark with a cowboy hat on his head. **Get well soon from me and Mark.**

**Thank you, I'll try.**

He texted again: **Learn how to drive, you nearly got yourself killed.**

I replied: **Dumb ass, lol.**

"I texted Kip to let him know about your wreck and surgery," Lilly said, looking at the picture of Mark.

"So, Lilly, don't tell Mom and Dad, but I'm moving in with Sydney. They would freak out if they knew, but it just feels right."

"Uh, I'm not saying a word to Mom and Dad. You haven't told them about all the crap I've done that they wouldn't approve of." She laughed.

"I think I'll bring Sydney and the kids over to Mom and Dad's for dinner or something when my ankle gets better. They won't be able to resist the kids. That could be my plan to weasel Sydney into their good graces." I laughed. But it was true, how could they not get attached to those kids?

"Will, I've spent the afternoon with Sydney and what I learned about her is she loves you. I mean, *loves* you. I'm glad you found her," she said, then got up and picked up her purse. "I've got to get to work. When you get discharged, I'll give you a ride home."

A hospital worker walked in and put a bag on my tray. "Surprise food delivery for you."

Inside was a chicken fried steak dinner and a piece of cheesecake. There was a sticky note on the top that read, "*Love, Sydney.*"

I texted her: **Thanks for dinner! It looks amazing!**

She replied: You're **welcome! I hope it's better than the hospital food you would have had to eat!**

I ate my dinner and before I fell asleep, I heard my phone ding one more time. It was Sydney again: **Good night, sleep tight, and don't let the bed bugs bite!**

# Chapter 16

## *Sydney*

### About a week later...

"As you can see, I like to surround myself with nice things," Will said, as we stood looking at his living room. He leaned his crutches against the couch and sat down.

I laughed. "I can see that! I'm impressed with the decorating skills. You have an incredibly eclectic vibe going on here."

It was obvious that home décor was at the very bottom of Will's priority list, not that I was judging. The color scheme could only be described as brown. The outside of the house was brown. The walls were brown paneling. Carpet-brown. A large wire spool, also brown, served as his coffee table. The dark brown couch was very worn and clearly older than we were. An aquarium, with brown water, was placed right on the kitchen bar. Odd place for an aquarium, but to each his own, as they say. It had about a fourth of the water left in it, but somehow live fish were still swimming in it.

Secretly, I hoped he wasn't terribly attached to most of these items, although I wouldn't mind upgrading the aquarium and giving the fish a life that they thought they'd never have.

Micah stood at the counter looking up at the fish, obviously concerned about their well-being. The glass was too dirty to see clearly. Elsie stood in a chair peering into it. "Mommy, the fish are hungry." I'm sure she was right. I dropped a pinch of fish food into the top for them, which they devoured immediately.

"Elsie and Micah, why don't you sit on the couch with Will while I gather up some things for him, OK?" Will wasn't going to be much help on crutches. He found some cartoons for the kids to watch, and Elsie climbed into his lap.

Will started to pull himself up. "I can help; it is my stuff after all."

"How are you going to do anything with your ankle? Just watch the kids, I'm fine. And we can come back to get the heavy stuff when Kip can help."

Will sighed and sat back down. I knew he hated just sitting there and not being able to get his own things loaded up.

"Mom, can we take the fish home too?" Micah asked.

Will looked at me and said, "It's ok. We don't have to take them. I haven't been the best fish dad."

"Yes, we are taking the fish home. It will be like on TV where we flip their house and they'll be so happy. We just need to wait for

Kip to help take it over there. But I'll add some water, that will make them happier for now."

Will's bedroom wasn't what I expected either. There was a king-sized bed with black and red bedding, at least the bedding wasn't brown too. Nothing at all on the walls, no lamp, no décor. The light switch didn't even have a cover on it. The only other furniture was a dresser that had some hats piled up on it. It seemed sad to me that this is where Will slept. It didn't give off a happy or peaceful feeling. If I had been over here before now, I could have helped him cheer the place up, make it more cozy for him, add some plants.

I bagged up all his toiletries and got the clothes out of his closet and drawers. Kip said he would help me get the bed and dresser sometime this week since Will wouldn't be able to do anything for a while.

"I should have some food in the kitchen that we can take." Opening the cabinets, I found that his grocery supply consisted of about 20 boxes of macaroni and cheese, a case of ramen noodles, and almost nothing else.

"Well, I mean, we'll be set on ramen and mac and cheese for a year." I laughed.

Seeing Will's house, it was easy to see that this was only the place where Will lived, but this was not something that he considered a real home. It wasn't a place that he took pride in or felt at peace in. I could imagine him sitting in this dark, lonely, undecorated, brown house and just feeling sad.

"How long have you lived here?" I asked him.

"Probably about three years. I don't spend much time here because I'm always at one job or the other. By the time I get home from DJ'ing, I only have a few hours of sleep before having to get to work at my regular job. At least I don't DJ every night." It was hard to believe that he could have been here for three years and had done absolutely nothing with it, nothing that made the house look like him. He hadn't ever made it into a home, and it made me sad for him because this house felt terribly depressing. I almost felt like I was rescuing him from this.

"Ok, only one thing left to do," I said. "I need to meet Mrs. Beasley."

"Ok, she's been excited to meet you and the kids." Will got his crutches and pulled himself up.

Mrs. Beasley's house was right next door to Will's. Her flowerbed was full of lilies, irises, and zinnias. I had a feeling she must have grown them all in her greenhouse. Her small yard was neatly mowed, and she had colorful flowerpots spaced perfectly on her porch, under a butterfly windchime. I just knew Will had helped her with all of this and I felt a little guilty taking him away from her. He would still take care of things for her, but she wouldn't have the same level of companionship that she had with him being right next door anymore.

Will knocked and opened the door. "Mrs. Beasley, it's me!" he called into the house. She came into the living room from the kitchen, pushing a walker. She was as cute as she could be. I was only 5 feet two inches, and I towered over her petite little body. Her short white hair was permed in tight curls, and she had dangly earrings in the shape of lady bugs that coordinated with her red leisure suit. I noticed she had an alert button hanging around her neck.

"Oh, my word! I'm so glad you all came to see me!" She walked over to Will, and he leaned down to give her a hug.

"Mrs. Beasley, this is Sydney, Micah, and Elsie," Will introduced us.

"I'm glad to finally meet you. Will has said so much about you!" I said, as she gave me a hug. She smelled like a mixture of rose scented perfume and soap.

"Well now aren't you just the most precious children? You look just like your mama," she said, looking down at the kids.

"I'm going to be free on my birfday," Elsie said to her. Mrs. Beasley smiled at this news.

"Now, Will, you go sit down and get off that ankle. Sydney, can you help me bring some cookies and tea in?" Mrs. Beasley asked me and started off to the kitchen.

"Kids, why don't you go sit down with Will." Mrs. Beasley had so many little trinkets sitting around, I didn't want the kids to touch something and break it.

Mrs. Beasley's kitchen was decorated with lady bugs, butterflies, and frogs. There was a sign on the wall over the back door that said Ethel's Kitchen. The vase of fresh purple flowers in the middle of the kitchen table gave off an organic floral scent. As adorable as her kitchen was, the most perfect thing I saw was a photo on her refrigerator. There was a magnet stuck on every corner of the photo. Clearly, she didn't want this photo to fall off. It was a picture of Will standing next to her in her yard. Will was towering over her with his arm around her shoulder. They were both beaming and looked so happy together that it made my eyes water.

"That picture was taken last year on my birthday. Will's like a grandson to me. He's a special one. You're a lucky girl," she said, putting a plate of cookies on the seat of her walker.

"Yes, I know. I knew it the first time I saw him. He's a keeper for sure," I said to her, still looking at the picture.

I carried the glasses of tea into the living room and Mrs. Beasley set the plate of cookies on the coffee table. The cookies reminded me of the tea cakes my grandmother used to make. The kids devoured theirs quickly.

In front of the window stood a tall birdcage that housed a grey cockatiel in it. It started whistling and Micah and Elsie went over to look at it.

"That's Karen. I've had her for fifteen years. She keeps me company," she said. I chuckled at the bird's name.

Next to the couch was a tall, round curio cabinet. Inside there were delicate angel figurines and a collection of piano shaped music boxes. While we visited, Mrs. Beasley told me she played the piano at church for most of her life until she finally retired from it about five years ago.

Will looked at me and hesitated before saying anything, then cleared his throat. "Mrs. Beasley, I need to tell you something. I'm going to be moving in with Sydney and the kids. I'm not here much anyway, so it won't be much different. But don't worry, I'm still going to take care of things for you, and I want you to still call me anytime you need anything." He looked at her, worried about how she was going to take the news.

"Will, now don't you worry about me, I'll be fine. I kind of thought you were going to say that. I've noticed you haven't been home much. You don't need to be paying rent if you aren't even there," she said, reassuringly. Mrs. Beasley was so awesome.

"Make sure you do not hesitate to call me. Anytime. And I'll still come to help with the greenhouse and your yard, just like I always do. None of that is going to change," he said to her. I knew he was good to Mrs. Beasley but seeing him with her made him even more attractive to me. Men who took care of their elderly neighbors were the best kind.

Mrs. Beasley gave the kids cookies to take home with them and we promised to come back to check on her soon.

"My parents invited us over for dinner this weekend," Will said on the way back home. "I think my mom's making meatloaf."

"That sounds good. Is it ok to bring the kids?" I asked.

"Of course it is! We are a package deal. But my parents love kids. I still think we shouldn't tell them that I moved in with you, though. They are incredibly old fashioned, and I'd certainly rather not hear the lecture on how we are living in sin." He laughed. I understood that because my family was the same way. The only ones I told about it were Leanne and Ashley and neither of them judged me on it.

When we got home, I unloaded Will's things and took them into the house. Will went into the kitchen and started dinner; he could stand at the stove on his crutches. It was a no-brainer that mac and cheese would be involved. He already knew about the bean requirement and put a small pan on the stove for Elsie's mandatory side dish and decided on sausage with barbecue sauce to go with it. He couldn't wait to be off his crutches so he could make pulled pork for us. Apparently, he was incredibly proud of his secret recipe. He loved to grill but hadn't done it in a while.

"Alexa, play 80s rock music," he said as he cooked. He had made our home so much more fun since he had been there.

There were two closets in my bedroom. One had been Jeff's. Will's clothes filled that closet now. His shoes and boots neatly lined up on the floor under the clothes. The empty side of the bathroom was now filled with Will's things. The clothes from his drawers would have to stay in bags for now until Kip could help with the dresser. Looking around the closet and bathroom and seeing Will's things there made me happy. They looked like they belonged there, like they should have been there all along.

From the kitchen, Will was singing as he cooked dinner. I loved it when he sang. Somehow, he managed to get Micah to set the table. Elsie was sitting at the table with a coloring book, her squeaky little voice singing along. This was what perfection looked like.

# <u>Chapter 17</u>

## *Will*

### The next weekend...

"I'm nervous about dinner tonight," Sydney said, getting the pie out of the oven. She insisted on taking something even though my mom said it wasn't necessary.

"There's nothing to be nervous about. It's going to be fine," I tried to reassure her.

"What if they don't like my pie? It's the only pie I know how to make." She made a lemon cheesecake pie with cherries on top. It looked delicious.

"I'm sure they will love the pie. Stop worrying so much," I said and laughed. She had herself so worked up over this. "Don't forget that I met your whole family on Easter, and I lived to tell about it."

"I know, I know," she said, sighing loudly.

Sydney gave the kids a final inspection and looked at herself again in the mirror. "We can take my car," she said, grabbing her keys and her pie.

Panicked at the thought of Sydney driving me again, I said, "No, no. We can take my truck," I said to her, grabbing my own keys. It had been a couple of weeks since my surgery and although I was still on crutches, I was driving again. I didn't need my left leg to drive, anyway. If the truth were ever told, Sydney's driving was truly terrifying. She was a nervous driver, didn't drive on the interstate, and didn't turn left on most streets. Some of the scariest driving I'd ever witnessed was when she drove me around after my surgery. I'm not usually an anxious person, but I truly felt a panic attack coming on the last time she drove. I was relieved to be able to get back behind the wheel again and drive us myself.

When we arrived at my parents' house, we walked in and found them both in the kitchen.

"Smells good!" I said as they both turned around.

"You're here!" my mom said, wiping her hands on her apron.

"Mom and Dad, you remember Sydney. And this is Micah and Elsie!" I said, as the kids both stared up at my parents. Sydney had chosen a green floral sundress and matching green hair bow for Elsie to wear. Micah wore navy shorts and a green and navy plaid shirt.

My dad got down on his knee, smiled at them, and said, "Well hello, Micah and Elsie! How old are you?"

Elsie spoke up first. "I'm gonna be free on my birfday," she said proudly.

"Wow! What about you, Micah?"

"I'm five," Micah said in almost a whisper.

"I made a pie for dessert," Sydney said, setting it on the kitchen counter.

"Oh, that looks delicious!" my mom said to her.

"Is there anything I can do to help?" Sydney asked, looking nervously around the kitchen. Sydney never liked having to help in the kitchen because she said she had no idea what to do in there, especially in somebody else's kitchen.

"No, I'm just waiting on the meatloaf, and we'll be ready," my mom said, and I knew that was exactly what Sydney hoped to hear.

I didn't know Lilly was coming, but I heard her voice coming down the hall. She showed up carrying an unfortunate-looking Beatrice. Beatrice was sporting a pink ballerina dress which matched her pink rhinestone collar. Her tongue, as usual, was hanging out about an inch from the side of her mouth. That dog just gave me the creeps. Lilly even let it sleep with her. I wouldn't be able to sleep knowing that hideous thing was even in my house, much less sleeping in my bed with me.

Even more disturbing than Beatrice joining us for dinner, my mother's older sister, Aunt Harriet followed behind. I couldn't believe Lilly didn't warn me that she was bringing Harriet, or I would have properly prepared Sydney. Our aunt wasn't overly pleasant with anyone and could best be described as grumpy. Once for Christmas, she wrapped an IOU as my gift because I'd forgotten that she lent me $75 two months before and never repaid it.

Once the remaining introductions were completed, Lilly put Beatrice outside and we all sat down at the table.

"There's meatloaf, corn casserole, and salad. I hope everyone's hungry!" my mom said, passing a plate of rolls around.

"I don't want any of that corn crap," Harriet said. Lilly and I exchanged a look and tried not to laugh. Sydney tried to act like she hadn't noticed anything at all.

"The *casserole* is very good, Harriet," my dad said, scooping some out of the dish for himself. He was one of the nicest people I knew, but even he could have a hard time being nice to his sister-in-law sometimes.

"Mommy, she said crap," Elsie said, looking at Sydney with big eyes.

"Here, Elsie, try your roll," Sydney said, putting some butter on it for her, attempting to distract her from the "corn crap" discussion.

Lilly changed the subject quickly. "So, Will, I have a question for you. Have you thought about getting a dog anytime soon?" She looked at us. Lilly knew we were living together but directed her question at me so that nobody else knew we were living such a dishonorable lifestyle.

Sydney and I looked at each other. I knew Sydney had been wanting a dog. She talked about it a few times lately. I'd wanted a large dog that could protect Sydney and the kids if I wasn't home. Sydney, however, had been wanting something smaller like a dachshund or a pug. I had a feeling she would be the type to dress it up, just like Lilly does with Beatrice. I could already see it now; I'd be the guy at the park with the chihuahua in a pink dress.

"Are you getting rid of Beatrice?" Sydney asked.

"Oh heavens no. I'd never dream of giving away that little gem," she said, looking at Beatrice who was standing at the sliding glass door, hoping to be let in. "However, I do have a friend that has a dog who is a fellow member of the Ugly Dog Community. He has been having some health issues that are preventing him from being able to give his dog the attention he needs.

This excited Sydney, she had a weakness for ugly dogs. "Oh! What breed is it? Do you have a picture?" The way she looked at me told me we were about to be the owners of an ugly dog.

"He is a two-year-old Chinese Crested mix. We aren't sure what he is mixed with, but we think maybe Yorkie. His name is Meatball Face." She got out her phone and started scrolling through photos.

"Here he is! Isn't he adorable!" Sydney looked at the phone and the "oooohs and aaaahhhs" started.

Of course, a Chinese Crested mix. If it looked anything at all like Lilly's dog, I was going to have nightmares about it.

"Will, just look at him! Have you ever seen anything so pitiful but still so cute at the same time?!" She showed me the picture. This thing was ghastly. It looked like it had mange or something. He was grey and brown and had long hair in some places and almost bald in others. The longer hair stuck out every which way and looked coarse. I'm not sure how Sydney and I were looking at the same picture considering our drastic differences in opinion over the appearance of this four-legged creature.

"I can honestly say I have never seen anything quite like it," was the only response I could come up with. Lilly showed Elsie and Micah the picture, too. They both laughed at him.

"Meatball Face is used to children, and he gets along with everyone, including other animals and even cats. I told Dwayne I would help him find a good owner. I wanted to ask you first. If you want, you could always let him stay with you for a few days and see if he will work out."

Sydney looked at me with huge eyes. "What do you think? You've been wanting a dog." We couldn't say much without hinting that we lived together, but I knew the wheels were spinning in Sydney's head. The kids would love to have a dog, and the yard was more than large enough for him to get plenty of exercise. I already knew we were going to be Meatball Face's new parents.

"What do you think, kids? Do you like Meatball Face?" I looked at the kids.

"Yes!!" they both exclaimed in unison.

After Lilly's phone was passed around the table, my aunt and both my parents shared my opinion of Meatball Face's appearance.

"Why would you want a dog that looks like that?" Harriet asked.

"He's cute, in his own special way, just like Beatrice," Lilly said to her.

Lilly texted the owner, Dwayne, to set everything up. Meatball Face had everything he needed already so we only had to pick him up. We decided we could go get him right after we left my parents' house.

"Who's ready for pie?" my mom said, getting up from the table.

"I'm always ready for pie. But don't let Elsie have any," my dad said, smiling at Elsie. She giggled, knowing he was joking.

Harriet watched the kids eat their pie for a minute and then, to my horror, said, "Sydney, do the children have a father?" Sydney's face looked completely shocked. Did she actually just say that in front of the kids? I couldn't believe it, but then again, I could. Harriet had a way of simply saying whatever came to mind with no regard for how it came out or who it offended.

"Yes, they are divorced," I spoke up for her. "Does anyone need more tea?" I said, holding up the pitcher, trying to change the subject. I already knew my aunt's view on divorce.

"I've never understood young people this day and age. They just get married all willy nilly and then just go get a divorce when they get tired of each other. Marriage is supposed to be a commitment until death, but nobody wants to put in the effort anymore." I couldn't believe this. Sydney was rendered speechless and looked at me with a panicked look on her face.

I started to speak up and respond to my aunt's inconsiderate comment, but my mother beat me to it.

"Harriet! Everyone has their own circumstances and that is none of our business." Harriet had been widowed in her early 50s after her husband died in a boating accident. She never wanted to even date after that. "I'm sorry, Sydney," my mother apologized and started clearing the table.

"Sydney, why don't you take the kids outside to play with Beatrice and I'll help mom in the kitchen," I said, trying to give her a way out of the awkwardness.

"I can get it, Will, you don't need to be up more than necessary on that ankle," Mom said.

I got my crutches and followed as Sydney went with Lilly to take the kids outside.

"Sydney, I'm so sorry about that," Lilly said to her.

"Yea, our aunt doesn't have a filter. At all... She's very old-fashioned, but that doesn't make it ok. I'm sorry," I said. I was used to this type of thing, but that didn't mean Sydney and the kids should be subject to it.

"It's ok," Sydney said and gave Beatrice's squeaky toy to Micah to throw for her. I could see her eyes watering. I felt awful for her because I knew some of what she had been through with her ex-husband, and it had to be hard to hear somebody say she should have stayed in that situation for the rest of her life.

My dad poked his head outside. "Anyone up for a game? We just got the one where you put a card on a headband on your head and you have to guess what the card says."

"No, Dad, that sounds like fun, but I think we are going to go to Lilly's friend's house and pick up my new son, Meatball Face." I was seriously not looking forward to picking up that hideous thing but Sydney sure was, so I was willing to give the little guy a chance. Maybe he would grow on me.

We gathered the kids and said our goodbyes. "Thanks for dinner, it was delicious!" Sydney said to my parents as we walked out. My parents hugged each of the kids and sent them off with a bottle of bubbles.

Lilly had already arranged with her friend, Dwayne, for us to go to the house and pick up Meatball Face. Dwayne, apparently, had significant complications with his diabetes and was going to have to have part of his leg amputated. His ongoing health issues were making it difficult for him to care for a dog and as much as he loved him, he decided it was best for both him and Meatball Face to find him a new owner that could take better care of him.

The front door was closed, but I could see a scraggly head sticking up just enough to see over the side window. He started barking when we walked up. Dwayne opened the door for us, he was sitting in an electric wheelchair.

We introduced ourselves to Dwayne and then to an exceedingly excited Meatball Face. He was even more unfortunate looking than he was in the photo, but he seemed extremely friendly. The kids and Sydney all got on the floor with him while he licked all their faces.

"I adopted him from the animal shelter when he was six months old. I was intending to get a German Shepard mix that I'd had my eye on, but then I saw him, and he was just so pitiful that I simply couldn't resist him. You should have seen him sitting in that cage looking all sad. I just couldn't leave him there. He may be ugly, but he's as good as you can get." Dwayne wiped his eye with the back of his hand. It was obvious that this was incredibly difficult for him, rehoming a dog that he clearly loved very much.

"Sir, I know this is extremely difficult for you. It looks like you've given him a great life so far. We'd be happy to bring him by anytime you want. I'm sure he'll miss you too."

We agreed to text Dwayne with updates and send pictures. He gave us all the instructions. Apparently, Meatball Face was on a special sensitive stomach diet, took allergy medication, and had a medical condition that required having his anal glands expressed by a vet every six weeks. It was this type of care that made it hard for Dwayne to keep up with anymore.

Once the truck was loaded with a doghouse, dog bed, and all the other dog care essentials, we made our way home with a homely but happy Meatball Face sitting in the backseat between Elsie and Micah. I felt better about him after seeing how well he did with the kids and how happy he made Sydney. My only request is that he sleep somewhere other than in our bed, preferably in a crate, in a different room entirely.

# Chapter 18

## *Sydney*

Elsie's 3$^{rd}$ birthday was coming up and I'd always wanted to make the kids' birthday cakes, but I didn't know the first thing about decorating cakes. My mom always made our cakes when we were kids, and I always loved them. My favorite cake that she made me was in the shape of an open book and I still remember how good it tasted. It seemed more special to me when the cake was homemade and decorated by somebody that loved me. I wanted to do that for my kids and give them something special to remember. I'd mentioned this to Lilly at dinner the other night and she suggested she teach a cake decorating class for me and whoever I wanted to invite. Her bakery had a classroom in the back where she did weekly classes, but she would do a freebie class just for us. I loved the idea and invited Ashley, Leanne, Kennedy, and Jamie. Inviting Jamie was a no brainer because this is the kind of thing she lived for. She'd been begging me to take a pottery class with her, but I hadn't had the time to do it.

I only had Elsie with me that day because Will was planning to take Micah with him to Mimi and Pops to begin working on their deck. He was off his crutches and in an orthopedic boot. Against my better judgement, he decided to give it a try and see if he was able to at least get started on the deck. If I guessed correctly, he wouldn't last long with that boot, but he may be stubborn enough to prove me wrong.

I picked up Kennedy and headed to the bakery. She was excited about the class and had been looking online at all the cakes she planned to make once she learned how to do it. From looking at the pictures she showed me, I hoped she turned out to be as good at this as she thought she was going to be. This also gave her a chance to get out of the house and do something fun with other people. Kennedy had never had many friends; she had a hard time socializing and it was difficult to find others that had something in common with her. The few friends that she had in school didn't keep in touch with her after graduation.

Lilly's bakery was amazing. It was decorated with a French country cottage style, which I loved. There were dried pink and white roses in small glass vases on the counter along with skinny gold candlesticks with pink tapered candles. A gorgeous gold chandelier with clear crystals and strands of clear beads hung in the middle of the shop over some white antique style bistro table and chair sets. The bakery reminded me of what you might find in a historical tourist area or even as part of a quaint bed and breakfast.

"Lilly, you have done an outstanding job with this place! I didn't even know it was here, or I would have been in here every week. I'm always on the lookout for a cute bakery," I said to her, admiring every nook and cranny.

"Oh, thank you! I'm proud of how well it's done. I just love all the great people I get to meet," she said. Lilly gave Elsie and Kennedy both a cookie and some lemonade while we waited for the others to show up. She also took a picture of Kennedy, Elsie, and I sitting at one of the little tables together. The décor in the bakery was a perfect backdrop for the photo, and it was one for a frame for sure.

I had a feeling she made an incredible cream cheese Danish. At this rate, I'd be reaching for my stretchy pants soon. I was bound to become a regular at Lilly's bakery.

Leanne, Ashley, and Jamie all pulled up about the same time and after I introduced everyone, we walked into the back to start our class. Lilly provided everyone with an 8-inch cake and enough icing and supplies to decorate it.

"How did you learn to decorate cakes, Lilly?" Jamie asked her, examining her supplies.

"My mom taught me. She used to make our cakes when we were kids. Then she taught me how to do it when I got older. She was literally the inspiration behind this bakery," Lilly said. Sweet! Now the bakery even had a Hallmark movie vibe.

"Decorating cakes must have been the big trend in that generation because it seems like all the moms knew how to decorate cakes. Our moms baked and decorated all our cakes when we were little too," Leanne said. It was a fun memory for the three of us. Our moms would decorate our birthday cakes together sometimes. I felt kind of guilty just ordering Elsie and Micah's generic looking cakes from the grocery store, but now maybe I could learn and continue the tradition. Homemade, to me, meant a box mix, not something completely from scratch. I just wanted to decorate the cake for them. I'd never aimed to be an overachiever in the kitchen.

Lilly made cake decorating look a heck of a lot easier than it actually was. We started with some very basic techniques, but with practice, we might be able to get by with some basic decorating. I thought I might be able to manage making Elsie a doll cake, the kind you stick the doll in the middle and decorate around it. The good thing is Elsie was too young to care how good it looked, she would be more concerned with the color, how it tasted, and the fact that a doll was in it.

"I want to practice all year so I can make Luca's cake," Ashley said, admiring the flowers she piped on her cake. She'd added little swirlies on it. She was more artsy than the rest of us were as we were not skilled enough for swirlies.

"I'm not going to be making anyone any cakes," Leanne said, looking at her sad little cake. "Look at this monstrosity," she said, pointing at it. I couldn't quite make out what she had done, but there were different colors of blobs grouped up together that didn't resemble anything.

Kennedy did not end up enjoying cake decorating as much as she thought she would. She quickly squirted some icing in the middle of her cake, called it good, and then started cleaning everyone's messes up for them. She enlisted Elsie as her assistant and gave her some wet paper towels. Elsie walked around wiping things that didn't need it like the wall, a table leg, and Jamie's purse. When we were through with our cakes, Kennedy cleaned up our trash, wiped down and sanitized all the tables perfectly, swept the floor, and washed our tools for us.

"Everything is sanitized and ready for your next class," Kennedy said.

"Wow, Kennedy, you didn't have to do all that, but thanks!" Lilly told her.

While we gathered our things up to leave, Lilly pulled me aside. "Sydney, does Kennedy have a job?" she asked.

"Not right now. She's had a few jobs, but they haven't lasted long because she gets overwhelmed too easily and ends up having meltdowns and needing to be picked up from work. Why?" I'd already told Lilly about Kennedy's autism, so she already understood the situation.

"Well, I thought she might like to work up here at the bakery with me a few days a week? I could have her clean, help get supplies ready for the classes, things like that. It doesn't get too crazy here and its usually only a couple of us working at the same time. It might be the setting she needs to keep her from getting overwhelmed."

"Oh wow, Lilly. Are you sure? I can talk to her about it on the way home. If she likes the idea, I'll talk to my mom, and we will have to work out transportation for her. But this might be the perfect thing for her." This really would be perfect for Kennedy. I was so glad Lilly thought of it. Kennedy took pride in her work when she had jobs before. She could be a remarkably hard worker when she was in an environment that suited her needs. Drama with other employees was a thing too, but I didn't see that being an issue here at all.

......

On the way to drop Kennedy off at Mom's house, I approached the bakery job subject. My mom tried everything with Kennedy. She had her in vocational programs in high school that were geared towards students with special needs. She also utilized the community workforce program for people with disabilities after she graduated. Those programs were helpful, but Kennedy just couldn't keep the jobs long. She had done some small cleaning jobs for family; she had been a sacker in a grocery store and did janitorial work at a couple of fast-food places. There never seemed to be just the right place for her. Holiday seasons were the worst because it got too hectic and loud. One place brought in a piano during the Christmas season and that sent her over the edge.

"Did you like the bakery?" I asked her, hoping she said yes.

"Yea," she said. "I don't want to decorate cakes, though."

"That's ok. You don't have to, but do you think the bakery is a place where you would like to work?"

"Like an assistant manager?" she said. She usually didn't have particularly realistic ideas about the jobs she was qualified to do.

"No, I mean you could clean, get supplies ready for classes, things like that. Lilly asked if you would like to do that. She saw how good you were at helping today."

"How much does it pay?" she said, in a tone that indicated she had some bargaining power.

"I don't know, but you aren't going to get rich doing it and if I remember correctly, you aren't earning any money at all right now and I know you like to shop." She loved to shop. If she had money, she wanted the most she could get with the money she had. And that didn't mean quality items, she wanted quantity. Dollar stores were her favorite. She was kind of a hoarder, and her room was filled with bins and organizers full of odd little things she collected.

She thought about it for a minute. "Yea, I'll try it. Do I get free food?" She was always on the lookout for free food.

"I don't know. We can tell Lilly you will do it, and we can work out the transportation with Mom." Driving wasn't an option for Kennedy so that was one struggle we had when she did have a job. We had to coordinate with her schedule, and we would all pitch in and help to make it work out. She'd tried public transportation, but that caused her too much anxiety and usually resulted in a meltdown.

.......

We talked to Mom and Raymond about it, and everyone agreed that this may be just the thing for Kennedy. We told Kennedy that she needed to be the one to tell Lilly that she would like to work there. It was her job after all, and she needed to be the one to communicate with her new boss. We practiced some role playing with her for about half an hour and we were finally ready to make the call. I put the phone on speaker so I could prompt Kennedy if she needed help.

The phone started ringing and Lilly answered. "Hello?"

Kennedy waited too long to say anything.

"Hello?" Lilly said again.

I prompted Kennedy to say hello. Then she surprised us all. "Hi, this is Kennedy Scott and I'm calling to accept the bakery position," she finally said. Nailed it! That was not at all the script we practiced but it still worked perfectly.

Lilly went along with Kennedy's formality. "Ms. Scott, I'm pleased to have you on board. I look forward to working with you!"

We all congratulated Kennedy on her new job, got a schedule from Lilly, and worked out transportation.

On the way home I called Will to see how he faired with his deck making project and to give him the big news about his sister being Kennedy's new boss. Apparently, he made it about two hours before his ankle started to hurt. Pop was having him sample his secret barbecue sauce recipe which we all suspected was just a regular store-bought sauce that he poured into a squirt bottle. They were about to head home.

Our families were fitting together. Will was off on his own with my family, I was off doing something different with his sister and Kennedy was going to be working for her. I thought about this being a sign that everything was how it should be.

I was almost home when Will called. "Sydney, Pop fell, and I think he's hurt. I called 911."

# Chapter 19

## *Will*

### Three hours earlier...

Mr. Richardson, well... Pop, as he insisted that I call him, brought out the plans for the deck that we worked on together last month. He had drawn them himself and every detail was meticulously planned out. Pop's lung function was diminishing and even with a portable oxygen concentrator, he could barely walk more than the length of one room. Before I broke my ankle, I'd built a ramp at his back door for his electric scooter.

I could tell we didn't pick the best day to work on this project because he was clearly not in a good mood and started barking out orders to me as soon as I got there. I had so much respect for the man that I tried to not take it personally. He also seemed to be struggling to breathe more than normal, and he was coughing quite a bit. Sydney had talked about Pop a lot lately and worried about him constantly. I'm sure it was hard for her to watch this man, who had been such a powerful force in her life, on the verge of not even being able to care for himself.

The supplies for the deck were delivered to the house the previous day. I marked off where Pop wanted the deck and started setting the posts. Since Micah liked watering, I put him in charge of helping to soften the dirt by holding the water hose over the spots I had marked for the post holes. Once the posts were all set, I started measuring the wood for the frame and joists.

"You need to cut that piece to six and a half feet," Pop said as I took a 2 by 4 to the saw.

"No sir, I believe we need to cut it at six and three fourths," I said, trying to not be disrespectful, but I knew exactly what it needed.

"Cut it at six and a half like I said," he ordered, then coughed again.

Although I was wasting a perfectly good piece of lumber, I did as he instructed, knowing full well that it was not going to work. And what do you know, the piece was too small.

"Do you not know how to read a tape measure?" he asked, seeing that the piece did not fit. Obviously, this measurement error was going to be my fault.

"Yes, sir. I know how to read a tape measure. I cut it at six and a half feet like you wanted." I pulled out the tape measure and measured it again for him. I figured he needed to see for himself. "See?"

"Well, cut it again the right size," he said and then drove off on his scooter, not wanting to accept defeat. I imagined that in his prime, he was probably almost never wrong, and I felt a twinge of guilt for not just humoring him.

Micah grew bored as soon as his post hole watering duties were finished, and Mrs. Richardson put him to work watering her flowerbeds. Like Pop, she had also asked me to call her Mimi rather than Mrs. Richardson. I must have a grandson quality about me or something.

"I'm sorry Rusty is in a crabby mood today, Will. He's not been himself for the last few days. I really don't think he feels good," Mimi said to me, turning off the water hose.

"Oh, it's ok. I think it's hard for him to watch somebody else build this deck when he is so used to doing everything himself," I said and finished cleaning up my mess while Mimi and Micah went inside to make root beer floats.

Their yard was immaculate, and not only the yard. Everything from the street to the back fence was perfect, proof that they took immense pride in their property. The flowerbeds were a rainbow of colorful flowers, and a row of massive purple Crepe Myrtle shrubs lined the fence along the driveway. They had lived on that piece of property for 40 years and had built everything themselves from the ground up. In all the years he had lived there, the deck was the first project that Pop had to watch somebody else build rather than building it himself.

I went inside and found Pop sitting in his recliner. "I've done all I can until the concrete sets up."

"Okay, Will, go grab a beer for both of us from the icebox." Fortunately, his demeanor had improved.

When I returned with the beers, he had me follow him into the guest bedroom. In the closet there was a large gun safe. He gave me the combination and had me open it.

He pointed to an extremely nice 12-gauge shotgun and said, "That's yours."

"What?" I asked, confused.

"I'm giving it to you." Then, reached over and grabbed a hunting vest and a case of shotgun shells. He handed those to me as well. "Dove season is coming up in a couple months, I wouldn't mind having some dove if you go hunting." He was out of breath from standing longer than he should have been.

In all my life I'd never heard of anyone giving their granddaughter's boyfriend such a nice gift and for no apparent reason. I thought about Easter, when Leanne and Sydney told me about how protective he was and how he hadn't liked any of the guys his granddaughters dated or married. I wondered what I did that was so different from the others.

"I need to sit down a minute," he said, sitting down on an antique looking rocking chair next to the bed.

"Would you like me to bring your scooter in?" I asked him, not wanting him to overdo it by walking back to his chair.

"Not, just give me a minute," he said. After he caught his breath, he pointed to a black and white photo of him and Mimi that was hanging on the wall. "That picture was taken right after we got married. When I met Louise, she was only 18 years old, fresh out of high school. I took one look at her, and I just knew. And do you know how long we dated before I asked her to be my wife?" he asked.

"Six months?" I asked.

"Two weeks. We dated for two weeks, and I didn't see any point in waiting any longer. When you know, you know. So, I bought a ring at McMurry Jewelers, asked her to marry me, and we've been together for 54 years," he said. "And can you believe McMurry's is still in business after all these years?" He laughed.

I shook my head. "That's amazing, Pop. You two really beat the odds." I wondered why he was sharing this story with me. I was sure he liked me, but was he hinting at something?

Pop stood up, but stumbled and fell sideways, hitting his side on the corner of the dresser on the way down. A lamp on the dresser fell off on the floor and broke.

Mimi heard the crash and hurried in. "Rusty!" she said, rushing over to him. He was on the floor leaning up against the dresser, struggling to breathe. I gave him his oxygen cannula, which was lying on the floor next to him, and tried to help him up, but he let out a yelp, holding onto his side when I tried to move him. Rather than hurting him any worse, Mimi and I agreed that we should call 911.

...........

The fall left Pop with two fractured ribs, which could be managed with pain relief. However, tests also revealed he had pneumonia, explaining his increased weakness and difficulty breathing. He was admitted to the hospital with IV antibiotics, which Pop was not happy about. He tried to smooth-talk his way out of it by telling the doctor that he had to stay home because his wife was a sleepwalker, and the last time it happened, she nearly burned the kitchen down frying an unopened can of tuna.

I'd waited in the waiting room with the kids, but they were getting restless. I didn't have anything to keep them occupied so I gave them my phone to watch videos on. Finally, Sydney came in.

"I think the kids need to go home. I can take them home and come back to get you when you're ready," I told her, taking Elsie's hand.

"We can leave in just a minute, but first, Pop wants to talk to you. I'm not sure what it's about," she said, with a puzzled look on her face.

I left the kids and Sydney in the waiting room and walked into Pop's room. "Close the door behind you, Will," Pop said. OK, this was rather concerning. What could he need to talk to me about that required such privacy?

"Sydney said you needed to talk to me. Is there something I can help you with?" I asked.

"I've had something in my pocket that I was going to give you today, but I fell before I could hand it to you. Can you get me my pants?" He was already in a hospital gown. I found his pants on the counter and handed them to him. He took an envelope out of his back pocket. "You can open it when you get home, but you have to promise me you won't let Sydney see it."

"Yes sir, I promise." I took the envelope. "Get to feeling better soon, Pop. You scared us today," I said and went to find Sydney.

"What did he want to talk to you about?" she asked.

"He needed to talk about the deck. I'm going back over to work on it tomorrow." Only half a lie. I honestly was planning to go work on it the next day.

On our way out of the hospital, we saw Sydney's brother coming in.

"Hey! They just got Pop into a room. He's not being a good patient," Sydney said to him.

"Yea, I know. He called me and tried to get me to smuggle in some cigarettes," Eric said. "Instead, I brought him some paper and drawing pencils to give him something to do." He looked at me. "Hey, uh, thanks for taking care of things with Pop today."

"No problem, he's a good man. Stubborn as hell, but a good man." I laughed.

The envelope was burning a hole in my pocket the whole drive home. What could it be? I imagined it could be some instructions for the deck, the combination to his gun safe in case I forgot it, or information on the shot gun he gave me. I couldn't imagine why any of that would have to be a secret.

As soon as I stepped into the front door, I made a bee line for the bathroom and locked the door. I stared at the contents of the envelope long enough that Sydney started knocking on the bathroom door making sure I was ok.

"I'm fine, just a little upset stomach," I hollered.

For the last couple of weeks, I'd been doing a lot of thinking and as crazy as it seemed, I knew what I wanted to do. Would everyone else think it made sense? Probably not. Nobody other than Pop, apparently. It seemed I had more in common with that man than I realized, and he knew me better than I thought he did.

Inside the envelope was a sale flyer for McMurry Jewelers, a check written out to me for $1,000, and a piece of yellow notepad paper that read "when you know, you know."

# **Chapter 20**

## *Sydney*

Pop remained cantankerous throughout his hospital stay. Being told what to do while being confined to a hospital bed didn't do anything for his attitude. The fractured rib/pneumonia combo was hard on him, but he had improved enough to go home. Mimi didn't drive much anymore, and the traffic in the area that the hospital was in was more than she could handle; therefore, Leanne volunteered to give him a ride home since it was more convenient for her than for anyone else. I wouldn't be surprised if the hospital staff were delighted to see him leave after the grief he gave them during his short stay.

Will, Eric, and Antonio all worked together on the deck Sunday and completed the project exactly the way Pop drew out on the plans. My mom and I helped Mimi decorate it. Mimi and Pop liked colorful things, so we helped her pick brightly colored pots in different sizes which we planted flowers and plants in. We also helped her pick a small, sturdy, white wrought iron table with matching chairs and a porch swing with blue cushions. Jamie helped me make a door mat that read "Mimi and Pop's porch." Everything looked cheerful but serene at the same time and I could already picture Mimi sitting on the porch swing with her coffee in the early summer mornings before the day heated up. Pop would most likely enjoy it most in the tranquil evenings when the sun started to go down, to unwind from the day.

In the past few months, I had seen Pop's health go downhill quickly and couldn't help worrying that he wouldn't be able to enjoy his new deck for much longer. That broke my heart, Pop was like my hero, and selfishly, I wanted him to be here forever. To me, he could do nothing wrong, and I always thought of him as the smartest person I knew. Realistically, I knew there would be a day when he wouldn't be here anymore, but that was simply not something I could stand to think about.

Shortly after Pop returned home, Mimi called and confirmed that he had approved of the finished deck. She said his face lit up when he saw it and he was already talking about having one of the guys grill burgers or steaks to eat outside. Pop's specialty had always been outdoor cooking, and I hadn't found anyone that could top his steaks. Pop and I were both steak snobs and shared a belief that steaks cooked more than medium rare were just not fit to be eaten.

That evening, Will and Micah went out to work on their latest project. Will had been working on building a flower bed in the corner of our front yard. It was going to be large, and our plan was to plant lots of perennial flowers that would multiply and return every year. He recruited Micah to help him. Micah had never had a much of a father figure with Jeff. He had learned more from Will in these past couple of months than he had learned in his entire life from Jeff. From the kitchen window I watched with a smile on my face as Will and Micah dug a trench where the border would go in. Micah worked next to Will with a small shovel, not making much of a dent in the dirt but that didn't matter. Then, Will cut some landscape timbers and let Micah help arrange them around the flowerbed. Will and Micah had formed a bond through the projects that they had worked on together. It was the most wholesome thing I'd ever seen.

Elsie and Will also had developed a special bond. They both loved to sing, and they would sing songs together. Elsie liked all kinds of music and, in the evenings, when Will was cooking dinner, he would pick songs that Elsie knew and tell Alexa to play them. Elsie would sing and dance around the kitchen while Will cooked. Sometimes Will would pick her up and dance around the kitchen with her. The sound of Elsie's high pitched squeaky voice mixed with Will's low voice was too cute for words.

Nothing Will did could make me love him more than seeing him with my kids. He wasn't just what I had been needing all these years; he was what the kids needed too. A few months ago, we didn't even know him, and now he was already so much a part of our family that I couldn't imagine not having him here with us forever. The kids and I were great on our own, but we were even better with Will.

After dinner, Will and I sat outside watching the kids play with Meatball Face. We had eaten our dinner on the back patio. Even though it was summer, I'd made one of my new favorite crockpot meals, chicken burritos. When Will moved in, he brought with him a crockpot and as a result, I had become an enthusiast of the "dump it and forget it" method of cooking. It worked great for me with my limited cooking skills. Fortunately for everyone, Will had taken over most of the cooking responsibilities.

While I ate, I stared at my plate and compared my chicken burrito to my own life. Another thing about me was if I was going to do any deep thinking, it was going to be while staring at food. I thought of me and the kids being like the burrito meat. Burrito meat is good on its own, add a little cheese and eat in a bowl with a fork, perfectly fine, nothing to complain about. But rolled all up in a warm tortilla, nice and neat, then the burrito is complete. One perfect little bundle. Will was our tortilla.

Will sat quietly watching the kids for a while, then finally spoke up, "How would you feel about a little weekend trip to New Mexico this weekend, just the two of us?"

"Oh, heck yea, that sounds heavenly!" I hadn't been to New Mexico in years and a weekend away with Will would be incredible. I loved traveling, but I hadn't been able to go anywhere much since I was a kid. Jeff never wanted to go anywhere, at least not with me anyway.

"I'll need to find somebody to watch the kids. I can ask Lanie, though." Lanie was the next-door neighbor and watched the kids for me sometimes. She was the perfect babysitter, and I trusted her completely. "Where do you have in mind?"

"My grandparents used to live in Mannington Lake, it's near the Guadalupe Mountains. I used to spend a lot of time there when I was a kid. I thought it would be fun to take you. It's only a three-hour drive; we could leave Friday after work and be home Sunday afternoon."

"Sure! How fun!" I said, then I had a moment of panic. "Oh, wait. So… If it's near the mountains are there bears there?" Bears were one thing I simply couldn't deal with. I was terrified of them; I'd even had recurrent bear dreams for years. The dreams were always the same. A bear would be trying to get into my house, but the door couldn't be locked, and the bear was able to open the door. They never hurt me, but they were always able to get in. And if other people were around in the dream, I was the only one who seemed concerned. I truly believe there's a meaning behind these dreams, even if I can't quite pinpoint what it is.

"They have them, but I've been going there my entire life and I've never seen any. We will be in a populated area where bears wouldn't be anyway," Will said, reassuringly.

"Let me check to be on the safe side in case there has been an influx of bears since you went last." I picked up my phone and googled **Are there bears in Mannington Lake.** Fortunately, google agreed that bears are rarely seen. "Ok, let's do it! But you have to promise me that we aren't going to go venturing out into the wilderness. Who knows what could be lurking in there." I've never understood how so many people can go hiking and camping in the wilderness and never seem to be concerned about the wild animals and creepy crawlies. One of the many things I was not cut out for was wilderness adventures.

Will laughed. "You were raised in the country with farm animals, you're perfectly comfortable around cattle, but you won't step foot into the wilderness."

"Um, there is a huge difference. Farm animals aren't dangerous, Will. And a bull is not a predator and certainly is not looking to eat limbs that it has ripped from my limp, lifeless body," I said, not at all joking.

Will chuckled. "I'm pretty sure that isn't a bear's intention either, but ok… I promise not to take you into the wilderness even though wild animals are most likely not waiting to rip off any of your limbs. But on a lighter note, there's a bed and breakfast downtown. I've never stayed there, but it looks like something you would like. I already checked the website, and they have availability for this weekend."

"YES! That's perfect!" I've always wanted to stay in a cute bed and breakfast, but I never got to go anywhere when I was married to Jeff. It seems he only went on vacation with the little girlfriend he kept on the side. I'd imagined a quaint little place that had homemade pastries in the kitchenette, specialty teas and coffees with cute little mismatched cups, and a handmade quit on the bed. But truthfully, we could stay in a storage shed and it would still be perfect as long as I was staying in it with Will.

I called Lanie and she happily agreed to do it; she adored the kids. Ever since the kids were born, Lanie had been the only babysitter I had ever had outside of family, and the kids were comfortable with her. She said she would stay at my house to make it easier for the kids and she could take care of Meatball Face that way too.

"What do we need to pack?" I asked him.

"Clothes for hot weather and tennis shoes for sure. And maybe something to wear if we go somewhere nice for dinner."

After we went back inside the house I made a packing list:

**Wasp spray** (Will still had not gotten an epi pen...)

**Bear spray** (Can't be too careful)

**Bug repellant**

**First aid kit**

**Asthma inhaler**

**Clothes**

Friday could not come soon enough. A little getaway with Will seemed like a dream come true. I hadn't left Willow Creek in ages, and as much as I adored the kids, a weekend alone with Will was exactly what I needed. I wanted the weekend to be special, something we would remember forever. I had a strange feeling that it was going to be just that, like we would look back years from now and still remember what we did on that weekend. And although I didn't know exactly how I wanted this to play out, I was one hundred percent positive about what I wanted to do to make it that way.

# Chapter 21

## *Will*

### Weekend at Mannington Lake...

When you know you know.  That's what Pop told me.  I'd already known.  I'd known when I first met her that night at the Iron Bar, but when I went to her house for Easter, that's when I knew she was the one I wanted to grow old with.  I guess it's true what they say about opposites attract because we were complete opposites, but we had chemistry that worked.

There wasn't anything I didn't love about Sydney.  Sure, I was attracted to her looks, but it wasn't just that by any means.  There were a lot of big reasons why, but there were also plenty of little things I loved about her.  She could be sarcastic but also had an amazing sense of humor and a good heart.  Her ridiculous lawyer joke and her drunken rhyming didn't bother me, but it also made me thankful she didn't drink often.  I never heard her sing for real, but she would burst out in song at any given minute with just sound effects instead of words. I liked that she was a country girl at heart even though nobody would guess it by looking at her. I loved her spontaneity. One moment she was saying she wasn't lifting a finger the whole weekend, but fifteen minutes later she would be heading to the hardware store to buy supplies to paint the bathroom. I liked that she tried to act tough, but she was also terrified of escalators or stepping up higher than the third step of a ladder.

Before Sydney, I was simply going through the motions. Then Sydney came along and gave me a reason to live. She and the kids became my purpose. I'd never thought much of myself, yet somehow Sydney saw something in me and believed in me.

Two days ago, I cashed the check that Pop gave me and went to McMurry Jewelers. I still couldn't believe that Sydney's grandfather was the one to get this all started. The owner, Sandra, was amazing and helped me pick the perfect ring. As soon as I saw it, I knew instantly it was the one. It was gold with an oval diamond and tiny leaves engraved on the sides. I thought it was appropriate due to Sydney's love of plants and natural things.

Lanie came over at 5:30, we told the kids bye and left a list of emergency phone numbers on the refrigerator along with instructions for Meatball Face's allergy meds. We loaded our things in the truck and headed to New Mexico with the snacks Sydney packed for the road since we didn't eat dinner before we left.

"So, I've been reading up and I found out that if we see a bear, we are supposed to make a lot of noise and make ourselves look big," she said, opening a fried apple pie.

"OK, thank you for your diligence in keeping us safe." I chuckled. I didn't want to tell Sydney this, but mountain lion sightings in Mannington Lake were much more common than bear sightings. I didn't imagine this news would be any more settling for her.

"I don't know why you think this is so funny. I've seen videos of a bear walking along the sidewalk right in the middle of town, terrorizing innocent pedestrians who merely wanted to go get a smoothie. Oh, and don't even get me started on all the stories I've heard of bears opening the door to people's houses and going right inside. Imagine being in the kitchen making a tuna casserole when suddenly there is a bear just moseying in as if it lives there? It's like in the dreams I have," she said.

"How long has it been since you've been to the mountains?" I asked her as they started to come into view, looking dusty blue from far away.

"Gosh, I was probably about twelve years old the last time we went. We used to go with Mimi and Pop. My mom gave us brand new, sharpened colored pencils and activity books for the ride. I remember we stayed in a log cabin, and I had my own room instead of having to share with my siblings. Eric and I would play in the creek and hunt for bugs and snakes. I wasn't afraid of anything back then for some reason. My dad and Pop grilled burgers and hot dogs and we made smores. The only thing we didn't do was break out in a round of campfire songs. It was kind of a Brady Bunch sort of vacation, but it was so perfect, and I'd give anything for a replay of it," she said, and it looked like her eyes were watering.

When we checked into our room that evening, I could tell Sydney already loved it from the way she looked when we drove up.

"You've got to be kidding me! It's adorable!" she said and started a tour of the room. "Look! Baked goods!" she exclaimed, surveying the refrigerator. Then she went into the bathroom and shouted gleefully, "There's bubble bath and eye masks!" It was obvious that I'd chosen the right place for this weekend.

I noticed a bottle of wine with two wine glasses on the counter, perfect. A large vintage-looking king-sized bed stood on the other side of the room against a cobblestone wall, also perfect. Both bedside tables had three brass candlesticks which I had every intention of lighting.

--------

The next morning, after an unforgettable night, Sydney woke me up with a cup of coffee, still wearing my T-shirt. She always wore my T-shirts to bed now. We partook of the baked goods that she was so excited about and then headed out so I could show her around. The ring was in my pocket just in case the moment seemed right, but my plan was to ask her during a romantic picnic that night. I knew of a spot out by the water that would be beautiful at sunset, when things were calm and quiet. I had always been afraid of rejection, and I was getting worried that this may be way too soon for Sydney. I had a feeling she wanted the same thing I did, but that didn't mean she wanted to jump in so fast. What if she was fine with just living with me in sin, as our families would say, and wanted to wait a few years before we made it official? This could potentially freak her out and ruin the whole thing.

The first place on the Mannington Lake tour was my grandparents' old house. I showed her where they lived, where I'd spent a lot of time when I was younger. Then I showed her the park across the street from their house where I used to play. The park had never been updated, and it was still exactly as it had been 20 years ago, complete with the rocket shaped metal slide that we played on and somehow lived to tell about it. During the summer we endured burning the backs of our legs on that scalding hot slide every time we went down. From the looks of it now, the slide also provided an increased risk of contracting tetanus.

After Sydney did a thorough inspection of the safety issues surrounding the slide, we sat on the swings. "I love seeing the places you enjoyed when you were little. It's sweet," she said as she swung on the swing. "I like this park, it's peaceful. Dangerous as it can be, but peaceful. I'm sure it's so quiet because parents won't let their kids play here due to the risk of hospitalization," she said and smiled. I'm sure that was true, I was surprised they hadn't at least torn down the hazardous play equipment, but the town was not overly populated and very few kids ever played here even when I was a kid.

When we left the park, we drove past the house where my great grandparents used to live and then we went to the cemetery where they were buried. Then we went to the beach at the river where I used to go swimming. Sydney was completely emersed in the whole experience and she seemed to enjoy seeing where I spent so much of my childhood. I loved that she cared about it.

We were both getting hungry for lunch and Sydney spotted a little run-down looking restaurant. The sign was so faded I could barely read it, but it appeared to be a local Mexican food restaurant. "Oh! can we eat there?" she asked. Sydney was something of a food critic and was known to eat foods that I would never dream of, but this seemed sketchy.

I looked at her, puzzled. "Really? It looks kind of run down." I didn't know if we should risk our gastrointestinal health, especially with the romantic night I had planned. I had a feeling that explosive diarrhea could spoil the mood.

"The little hole in the wall places are the best places, trust me on this one," she confidently said, and I hesitantly pulled into the parking lot.

She was right. The food was amazing, authentic Mexican food. The service was beyond spectacular. The owner, Mike, came out and talked to us for a minute, making sure the food was to our liking. Sydney let him know that she would be adding the sour cream chicken enchiladas to her list of top favorites, and that we would definitely be back.

A man and woman, probably in their 70s, were seated at the table next to us. The man kept looking over at us. Sydney noticed too. She texted me from across the table.

Sydney: **He keeps staring at us.**

Me: **Ask him why.**

Sydney: **No! You ask.**

The man finally leaned over toward our table and spoke up. "Um, excuse me, I couldn't help noticing you ate the enchiladas. Were they good?"

"Yes, sir, very good," I replied.

"Did you get chicken or beef?" he asked.

"Chicken, sir."

"Oh, good. I was going to say the chicken is the best. My name is Thomas. And this here is my wife, Carol." He continued talking to us as his wife waved and smiled.

"Hello, nice to meet you. I'm Will, and this is Sydney," I said while Sydney waved, trying to go back to eating.

"Are you guys from Mannington Lake? I haven't seen you here," Thomas continued talking again.

"No, we aren't. Just visiting," Sydney told him politely, trying to take another bite but clearly afraid he would start asking questions again.

"Do you mind me asking what you are doing here then?" Thomas was a nosey one.

"Thomas, they are trying to eat!" his wife finally chimed in.

"It's fine, ma'am. We're just visiting, thought it would be a nice weekend getaway," I replied, trying to not laugh.

After a few more minutes of interrogation, Carol was able to herd Thomas out of the restaurant. Something about that couple was so sweet. I wondered if someday that would be me and Sydney. One of us having to monitor the other one and keep them in line. I smiled just thinking of it.

"Well, the citizens of Mannington Lake are rather inquisitive." Sydney giggled.

"That they are." I laughed, finally finishing my meal. "Ok, you were right. These are the best enchiladas I've ever had," I said, scraping the last bits off my plate.

"I feel like places like this are more concerned about the food quality and customer service and less worried about how it looks from the outside. I always love a mom-and-pop place way more than a chain restaurant, plus it's just good to support the local businesses. So, where to next on the Mannington Lake tour of Will's childhood memories?" she asked, finishing her drink.

"It's my favorite place here, the place where my granddad used to take me fishing. Don't worry, it isn't in the wilderness. There are usually a lot of people there fishing and riding boats. No chance of bears, I promise," I told her before she had a chance to question the probability of bear sightings.

I was seriously getting nervous. Our next meal would be the picnic. What if I was jumping the gun on this? The ink on her divorce papers was barely dry, and she might want to wait a while before getting into another marriage. I couldn't assume she was already certain that we are destined to still be together when we are 70 years old and reminding each other to take our bedtime pills.

Sydney was quiet on the drive to the lake and seemed nervous. I assumed she was questioning my honesty on the whereabouts of bears at the lake. I'd never heard of anyone with such a bear phobia. "Everything ok?" I asked her.

"Yep! Just deep in thought is all," she said.

I parked the truck at the lake after we got out, the ring was burning a hole in my pocket as I thought of what was to come in only a few hours. We walked along the sidewalk on the edge of the water, holding hands. I thought it was funny that Sydney never even unpacked her bear spray or her wasp spray that she had sworn we wouldn't ever be without.

"This is the spot where we used to like to fish," I told her, and we stopped to look over the lake. The spot was a little quieter and it was a good place to fish because the boats didn't come this way. The trees provided enough shade that the heat wasn't as intense as it was in the sun. There was a bridge a little further down. On the side of the bridge somebody had taken red spray paint and painted "Lupe + Felicia" in huge letters that could be seen from a distance. Sydney found this entertaining and took a picture of it.

"I hope Lupe and Felicia are still together," she said, staring at their names graffitied on the bridge.

"They seemed to assume they would be." I laughed.

"I love it here! Let's go sit under the bridge. It looks so peaceful," she said and led me to sit on some large rocks.

"This is beautiful. I wish we had places like this in Willow Creek. I'd take the kids there all the time," she said, taking in the scenery. She looked incredibly beautiful sitting on that rock, just natural and more at ease than she had been in the truck on the way over here. Maybe I won't wait until tonight. Maybe this was the moment.

I started to put my arm around her, but she turned and looked at me. "Will, I'm about to sound cheesy so please forgive me in advance. I'm not good at this but I have something to say."

"OK, I forgive you for the upcoming cheesiness," I said, wondering what it was about.

"Ok, here goes. I love you. I mean, I really, really love you. I love the way you look at me as if I'm gorgeous even when I just got out of bed. I love that you help little old ladies plant tulips. I love that you act like it's an emergency when my tires are only slightly low. I love that you sing the Veggie Tale cheeseburger song even when the kids aren't even in the same room." She paused and wiped her eyes, which were now watering. "And I love that you would protect me with your life without even hesitating, even though I would try to stop you. I love the way you are with the kids, as if they were yours. You are the most kind, generous, selfless man I've ever known. I know we haven't been together for very long and you might think it's too soon, but when you know you know, and I know." She paused and took a deep breath. "Will you marry me?"

My heart skipped about four beats. All this time I was worried that she might think it was too soon but here she was, doing exactly what I intended to do all along. I slowly pulled the ring out of my pocket, opened the box, and said, "Yes, Sydney. I will absolutely marry you."

# Chapter 22

## *Sydney*

Yesterday seemed like a fairytale, or even a Hallmark movie because it was too perfect. The fact that Will and I both went on this trip with the same intention was insane and a sure sign that we were meant to be. I cannot believe he literally had an engagement ring in his pocket the entire time that I was building up the courage to ask him myself. Nobody was going to believe this story when we told it.

I've never been the type to care about old fashioned gender roles and I certainly do not believe that it is only acceptable for the man to propose to the woman. During the past few months, I'd developed a confidence I never had before and I firmly stand behind my new belief that if you want something, go get it. Man or woman, it doesn't matter. I intended to teach this to my kids as well. I've never understood how basically all my female friends that were in male/female relationships would wait to be asked to the prom, and to homecoming, or on a date, or to marry somebody. I knew that I wanted to marry Will, so I asked him. That simple. I'm sure all our family and friends will gasp at this when we tell them. The important part is that Will said yes, and even more importantly, he already had that gorgeous ring with him because he was planning to propose that very night. I simply beat him to it. It seemed like the perfect time and place, sitting there under the Lupe and Felicia bridge, in the same area where he had such wonderful memories of fishing with his grandfather.

One day I might look back and wish I'd held out and waited for Will to ask me to marry him. I've never been proposed to. Jeff and I simply decided to get married one day while we were watching TV, nothing romantic about it. But for now, it will just add to the excitement of our whole relationship because it's different than what has happened with any of our friends and families' engagement stories.

Will planned the most romantic night last night. I thought we were going to a restaurant and while I was getting ready, he left to pick up a few things. He came back with a beautiful bouquet. Mannington Lake didn't have many florists, and only one of them had pink tulips in stock. It was sweet that he thought of this because pink tulips were the flowers that he gave me on our first date. Instead of a restaurant, Will prepared a picnic at sunset in a quiet spot near the water. He packed peach wine for me and a local beer for himself. For dinner, we shared a delicious charcuterie board that he had pre-ordered a few days earlier. I knew Will might have preferred just about any other meal, but he knew how much I loved it. I made them at home sometimes to eat during game nights, but never as fancy as the one Will brought. Cheese and fruit just hit differently when they're aesthetically displayed on a wooden board.

Today, Will and I planned to stop by his brother's house on the way home. It was only about half an hour outside of Mannington Lake. They hadn't seen each other since Christmas, and he wanted to introduce me. I was nervous to meet them. By what Will told me, they seemed higher on the social ladder than we were, and I wasn't sure I would have anything in common with them. Will told me that Toby is a college golf coach and co-owner of the local golf course. His wife, Kayla, is a sculptor and owns a fine art gallery. They are outdoorsy people, and liked camping, fishing, shooting, sports, basically everything that Will loved but that I stayed as far away from as possible. He also told me they have a labradoodle named Eevee René. I loved it when people gave their pets a middle name.

When we arrived at their house, I was in awe. It was a large white colonial style house on a hill with a breathtaking view of the river and distant mountains. The house was brand new, and they had only been there a few months. The inside of the house was decorated with timeless, tasteful décor with the main color being the green from their plants. It literally looked like something an influencer would post on Instagram. I wondered if they did this themselves or if they hired a decorator. It was truly impressive and extremely clean. If you dropped a cookie on their floor, the five-second rule almost seemed unnecessary. Outside, Will was drooling over the new smoker they had in their huge outdoor kitchen. I'd never seen anyone with so much cooking equipment on their patio. They also had a kegerator so they could drink beers on tap, which Will was also incredibly impressed with and helped himself to some.

Kayla and Toby took us on the grand tour of the rest of the house, and I made some mental notes of décor ideas for my own house; the few ideas that I could actually afford. Eevee René had her own little area near the living room. It was the cutest thing I'd ever seen. She had a classy little black bed with wooden legs, a black and beige rug in front of her bed, a small end table with a lamp, and a picture of herself on the wall over her bed. There was a personalized basket of toys next to the end table. I was inspired to make Meatball his own area ASAP.

We sat outside on the patio for a while making small talk. Eevee and I had already become friends, and she sat with her head resting on my knee as I scratched her neck.

Beaming like a proud dad, Will showed Kayla and Toby pictures of the kids and one of Meatball Face. One of the pictures was of Will and the kids eating popsicles on the back porch, Elsie's dripping all over the front of her shirt. If anyone hadn't known better, they would have thought Will was the kids' biological father by the way he talked about them.

"So where did you two meet?" Kayla asked us.

"We met at the Iron Bar where I DJ," Will said.

"Well, I don't really go to bars much, but I was there with my cousin just so she could see her boyfriend," I said, hoping they didn't think I was a barfly.

Toby laughed. "It's fine, we aren't judging."

"Sydney has some new jewelry," Will announced, looking at my finger.

Kayla noticed my ring. Her eyebrows rose instantly. "Is that what I think it is?" she asked, leaning over to see.

"Yes!" I said, giving her a closer look at the ring. "Actually, we've just been engaged since yesterday! Nobody else knows yet," I told them both, smiling.

"She proposed and I said yes!" Will said. "Actually, I already had the ring, but she asked before I ever got a chance to." He laughed.

"Wow!" Toby said but his eyes didn't match his smile. "You two have known each other how long?" he asked, looking at us inquisitively.

"A few months. We met a little before Easter," Will told him, seeming oblivious to what I knew Toby was thinking. They were probably thinking the same thing everyone else was going to think as well, that we hadn't known each other long enough and that I was pregnant. Well, I wasn't pregnant, so they were wrong about that.

"So, a little over two months," Toby added.

After an awkward pause, Kayla was the first to speak up again, "Well, congratulations to you both! Have you thought about a date yet?"

Will and I looked at each other, we hadn't even discussed a date yet. "Um, we don't know yet. I was kind of thinking December, but I'm open to anything," I said. I always thought December weddings were pretty.

"You can stay a few hours before you leave, right? Why don't we go do something fun to celebrate?" Kayla asked.

Toby spoke up first, "How does everyone feel about going out to the shooting range? I got a new pistol, and I'd love to try it out. There's a barbecue restaurant right across the street that's pretty good. We could have lunch there after we are finished shooting before you have to head home."

"That sounds great!" Will said excitedly.

I panicked. I'd never shot anything other than a BB gun before. Pop used to let us shoot BBs at empty cans but that's the extent of what I could do. Maybe I could just sit out and watch them instead of making a fool of myself.

When we arrived at the gun range, we rented our space and bought some targets. Everyone else went first as I watched, trying to avoid having a turn. Guns had always scared me.

"Ok, Sydney, your turn," Will said to me.

"Oh, no, that's ok. I don't know how to shoot or even know how to load it," I said. Everyone else was clearly experienced in this and I was going to look ridiculous.

"I'll teach you," Will said.

Hesitantly, I agreed. He already performed a miracle teaching me how to drive a standard, maybe he could teach me this also. The difference was I had an audience this time.

I did not enjoy providing entertainment for everyone as they watched me, and I was going to be mortified if I totally sucked at it. I decided there was a 94.7 percent chance that I would, in fact, suck at it. Normally, I could simply laugh it off if I made a fool of myself in front of others, but it wasn't that easy for me to do in front of people I didn't know well. Instead, I only ended up with anxiety.

Will proceeded to show me how to make sure the gun was clear of ammo and how to hold the gun safely. Then he made sure I had my safety goggles and earmuffs on. I did appreciate the safety component to all of this, safety first was my motto. He showed me how to properly aim, load, and insert the magazine. Holding a loaded gun made me uneasy, but at that point I had to learn because all eyes were on me and there was no backing out.

For the next few seconds, my whole life's mission was suddenly to shoot the middle of the target. I took my time, trying hard to focus. Will stood back as I cocked the gun, took it off the safety, and squeezed the trigger. I proceeded to shoot about 10 rounds and then pushed the button to pull the target in. To everyone's shock and amazement, I had a good grouping with all of them right in the center of the target. I shot better than Will did, and he had been shooting for years. Once again, Will proved the impossible by teaching me something that I did not think I could learn. I wasn't sure if I would ever want to do it again, but at least I tried it and apparently, I was good at it. It made me laugh to myself because it was so random and unexpected, probably a classic case of beginner's luck.

After we finished at the range, we had lunch at the barbecue place where everyone was still oooh-ing and awwww-ing over the skills that I never knew I had. I earned the new nickname of Sharpshooter Sydney. Then we went back to Toby and Kayla's for Kayla's homemade cherry cobbler and vanilla ice cream on the patio. She seemed close to perfect so far.

Toby stood up and motioned for Will to follow him. "I've been having trouble with my lawn mower, can you take a look at it really quick?"

Kayla and I were left alone on the patio and talked about some ideas for the wedding. I found that Kayla is incredibly creative and had a lot of great ideas. She was going to come in handy.

A little while later, Will and Toby came back from the garage with strained expressions on their faces. "Well, we better hit the road. Sydney, are you ready?" he asked.

"It was so nice meeting you both, I had a lot of fun!" I said. "And you too, Eevee René," I added, giving her one last pat on the head.

"I guess we will see you at Christmas then, or at the wedding, whichever is sooner!" Kayla said, giving both of us a hug.

Toby gave Will a hug and we started on our way home. I'd never been around so much hugging until I met Will's family; they were all avid huggers which I would need to get used to.

"Well, that got awkward," Will said, backing out of the long driveway.

"What? I think they were surprised we are engaged already, but I thought it was fun! I liked Kayla! It will be fun to have her as a sister-in-law. She has a ton of good ideas for the wedding. And did you see the cute little spot for Eevee? We could totally do that for Meatball Face," I said, folding my target up neatly. I planned to keep it as proof of my marksmanship skills.

"Sydney, when Toby took me in the garage, it had nothing to do with a lawn mower. He was lecturing me about jumping into things.

I know he is only looking out for me, but I wish people could understand that I can make my own decisions without everyone telling me what they think about it."

"Well, I'm sure he thinks I'm pregnant or something. But whatever, it's fine. He's only worried about you and doesn't want to see you get hurt. 25 years from now when we are still married and happy, everyone will see that we knew what we were doing."

I believed there was no fixed timeline for knowing if you were making the right decision. Some people date for ten years only to end up hating each other a year after their wedding, while others with a two-year engagement break up three years later. Then there are other people like Mimi and Pop, who only knew each other for a whole two weeks, got married, and have been happily together for more than 50 years. Odds were that many of our friends and family would give us their unsolicited opinion of how we rushed into this, so we were going to need to get used to it.

# Chapter 23

## *Will*

I didn't have an opinion on when we should get married, the color scheme for the wedding, or the flavor of the cake. I figured my job as groom was simply to show up at the wedding on time, wearing the assigned clothing, and remembering to bring the ring. I assumed all decisions regarding the wedding were to be made strictly by Sydney. The wedding is for the bride, not for the groom. At least that is what I've learned from the weddings I've been to in the past and from what my married friends have told me.

The way Sydney asked my opinion on wedding details the entire drive home was an indication that she did not care about traditional wedding planning methods. Or maybe it was that I was wrong about how weddings are planned.

"How do you feel about navy and ivory for wedding colors? Oh, and do you want something more casual? We don't have to do anything fancy. What about cake? What flavor do you want for the groom's cake? I like December, do you? Wouldn't it be adorable to do tiny succulents for wedding favors?"

For each question she asked, I had no real answer. I responded with a variety of, "Yea, that's great! Perfect! Anything is fine with me!" Honestly, I didn't care about any of those things. Whatever she wanted was fine with me. We could get married in a public bathroom at 5:00 in the morning and it would still be perfect for me. I just wanted Sydney to be my wife. I'd even be fine with eloping or going to the courthouse, but I knew Sydney wanted a wedding.

"I really do not want anything big or fancy. Only a few friends and family. Is that ok with you?" she asked.

"That is perfect," I said. I was relieved. A small wedding with only a few people was better than I imagined.

"I feel like weddings now are like a social media competition or something. It's this huge production with all the parties and matching pajamas and rules for what you can wear to brunch and it's just too much. I feel like all the fluff takes the fun out of the wedding and just makes it stressful for everyone. I can't deal with all that."

"Who has to wear matching pajamas? And there are rules for what you can wear to brunch?" I asked.

"Oh my gosh. It's a whole thing. I don't know about the groom's people, but there are policies and procedures for what the bridal party wears for literally everything. I'm going to be rebellious and not even have a bridal party, only one single bridesmaid. She can wear whatever the heck she wants. I think just simple and not having to go by a bunch of rules and regulations is better for us, don't you think?"

"Sounds good to me." I liked the rebellious side of Sydney; it could get entertaining sometimes.

Sydney had already called Leanne, Ashley, and Jamie on the way home and told them all about how we became engaged. Then she texted them all a picture of her ring. The three of them were all supportive and happy for us. We decided to wait until we got back home to tell anyone else because there was a good chance that there would be some skepticism with a few.

. . . . . . . . . . . . . . .

That evening when we got back home, Sydney proudly taped her shooting target on the pantry door and took a picture of it for her "records" as she called it. Based on the thousands of pictures on her cell phone, Sydney needed a record of everything. Most of her photos were of Micah and Elsie, but she even had photo documentation of the daily progress of her Monstera leaf opening which was at least 30 photos.

During dinner, I told the kids I had something big to ask them. While they both sat wide-eyed waiting to hear the big question, I asked them if they would be ok with me and their mom getting married. Even though they were young, Sydney and I wanted to include them as much as possible since it affected them as well. Elsie didn't have much understanding of marriage. She mainly knew that a wedding was a party with a fancy dress and cake. Micah had a basic understanding of the concept of marriage in that it was a couple that loved each other and lived together and sometimes had a family. Fortunately for me, they both happily gave me the go-ahead with marrying their mom.

Earlier, on the drive home from New Mexico, I suggested that Sydney and I tell her grandparents our news when we got home. She wasn't as confident about telling them as I was, but she also didn't know about the envelope that Pop gave me.

After we talked to the kids, we went over to Mimi and Pop's. Pop didn't look good. He'd declined more lately, he'd been losing weight and getting weaker, and he looked as if he had aged ten years in just the past couple of months. He didn't like for anyone to baby him, though.

"So? Tell us about your trip to New Mexico! Did you have fun?" Mimi asked us while she got the kids a bowl of pretzels. It seemed that neither Mimi nor Pop believed that children could ever be without food or drink.

"Oh, it was so fun! Will taught me how to shoot!" Sydney said, excitedly.

"Not only did I teach her how to shoot, but she was better than I was! You should have seen her!" That was something I was still having a hard time believing, even though I watched it with my own eyes and would see the proof every time I went to the pantry.

"Of course she can shoot, she's my granddaughter! What else did you do?" Pop asked.

Sydney paused for a moment. "Well, I know it may seem a little soon," she said hesitantly, "but we got engaged!" She showed Mimi and Pop her left hand.

"Oh my! I'm so happy!" Mimi said and hugged us both. "I just knew it!"

"What took you so long?" Pop asked me, smiling from his chair.

"Your granddaughter proposed to *me* before I even had a chance to do it! I had the ring in my pocket!" I told him.

"You're both ok with it? I was afraid you would think we were jumping into it too soon," Sydney said relieved.

Mimi sat down and pulled Elsie into her lap. "I've told you how long Rusty and I dated before we got engaged. Two weeks! It worked for us! You two remind me of how we were when we were younger."

Pop looked at me and laughed. "You've had her cooking, right?"

"Yes, sir. And I've already planned to be the primary chef." I laughed while Sydney rolled her eyes and playfully hit me in the arm.

"We were thinking about having the wedding in December. It's only six months away, but I think I can get a small wedding planned by then," Sydney said.

Mimi and Pop looked at each other and Mimi's expression changed from happy to sad in an instant.

"I don't think I'll be able to make it to a wedding in December," Pop said, looking down at the floor. "I sure would like to go through."

Sydney looked at me and I knew what she was thinking. We would be moving the wedding up sooner. It was getting increasingly difficult for him to get out of the house anymore. He typically only got out for medical appointments, and even that was almost too much for him to handle.

"We can move it up! I really want you both to be there. Do you think September would work?" she asked him.

Pop shook his head slowly. "How about next month?"

"Rusty, that's too soon. They can't plan a wedding that fast," Mimi said with a pained expression on her face.

I eyed a folder from a hospice company sticking out from under a notebook on his end table. He caught me looking at it and casually straightened the notebook to hide it. Sydney didn't see it.

Sydney looked at me with panic in her eyes at the thought of planning a wedding for next month, but we nodded at each other in agreement. Sydney wanted her grandparents there and we would do whatever we needed to do to make that happen.

"Of course. Next month it is!" I said, unsure of how we would pull it off, but clearly, we needed to do it fast if Pop was going to be there.

Mimi followed us out the door when we left. "I'm sorry Pop pressured you. He probably shouldn't have done that, but he does want to see the two of you get married. He's been talking about how much he likes Will ever since Easter."

"It's ok, we'll make it work. It makes me happy that he likes Will considering how he hasn't liked anyone else any of us have dated or married." Sydney laughed.

The kids climbed into the car with their bags of animal crackers and their five-dollar bills that Pop gave them. The kids always seemed to leave Mimi and Pop's house with gifts and prizes. For as young as they were, they were both getting quite a stash of dollar bills in the little personalized banks Sydney was using to save their money in. Sydney collected their bags of animal crackers before she got in.

. . . . . . . . .

"So, we are going to tell everyone we are engaged and that the wedding is next month…" she said slowly as she unlocked the door and walked into the house. "Everyone is going to think I'm pregnant."

I'm sure it would be the first thing everyone thought. But we did set ourselves up for whatever negativity or assumptions people had so that was on us, but it was fine, I didn't care.

"Who cares what people think? It's our life, not theirs. We know what we have, we know we love each other, and it doesn't matter what other people think, right? We'll prove them wrong."

"You're right. We've pretty much gone against the norm ever since we even met. We might as well keep it going that way." She walked over to the calendar on the refrigerator. "How about Saturday, July fourth?"

"Fourth of July? I'll lose my independence on Independence Day." I laughed. Sydney smirked and rolled her eyes at that.

"So, if we do the fourth of July, it will be perfect. We will be off work for every anniversary unless we work somewhere that doesn't close on holidays."

"And it keeps the holiday theme going. The first time I came over was Easter, then we get married on the fourth of July. You're right. It's perfect," I said. "And it will be hard to forget our anniversary," I added, chuckling.

Sydney took a roll of chocolate chip cookie dough out of the refrigerator and cut off a huge chunk to eat raw, her favorite snack. Then she placed slices of the rest of it on a cookie sheet and put them in the oven. Micah sat on the floor to watch them bake through the oven door window.

"Kennedy would have a fit if she saw me eating this. She does not condone eating raw cookie dough even though it says on the label it's safe to eat raw." She laughed and sat back down next to me with her heap of dough.

She gasped and sat up straight like she just had the best idea ever. "You know what else? Since we are on the untraditional bandwagon, let's get married at 10:00 in the morning! I mean, it's better than making our guests sit in puddles of their own sweat in the heat of the day in 100-degree weather. And since it's the fourth of July, they can have the rest of the day for their own festivities instead of being bogged down with our wedding. I mean really, nobody actually *enjoys* going to a wedding unless it's their own.

"Then, instead of any of the traditional wedding activities, we just can have some cake, and everyone can be on their way. No taco bar, no drunk people line dancing, no hour-long photo session. We can ask people to take candid photos on their cell phones and send them to us. How does that sound?" she asked me.

"That sounds like my dream wedding," I said to her. Actually, I didn't have a dream wedding and I'm pretty sure none of my friends did either. But Sydney's idea sounded perfect to me.

"Yay! I mean, we have one month to plan it so we certainly can't do much anyway. And honestly, have you ever noticed that sometimes everyone seems so stressed on their wedding day that it doesn't even look fun for anyone. I don't want a stressful day. I want us to be happy and enjoy the day. Something simple and easy and just have people there that are close to us. To me, that is the perfect wedding day."

We decided we would ask Kip to be my best man and Leanne to be the maid of honor since we wouldn't have even met if it weren't for her. Elsie and Micah would be flower girl and ring bearer of course.

The cookie timer went off and Sydney got up and scraped the cookies onto a plate and handed one to Micah. Elsie came in to collect her cookie, wearing a purple beanie on her head and snow boots with her shorts.

"Where are we going to have it?" I asked her as she handed me a cookie and sat on my lap.

"Oh, good question... I have no idea. I have a friend that got married on the patio at a yogurt place."

"I think I know a place, not as fancy as a yogurt place patio of course, but with some sweet talking to the owners, I think it will work."

# Chapter 24

## *Sydney*

"Um, there's raw eggs in that," Kennedy said with a disgusted look on her face as I licked cake batter off the spoon. "Don't come crying to me when you have food poisoning. But it's your funeral, I guess," she added and shrugged.

"I've been licking cake batter off the spoon my whole life and I haven't died yet," I said, getting the last scrape of cake batter before putting the bowl in the sink.

"We have a rule against that at work," Kennedy said as she picked up her work notebook to show me. When she started her job at the bakery, she made a very organized three ring binder which contained a map with the fire escape plan, an employee handbook, a calendar of Kennedy's work schedule, and contact information for the people who worked there.

I'd decided to make Elsie's birthday cake at my mom's house in case I needed help with it. This was my first decorated cake since taking the class at Lilly's bakery and I was either overly confident in my skills or just plain stupid because I would be taking this cake to Elsie's birthday party today and there was no backup plan. It was sure to be embarrassing if the cake was a total flop, but my mom may be able to help salvage it if my decorating skills were not as on point as I hoped they would be.

Our families would all be meeting for the first time at the party. They all knew about our engagement, so we decided the party was a good time for everyone to get to know each other.

When we told my mom and Raymond about our engagement, they had no negative comments, and they didn't even suggest that I was pregnant. They didn't act as excitedly as Mimi and Pop did, but I think they could see that Will fits so well with me and the kids and our lives are way better than they were a year ago. My mom even offered to let me wear her wedding dress that she married Raymond in. We were the same size and with the style of the dress, it probably didn't even need to be altered.

Both my dad and Eric thought it was ridiculous that Will would propose so soon when we had only dated for two months. Then, when they found out it was me that proposed, they decided I'd completely gone certifiably insane.

Even though none of my family assumed I was pregnant—at least I don't think they did—Will's family, except for Lilly, all jumped to that conclusion in an instant. As a matter of fact, "Is she pregnant?" was the first thing most of them said when they found out. It was hurtful; although, I can't say I blame them. They didn't even know me well and that wasn't their fault. But it made me feel like they didn't see the value in our relationship and that he would only want to marry me because of a pregnancy and not because he loved me. Even if I were pregnant, I do not believe that is a reason to get married. You get married because you love each other. Marriage isn't built on obligation.

The cake turned out halfway decent. I picked up the doll cake topper, stuck it in the middle, and piped swirls all around the cake to make it look like a dress. Then I made some cupcakes with the same color icing to go around it. I was surprised at how good everything looked.

"See there? Not bad for somebody who doesn't have any talent!" Raymond joked and nodded approvingly at the cake. He always said that to me when I did anything that turned out good because I used to always say I wasn't talented at anything.

"It's actually not bad, but Lilly could have done better, though," Kennedy said, looking at my handiwork.

"Wow, Kennedy," I said even though I wasn't actually offended. She says what she means and it's true that Lilly could do better.

"Kennedy, that isn't nice. Sydney did a great job, and Elsie is going to love it," Mom said, coming to my defense.

I gathered the cake and cupcakes and loaded into the car to go home and get everyone ready for the party. As I was about to start the car, my phone dinged.

**It didn't take you long to get engaged.**

My stomach turned into a knot. It was Jeff.

Jeff's text didn't deserve a response. I wasn't sure why he was contacting me now when it had been several months since I'd had any contact with him. For the first few months, I'd tried texting and calling him to try to find out what his plans were for seeing the kids. According to our divorce agreement, he had a right to scheduled visitation. But he never answered my calls, and he usually ignored my texts. Any responses he gave were always vague, and he never committed to anything. Finally, I gave up trying.

......

Back at home, I finished getting things ready for the party and wrapped Elsie's gifts. We got her puzzles, books, doll accessories, and a little doll that she saw at the store a few weeks ago and hadn't stopped talking about. This was the most hideous looking doll I'd ever seen, but Elsie just fell in love with it.

Instead of putting a damper on Elsie's big day, I didn't mention Jeff's text. I'd tell Will about it later.

We loaded up in the truck and headed to the party. The afternoon was terribly hot, and it took a while before the air conditioning started to work. Had I known better, I would have let the air conditioning start to cool off the truck before I put my cake masterpiece in it. I held the cake in my lap with the cupcakes in the backseat. The cake was starting to glisten in a way that I didn't think it should.

The Jump N Bounce Barn was everything parents dreaded but kids love. We were greeted at the door by a man in a cow costume who wished Elsie a happy birthday. Inside, we were told to leave our shoes on the shelves, and we were guided to party room number 3 where I set the cake and cupcakes in the middle of the long table. To my horror, the cake was starting to resemble one of the ugly cake memes you see going viral on social media. The icing was sliding down the sides and puddling at the base. Where the pretty swirls once were, now there was visible cake that looked like a pink milkshake had been poured on it.

"The cake! Will, look! I can't let anyone see this!!!" I cried, pointing at the disaster in front of us. Somehow, the cupcakes didn't look too bad.

"Just tell them Elsie decorated her own cake?" he suggested, amused.

"This is not funny! Your parents are going to see this! Crap! So is Lilly and Elsie's friends' parents!" I was on the verge of tears. And of course, at the most inopportune time, Lilly herself comes into the room and walks over to us.

"Hi!" she said before noticing the cake. "Oh!" she exclaimed, clearly trying to keep her facial expression in check while observing the cake.

"Yea, it was too hot in the truck and the cake melted. Can we fix it?"

"Ummm. I'm afraid that's goanna be a no," she said as Kennedy walked up to us.

"What the heck?" She scoffed, staring wide eyed at the heap of cake and melted icing before her.

"Nothing to see here," I told her, not wanting to draw attention to it while we tried to plan our strategy.

We salvaged the cake debacle by scraping off the remaining icing and making it look intentional, like a trendy naked cake design.

While we worked on the cake, Lilly updated me on how Kennedy was doing at work.

"She's doing a fabulous job, Sydney! I think it's just the right place for her. I can see how she wouldn't do well in something fast paced or crowded. She keeps everything clean and organized, and she's doing much better greeting people when they walk in the door. I'm thrilled to have her there." That was excellent news. I was so glad we found a good place for her to work. And she loved having money to spend.

Once the icing fiasco was resolved, introductions were made between the two families, and we sat down for the naked doll cake and cupcakes. Then, Elsie opened her gifts, and everyone moved into the play area.

An hour later, weary parents gathered their children and wished Elsie their final "happy birthdays." It's a good thing the time allotment for a party was only two hours, I don't think any of the adults could endure much longer than that.

Our families both got along remarkably well, and everyone remained on their best behavior...until the awkward moment when Kennedy stood up to make an important announcement to the entire group.

"I need an appointment with the gynecologist," she stated loudly and firmly.

This random statement made my mom nearly spit out her drink and sent Eric into a fit of silent, convulsing laughter to the point he was crying and had to leave the room. It wasn't the fact that she wanted to go to the doctor that was funny, it was the way she very matter of factly stated it to everyone there, including the men, as if she was about to give a toast.

We even managed to squeeze in a bit of wedding planning during the party. Barbara and Lillie volunteered to make the wedding cake and the groom's cake. Will decided on German chocolate for the groom's cake, and I told them they could make any flavor of cake that they wanted to for the wedding cake. I trusted their judgment on it, and I wasn't picky.

We decided to have the wedding in Will's parents' back yard. Leonard panicked just a little bit when we asked him, and even though we told him not to stress about the yard, he made plans to go straight to the store after the party to buy fertilizer. He insisted that the grass would be green and pretty in time for the wedding. It had been so dry and hot lately that everyone's yards were turning yellow.

One of Raymond's friends was an ordained minister. Raymond called him during the party, and he agreed to perform the ceremony for us. I would make the bouquets and all the decorations. Our wedding was coming together perfectly!

Most importantly of all, both sides of our families were able to see Will in action with the kids. He had as much fun as the kids did, throwing them into ball pits, refereeing races down the slides, and helping them make baskets on the short basketball goals. It was good for everyone to see that he was good with the kids and even though he wasn't theirs biologically, he was happy to fill that seemingly vacant position.

......

I'd been so busy at the party that I hadn't thought about Jeff's text until we got home. We'd only been home about half an hour when he texted again.

**Those are my kids, not your boyfriend's.**

What the hell was this? He hadn't seen or even asked about them since moving to Colorado with his girlfriend, almost a year ago, even before our divorce was final. And now he's suddenly worried about them? I wasn't about to engage in this with him. It was just like him, always ready to twist things around and make it look like I was the one in the wrong.

Will saw me frowning at my phone. "What's wrong?"

I checked to make sure the kids weren't in earshot, but they were both in Elsie's room playing with her new things. "I don't know what to make of this," I said, worried and confused. "But I have had two texts from Jeff today." I showed him both the texts on my phone.

"Wow," he said. "Who does this asshole think he is?"

"I don't even know how he knows about you. We haven't really had any communication in months, unless he has a friend giving him information about me or something."

"Is he still in Colorado?"

"I don't even know. He doesn't have much family, but the ones he has all live in Colorado. I blocked him on all my social media when we got divorced, and I don't follow him on anything. He never would return my calls or texts back when I was trying to work out visitation."

Even though his texts weren't overtly threatening, those two messages caused so much anxiety that I couldn't sleep all night.

Michelle J. Mann

# Chapter 25

## *Will*

### Monday...

Sydney didn't receive any more texts from Jeff since Saturday; however, she remained on edge through the rest of the weekend. Even though the texts weren't threatening, she said she just had a gut feeling that there would be more coming, and that Jeff had something up his sleeve that she should prepare herself for.

We asked a few of the neighbors to keep an eye on the house, especially if they saw a black truck since that was the last truck that Sydney knew him to have. I told her to call me immediately if he were to show up at the house or threaten her in any way. She already had a video doorbell on the front door, but I went ahead and put a camera on the backdoor too. Luckily, she would be at work all day today.

On the way to work, I thought about how my family felt about the wedding. My parents did a great job of hiding their real feelings at the party, but I knew in the back of their minds, they still disapproved of our engagement. There's no way they could have had a change of heart that quickly.

It isn't that they dislike Sydney. They aren't the type of people that necessarily dislike others, they tend to see the good in people that others don't always see; however, things seem to be different when it involves their son's future wife. I just wish they could see all the good in Sydney, the things I see in her and the reasons why I don't want to wait to be her husband.

What irritated me most is that in all the things I'd ever done throughout my entire existence, finding Sydney was what turned my life around like nothing ever had and yet it seemed like only a few people were truly happy for me. There was not one single cell in my body that doubted that she was the only one on earth for me, and it was looked at with disapproval from some of the people we loved. All I could hope for was that in time, they would come around, and they would understand that we knew what we were doing.

I told myself I wasn't going to worry about what other people thought about it. Sydney and I agreed to move the wedding up to next month based on Pop wanting so badly to attend. We didn't need to explain our reasons for having the wedding so quickly. That was between us and Pop, and we would move it up to today if that was the only way he could come.

When I pulled up to the office, Lisa's car was parked in the front. She didn't come to the office particularly often, but when she did, she usually brought us food. I didn't stop for my breakfast burrito this morning so I hoped that would be the case.

Sure enough, she handed me a donut when I walked in. "Good morning, Will! I know you like the blueberry cake ones, so I saved this one for you."

"Lisa, you're too good to me," I said, taking the donut from her.

"I'm glad I caught you before I left, though. Gerald and I are having a barbecue on the 4th of July and hopefully we will do some fireworks too. You and your girlfriend are invited. I hope you can make it!"

"Aw, thanks for the invite, but we can't make it," I said. Since Gerald hadn't had anything nice to say about Sydney and I being together, I hadn't been in a hurry to tell him about our upcoming nuptials.

"Why not?" Gerald asked with his mouth still full of donut.

"We have a wedding to go to."

"Oh, who's getting married?" Lisa asked.

"I am. Just a small wedding at my parents' house with a few close friends and family. We haven't sent out the invitations yet," I told them; both had looks of disbelief on their faces. "So, we'll be a little busy all day."

Here we go, I had a feeling this was going to spark another conversation about Gerald's feelings about Sydney and her 'deceiving intentions.'

"Oh wow! Congratulations, Will!" Lisa said and gave me a hug. She was much nicer than her husband, and I wasn't sure how they managed to stay married for as long as they had, but they do say opposites attract.

Gerald's face said it all. I wasn't surprised when he motioned for Lisa to follow him to the breakroom, as if I wouldn't figure out that they were going to talk about me. This would have been a great time for me to leave and head to the job site, but Gerald's truck was parked behind the work truck so I couldn't get out. Even though the breakroom door was closed, I could hear what seemed to be some arguing and shushing, followed by some more talking. They emerged a few minutes later; Lisa couldn't look at me.

"Look, Will, I know you don't want to hear this. I tried to warn you when you first started going out with her, but you wouldn't listen to me. And frankly, I'm not surprised at all that you two are suddenly getting married. You've been together like what, two months?" he said.

"Yes, so?" I looked at Lisa to see if she had anything to add, but she looked at the floor as soon as our eyes met. This felt more like a lecture from a dad to a teenage son and not at all appropriate for a boss to an employee.

"When you two first started dating, I had a bad feeling about this. And I think I was right. I mean, already getting married? It's obvious, Will. She's just looking for a dad for her kids."

Lisa tried to intervene. "Gerald, we don't know that..."

I sighed heavily. "Gerald, that isn't true, and this really isn't any of your concern as it has nothing at all to do with work. Can we just go, please? We are running late," I said, grabbing my keys and another donut and heading for the door.

"Hold on just a second, Will. Lisa and I talked it over and we agreed on something. If you postpone the wedding for a while, we will pay all the expenses for you to go on a trip to Cancun with us. You can use the time to rethink things and maybe come to your senses a little. We'll even pay you for the whole week, so you don't lose any income."

That pissed me off, but I remained under control, mainly for Lisa's sake. "Thanks for the offer, but I'm going to decline. I do not need to rethink things, and we will not be postponing the wedding."

"Look, it's a free trip. Have you ever been to Cancun? The resort is all inclusive and you can have all the tequila you want. Worst case scenario is you go on this trip, and you don't change your mind." Gerald continued to push.

"No, like I said, I'm good. I'd rather have Sydney than Tequila in Cancun," I said frustrated. "I'm really not sure why you are so worried about it."

Lisa finally spoke up, "I'm sorry, Will, Gerald just worries about you. We've known you for a long time and he doesn't want to see you get hurt. That's all." She looked at Gerald. "Let's drop it, though. Ok Gerald?"

He rolled his eyes and finally said, "Ok, fine. I guess we'll drop it. Let's get to work then."

This was the second time that Gerald had gone too far. This subject was outside of the boundaries of work, and it was unacceptable for him to continue to disrespect the woman I love. I need this job, but could I continue to endure this treatment from my boss? This was not a high paying job. I had to supplement my income with the DJ gig. I could find another job that pays at least this much or more in no time. One where I didn't get bribed with a vacation in exchange for not getting married.

"Yea, you're going to drop it, Gerald." I threw my work truck keys on the counter. "Because I quit."

"Dammit, Will." Gerald slammed his coffee cup down, sloshing coffee all over the counter.

"No, Will... Gerald didn't mean to insult you," Lisa pleaded.

"Yes, he did, Lisa. I won't have him talk about Sydney this way anymore. I'm done." I walked out of the office and slammed the door behind me.

I drove to the coffee shop down the street to calm down and think about what my plan was going to be. I needed to find another job quickly. I decided to wait to tell Sydney about my sudden unemployment until later in the day when I had a plan in place and hopefully, another job. I had several connections in the same type of work.

My phone dinged. It was Sydney. **Do you think the living room would look better painted Alabaster White?**

Oh, this wasn't a good sign. About a week ago I came home from DJ'ing to find a pile of carpet laying over the rail of the front porch. Sydney, it seemed, had suddenly determined that she no longer liked having carpeting in the hallway and proceeded to pull it up and pile it outside.

Her plan had been to lay vinyl flooring, stating she googled it, and it seemed self-explanatory. It wasn't, and I wasn't at all surprised about the painting project.

**Me: The living room is already painted white.**

**Sydney: Yes, it's cotton white, not Alabaster White. There's a HUGE difference.**

How different can two whites be?

**Me: You're at the paint store, aren't you?**

### Sydney: Maybe...

If there was one home project that I could spend for the entire rest of my life without doing, it was painting, but apparently, we would be dramatically changing our existing white walls by painting them Alabaster White instead. It's one thing to paint when you think it will look different, it's even worse to paint when you have no doubt it will not change a thing.

I called a friend of mine that works for a competing fencing company. He said they'd been busier than usual lately and could use the extra help. It wouldn't be permanent, but it would get me by until I found a new job.

I stopped by Mrs. Beasley's house before heading home. She needed me to change the air filters in her air conditioner. I invited her to the wedding while I was there and told her the invitation would be coming in the mail soon.

"Oh! I would not miss that for the world! That Sydney is just the sweetest girl. Oh, and those precious children! You're a lucky one, Will, but so are they." I sure did love that sweet little lady. It was funny how the oldest people seemed to be the most excited about me and Sydney.

She sent me home with some key lime cupcakes that were left over from the church bake sale and told me to bring Sydney and the kids over to see her soon.

Kip called me when I was almost home. "Hey, Will, we need to plan the bachelor party. Tell me what you want to do, and I'll make it happen."

"I don't know. Maybe camping? Or fishing? Water skiing? Bungee jumping? How about we schedule it for the day Sydney plans to paint the living room?" I said, not actually joking about being gone during the painting festivities.

"Ok, well, think about it and let me know. Also, I have a favor to ask you," he said.

"Ask away."

"I'm out of town right now and I need somebody to run by and check on Mark. Just check his water and see if he needs anything."

"Sure thing, I'll take Sydney with me. She is past due for a visit with Mark."

I hung up with Kip when I pulled into the driveway. I walked into what appeared to be a construction site in the living room. My ladder was set up near one wall, furniture was pulled out in the middle of the floor, the walls were bare, and an unopened can of paint was sitting on top of a large piece of plastic. Wow, she did not waste any time at all.

Sydney came out of the kitchen wearing an old T-shirt and shorts, with her hair piled up on top of her head. "Well, I decided tonight was as good a time as any to start the renovations," she said.

"I see that…" I said and chuckled at the word 'renovations.' She looked so cute when she was in home project mode, even if it was a painting project that would no doubt involve my services in reaching the high parts. I already knew she would not go over the second step on the ladder.

"Well, you see… the thing is that I was all stressed out about Jeff texting me and this is my therapy to get my mind off it. I can throw myself into a project and think about that instead," she said, starting to tape off the fireplace mantel.

"Ok, I get that. But before you get too far into this, Kip needs me to go check on Mark. I thought you'd want to go with me, but if you'd rather paint…"

She stopped taping and stood frozen for a second.

"Well?" I asked, smiling at the way she was so deep in thought about her dilemma.

Finally, she let out a long deep breath. "Ok, fine. We'll go see Mark tonight, but the painting will begin tomorrow night at 6:00 sharp," she said matter of factly which made me laugh.

We gathered up the kids and piled into my truck. We heard Elsie's squeaky little voice from the backseat as she sang along to every song that came on the radio the whole way. Micah sat quietly, holding the apple he took to feed Mark.

Mark had been lying in the dirt but got up when he saw us coming, anxious for some attention. Even though Mark was the tamest, calmest bull we had ever seen, he was still a massive beast, and we didn't want to take any chances with the kids. We always had them stand on the other side of the fence and we would lure Mark over to the fence, so they pet him, rather than taking them up to him.

Once Mark made it to the fence, I held Micah up so he could hand Mark the apple. He took it from Micah's little hand and ate it, which resulted in happy squeals from both kids. Then I picked up Elsie and held her to where she could pet Mark on the head.

Sydney went into the barn, grabbed a brush, and then brushed Mark's shiny black hair.

"Mark likes having his hair brushed as much as I do," she said. Sydney loved that bull so much. I stood and watched her. I thought she looked gorgeous brushing Mark, even in her old painting shirt and shorts, boots, and her hair a mess. It looked like all her worries about Jeff were gone and she was just in her own little world without a care at all.

Elsie and Micah stood on the fence while Elsie sang loudly, "And on that farm he had a bull, E-I-E-I-OOOO."

"Elsie! Stop singing!" Micah finally said, tired of his sister always being so noisy.

I stood back and took a picture with my phone. The kids on the fence and my beautiful fiancée in the background brushing a freaking huge bull, as if it is the most calming activity she's ever done.

We can deal with whatever does or doesn't happen with Jeff. I'll make sure of that. And we can handle all the negativity. Years from now, when we are still together and happy, nobody is going to care about who did or who didn't agree with it.

# Chapter 26

# *Sydney*

The living room transformation project started Tuesday after work, but I only got one wall finished and put back together. The plan was to work on it again yesterday after work, but I started feeling sick and having more asthma. I carried my cup and book into the bedroom because I couldn't bear to look at my unfinished painting project another minute, knowing I couldn't work on it until I got over this respiratory infection.

I'd felt sick enough that I had to take the day off work. I needed to keep my asthma from getting bad, too. It always gets worse when I'm sick and it isn't uncommon for me to have to go to the hospital. Will took the kids to daycare on his way to work because I planned to take some medicine, stay in bed, and hopefully get some sleep.

Before Will left for work this morning, he made me my favorite breakfast, avocado toast with a fried egg on top. He also made sure the refrigerator was stocked, so I had plenty of things to drink all day. He even took my temperature and checked my oxygen. It was so sweet; I'd never had anybody treat me this way since I'd been an adult.

I heard my text notification.

**Are you up to debriefing via text message?** It was Jamie.

Me: **Yes, what's on the agenda?**

Jamie: **Your boss is going to be the death of me.**

Me: **I'm not claiming her. What did your boss do?**

Jamie: **She told me I have to start being at work by 8:00!?**

Me: **Uh huh… You know we've opened at 8:00 for the whole three years you've worked there, right? lol**

Jamie: **Yes, but I've never once come to work on time, so I don't know why she's worried about it all of the sudden…**

Me: **Hmmm. OK, well, my cold medicine is kicking in so I'm going to take a nap.**

Jamie: **OK, but really quick, anything new from Jeff?**

Me: **Nope, haven't heard a word from him since Saturday. I guess he got over it and moved on.**

Jamie: **K, you better be back tomorrow or I'm faking a ruptured ovarian cyst and staying home.**

I put my phone down on the end table and hoped it would be quiet. I never silenced my phone when my kids weren't with me.

Meatball Face peered up at me, making it impossible to ignore his pitiful little face. I grabbed him and put him in bed with me, then took another couple of puffs of my inhaler before finally drifting off to sleep.

.......

The barking woke me up. I looked at the clock, 1:17PM. "Meatball, go back to sleep," I said and covered my head up. Then I heard the knocking, and the barking became more frantic. Probably just my one of my online orders, they usually knock once and then leave the package by the door. They knocked again.

"Dammit. Come on, Meatball." I picked him up and put him on the floor. He ran to the door.

I opened the door and froze. Jeff was standing on my porch, holding the screen door open. Every single bit of anxiety I used to have all came flooding back at once like a punch to my throat before I could even process what was happening.

That asshole stood there looking at me just like he used to. Towering over me like he was in charge of me.

"You ignored me when I tried to talk to you, so I came to talk to you in person," he said, his voice as arrogant and condescending as ever.

Wait, what? He ignored every single one of my calls and texts for months. He texted me twice last week and it was nothing that required or deserved a response, so I didn't. We were right back to him gaslighting me.

"You need to leave, if you need something, you can call me," I said, and tried to close the door. I could tell by his tone that it wasn't going to be a good conversation.

"It's also my house, and I'm not leaving until we get something straight," he said, pushing past me into the living room.

"I didn't say you can come in. What are you even doing in town and how did you know I was at home?" Had he been watching me? He shouldn't have known I wasn't at work.

"A friend told me your car was home. I called your office to be sure, and your boss, Mei, has no problem telling callers when her employees are out sick."

Dammit, Mei. How could she be so stupid?

"You need to leave or I'm calling the police." My phone was ringing but it was still on my end table in the bedroom.

"You always did look cute when you were pissed off," he said, stepping closer to me.

"Will should be home any minute, you need to go," I lied, stepping backward away from him.

"Speaking of Will, I'm their dad, remember? He doesn't have any business over here playing daddy."

I could hear my phone ringing again from my bedroom.

"Will has been more of a dad to them in the past few months than you have ever been since Micah was born." This was not a lie. There was no comparison between the two.

I started wheezing and reached for my extra inhaler on the coffee table. Jeff grabbed it before I could get to it.

"I'll make you a deal, I'll leave and give you your little inhaler back, but only if you do me a favor. If you'll stop fighting, it will make it a lot faster." he said and pushed me against the wall while he unzipped his pants. I was struggling to breathe while he put his hand up my shirt.

The phone rang again.

"Stop it!" I yelled and tried to push him away. Meatball Face started barking aggressively and tried to bite Jeff's leg, but yelped loudly as Jeff kicked him away.

Will kept a gun in a locked box on the top shelf of his closet. A couple weeks ago, he showed me where the key was and how to unlock the trigger lock. I needed a way to get to it. And I needed my phone and my inhaler.

I started panicking, not only because of what Jeff was doing, but also because it was getting so hard to breathe. I kneed Jeff between the legs and broke free, but only for a second.

"Bitch!" he said as he caught me by the arm. Then I felt the impact of his fist as it hit my face. My ears were ringing as he pinned me down onto the couch. I screamed again as he held my arms above my head and pulled my shorts down with his other hand. I tried to get my legs out from under him, but he had his entire weight on me, and I couldn't move. I was suffocating and couldn't do anything about it.

"Stop fighting, Sydney, you know you want it," he said, his foul breath inches from my face.

The front door swung open, and before I knew what was happening, Will had Jeff in a chokehold, swung him around, and threw him down on the floor. He sat on top of him and proceeded to punch him over and over so forcefully that Jeff's blood was splattering on the white walls, and I wasn't sure if he wouldn't kill him.

I found the inhaler on the floor and took several puffs of it. Once I was able to, I screamed as loudly as I could.

Moments later, two sheriff's deputies burst into the house and pulled Will off Jeff. Then they handcuffed both men. I was still in shock, my mind was racing, trying to process what just happened.

"Wait! Why is he handcuffed?" I cried, pointing at Will. "That's my fiancé, he saved me!" Will was out of breath with Jeff's blood splattered on his work uniform.

"Ma'am, we just need to talk to him and get everyone's story first," the deputy said, leading Will out on the porch.

The second deputy escorted Jeff outside and put him in the patrol car. Jeff's face was red with blood, and it looked like he could have a broken nose and some missing teeth.

Will's handcuffs were removed, and he was asked to stay on the porch while the deputy came inside to talk to me. I was shaking and just wanted Will with me.

"Ma'am, my name is Deputy Ortiz. I know you're scared, and you want your boyfriend to come in, but I asked him to stay on the porch until I'm through talking to you."

"He's not going to be arrested?" I asked, crying again.

"No, ma'am. I don't believe so. I just need to get your story on what happened and then he can come back in."

"Jeff is my ex-husband, and he pushed his way into the house. I was having asthma, and he told me I couldn't have my inhaler back until I 'did him a favor.' He tried to force himself on me and when I tried to get away, he punched me in the face and then he pinned me down and tried to take off my clothes."

"Ok, does your ex-husband have any rights to the house?"

"No, our divorce is final, and I got the house."

"Ok, then what happened after that?"

"Then Will came home and pulled him off me and they started fighting. That was right before you came in."

"Do you feel like you need to go to the hospital to be checked out?" he asked, looking at my face.

"No, I think I'm ok," I said, putting my hand on my face. I was going to have an ugly bruise. He took some photos of my injuries.

"I'm sorry this happened to you, your ex-husband is being arrested on charges of assault. This is the case number." He handed me a card. "Feel free to call the station if you have any questions, we're going to take some photographs of the scene," he said and left to tell Will he could come inside.

Will ran inside and wrapped his arms around me tight. "Sydney, are you ok? I wanted to kill that son of a bitch." He pulled back to get a good look at my face and scanned the rest of my body for injuries.

"I'll be ok. How did you know?"

"The doorbell notified me that somebody was at the door. I saw him on the video and called the police. I kept trying to call you. I can't believe it took them so long to get there."

"He wouldn't let me get to my phone! If you hadn't come when you did, I think he would have raped me. I couldn't get away from him." I started to cry harder. "And he took my inhaler, and I couldn't breathe! He wasn't going to give it back to me until I had sex with him." I was trembling while it all sank in what all just happened. He used to do this kind of thing to me in the past, but never to this extreme, and he had never hit me that hard before.

"He won't be here again; he can't be that stupid. If he does, he'll be leaving in a body bag, not a patrol car."

While Will went to pick the kids up, I took a hot shower and put an icepack on my face, which was puffy, red, and bruised. My eye was starting to swell up more also.

Micah and Elsie both carried gifts for me when they returned.

Micah handed me a bouquet of pink flowers wrapped in green tissue paper.

"He picked those out himself," Will said, going to the kitchen for a vase.

"What happened to your face, Mom?" Micah asked, staring at me.

"Just a little accident; it'll be fine, though. It hardly even hurts."

"I'm sorry 'bout your face, Mommy," Elsie said, giving me the stuffed ladybug she picked out for me. She continued to stare at my face with big, concerned eyes.

"For dinner, you will be dining on coconut shrimp with pina colada sauce, shrimp scampi, and popcorn shrimp, with a side of loaded baked potato. I'm not making it, but it will be delivered soon." Will spoils me to the maximum. That is my favorite meal.

"You hate shrimp," I said.

"The kids and I are having chicken strips and fries. Our order is coming separately," he said, handing me a glass of peach wine.

I smiled, probably for the first time the whole day.

"There's a whole roll of cookie dough in the fridge for dessert. You can eat the whole thing raw if you want," he said. He was clearly doing everything he could think to do to make me feel better after what happened today.

"Thank you, Will. You didn't have to do all this, I'll be ok," I said, cuddling up to him closer. "But I'm glad you did."

# Chapter 27

## *Will*

I checked the jail roster every day. Jeff was still sitting there right where he belonged. He wouldn't be there forever, and we'd need to deal with that. We would probably need to get Sydney's attorney to help us handle things because it was complicated with the kids. But for now, Sydney was doing okay, and I would do anything to make sure she stayed that way.

It was no secret that many of our family members weren't on board with our sudden and short engagement. There'd been quite a bit of gossip floating around both families. Most of them thought it was too soon and most of my family suspected that Sydney was pregnant, which she was not. I'd been tempted to send out a group text to my family requesting that only those that were happy for us attend the wedding, but Sydney talked me out of it.

"It doesn't matter what anyone else thinks. Like I keep telling you, one day, many years from now, when we are old and grey, nobody will even remember that they didn't approve. It's fine," she'd said.

Sydney's mom and Raymond volunteered to keep the kids all day so we could get things ready. They would take them to the rehearsal and to the dinner, but then they would take them back to their house to spend the night.

We spent the first part of the day getting everything ready for the rehearsal and the wedding. We picked up the chairs and arch that we rented and set those out. Then we set up the cake table and had everything else set out and ready to put in their places in the morning.

Sydney did a beautiful job with the decorations which she made herself including floral arrangements, bouquets, boutonnieres, and corsages. She'd chosen simple greenery with various ivory flowers. She had a knack for decorating and it saved us a fortune that way.

My dad fertilized the lawn after we asked him to hold the wedding at their house. He'd been diligently watering daily until it looked healthy and green. He'd planted flowers in the flowerbeds and placed potted plants around on the patio. The yard looked great.

It didn't take long to get everything ready since it was going to be such a simple wedding. Afterwards, Sydney went over to Ashley's house with Leanne so they could do their "spa treatments."

I thought it was brave of them to do that the day before the wedding because from what Sydney told me, there was usually some sort of disaster involved. Ashley was going to put some highlights in Sydney's hair as well. That alone seemed a little sketchy. I wasn't sure if Ashley even knew how to do highlights, but I'd heard enough horror stories from Lilly to know that things can go bad fast when dealing with hair chemicals. Afterwards, they were all going to get massages. I wouldn't see her again until the rehearsal.

With Sydney being gone all day, it left me just enough time to get her gift ready. I'd been planning a big surprise for her, and I was going to give it to her when we got home tonight. I'd known about this surprise for a couple of weeks, and it was driving me crazy keeping it a secret from her.

Sydney had been over at Ashley's for a couple hours when she called me, sounding frantic.

She was whispering, "I'm going to kill Ashley!"

"Why are you whispering and what's wrong?" I asked.

"I'm in her bathroom. I don't want her to hear me. I have freaking white hair!!!"

"Why do you have white hair?" I wasn't surprised. I knew it was a bad idea to let an untrained Ashley highlight her hair the day before the wedding.

"I'm sending you a picture."

A second later, I received her picture.  Her hair was very, very light.  She had dark blonde hair the last time I saw her.

"Wow!  It looks great!"  It honestly did not look as bad as she thought it did.  She still looked beautiful.  It was just a shock to her because it wasn't what she was expecting.  But she still looked great.

"Stop lying!  I look ridiculous!" she hissed into the phone.  "I have to go; I'll see you later. Bye."

We saw each other again at my parents' house for the rehearsal. She had on a green Boston ball cap with her hair in a ponytail.

"Sydney, your hair looks fine.  You don't need a hat," I told her. She always got highly insecure any time there was the slightest change in her appearance.

"You're only saying that to be nice," she snapped.

I laughed a little. "No, I'm saying that because it's true.  And are you wearing a hat tomorrow with your dress?"

"I haven't figured out the details yet," she said, looking annoyed.

Once everyone got there, we went through a quick rehearsal. The only people that needed to be there were the ones that were actually in the wedding party.  We invited parents, siblings, and grandparents to dinner, though. Mimi and Pop weren't going to make it to dinner, Pop wasn't feeling well, and he was trying to not overdo it so he could be at the wedding.

Sydney had made the decision to walk down the aisle alone rather than having anyone walk with her. Seeing her come down the aisle, even in that green hat, made me want to cry right in front of everyone. By this time tomorrow, we will already be married.

The kids looked as cute as they could be practicing their parts. Elsie was born to be a flower girl and played the part like the crowd pleaser that she was.

Kip walked over to me after the rehearsal. "What is the maid of honor's name? And is she single?" he asked, looking over at Leanne. "She's freaking hot!"

"That's Sydney's cousin, Leanne, and yes, she's single." I glared at him. "But don't be stupid with her, she's a nice girl."

After the rehearsal everyone headed to La Pimienta's where my parents reserved the private room for the rehearsal dinner. They chose it because that's where Sydney and I had our first date, and I appreciated the thought they put into it.

Kip stood up. "I would like to give a toast to the bride and groom." Everyone stopped talking and gave him their undivided attention. "I've known Will for ten years, and I've never seen him as happy as he is now. Sydney, you've taken this worthless piece of crap and turned him into a respectable human being. Thank you for doing what the rest of us failed miserably at."

"Cheers!" everyone said in unison and laughed as Kip sat back down.

Leanne stood up next. "Well, I'm not one to give toasts, but here goes nothing. Will, I knew the two of you were destined to be together that first day when you met. I've known Sydney since the day I was born, and I've never seen her this happy. I just want to welcome you to the family and congratulations to you both!"

I held Sydney's hand and put my arm around her. She had tears rolling down her cheeks. "Thank you, Leanne!" she said to her.

Everyone cheered again and then the least expected individual stood up and tapped her glass with her spoon. We could have heard a pin drop as the whole room turned completely silent.

"I would like to propose a toast in honor of the bride and groom, Sydney and Will. As the sister of the bride, I want to say how happy I am that Sydney has met someone that will protect her and do life with her. She couldn't ever find anyone better than Will. I'm so happy to have Will as my brother-in-law. Congratulations to both of you." Kennedy still stood proud and confident. I couldn't be prouder of her than I was at this moment. I knew how difficult it was for her to get up in front of everyone and do that.

Everyone cheered and tapped their glasses together. Tears rolled down Sydney's parents' faces. Tears were streaming down Sydney's face, but she had a huge smile.

"Thank you so much, Kennedy! That means so much to us!" she said beaming.

The dinner wrapped up and everyone started leaving. Leanne and Kip hit it off during dinner and decided to go out afterwards for drinks.

"Everything is ready for the surprise," Kip said to me discreetly.

"Thanks, man. I owe you one for this," I said and hugged him.

On the way home, I told Sydney I had a small gift waiting for her.

"I didn't know we were supposed to get each other gifts!" she said, looking worried.

"It's only a little thing, nothing big. Don't worry. I just thought it was something you would like."

When we walked into the house, I handed her a pink gift bag that was sitting on the counter. She eagerly pulled the tissue paper out.

"Oh…" she said, looking confused. "You got me a fruit basket?" she said, pulling the basket of apples, oranges, and pears out of the bag.

"I thought you would like it. You like fruit."

"Yea, I do. Thanks, Will!" she said, trying to be nice but clearly disappointed.

"If you don't like it, I have something else you can have."

"No, I like it," she said, trying to pretend like she liked her fruit basket.

"Seriously, there's more. Bring an apple with you for a snack and I'll take you to the other part of it. Here, put on this blindfold." I put a blindfold over her eyes and picked her up.

"What are you doing, Will?" she said, laughing.

I carried her around in circles so she wouldn't figure out where we were going. Then, I carried her around the back, opened the gate, and stood her back down on the ground.

"Ok, take off the blindfold," I told her.

She took off the blindfold and stood there, seemingly shocked as she stared at her massive gift standing in front of her, wearing a huge pink bow wrapped around his beastly neck.

"Mark?" she said, starting to cry. "You got me Mark? He's mine?"

"He sure is!" I said, beaming at her.

"How? Why? I don't understand!" she said, petting her new bull.

"Kip is moving into town, and he can't keep him. He and his friends were over all day getting everything ready. He is donating a barn for him too, but it will be a few days before we get it. Until then, he'll have this lean-to shelter."

"Will! I can't believe it! Oh my gosh! Thank you!! She jumped up and hugged me."

"Oh, and the fruit basket isn't for you. It's for Mark."

# Chapter 28

## *Sydney*

### July 4th

I'd be lying if I said Jeff wasn't on the back of my mind all the time since he attacked me. I'm only human. I can't erase what he did or stop worrying about what was going to happen when he got out of jail. But today was about me and Will. A day that we would remember for the rest of our lives, and I wasn't going to let anything ruin it for us.

Our suitcases were packed and ready to leave tomorrow. Micah and Elsie were going to be staying with my mom for part of the week and Leanne the other part. My dad and Emma came to town for the wedding and gave us an all-expense paid vacation to Cancun for our honeymoon. We'd known about it in time for both of us to take the week off from work. Both Dad and Emma were happy for us, and they both welcomed Will to the family. My dad had been a little shocked at first, but the rest of my family, came around when he saw how happy Will made me and the kids.

The trip to Cancun was perfectly ironic. Will told me about Gerald trying to bribe him with a trip to Cancun instead of marrying me. Now Will still got to go to Cancun, except with me, instead. It's crazy that somebody would be so against Will marrying me that he would bribe him with a vacation. And the whole reason that he didn't approve of me was because I was divorced with two kids. What a sad little life people must live to think that I am not worth marrying simply because I ended a bad marriage to begin a better life for myself and my two adorable little children.

Now, it was happening. It was 9:30 AM on the 4th of July. I'd never heard of anyone having a wedding at 10:00 in the morning, but here we were. But it makes sense, right? I mean, who wants to be all hot and sweaty, sticking to their seat in the middle of a heat wave? Nobody does. So, it's a win-win situation. We get married, and nobody has to die of a heat stroke sitting through it.

I stood in Will's parents' master bathroom, looking in the mirror. I was wearing my mom's wedding dress. I didn't even have to have it altered, it fit perfectly. My hair was still shockingly blonde. Somehow, I had hoped I would wake up this morning and it would have darkened just a little. Even though any fool will tell you that bleached hair isn't going to get any darker. My extreme lack of patience in waiting for a hair salon appointment always got me into

314

trouble. Now I'd be getting married looking like the spokesperson for hydrogen peroxide.

The bedroom door opened, and Jamie walked in, carrying a large gift bag. "Oh! You colored your hair!" she said, trying not to stare.

"Ashley did it and it's lighter than I thought it would be. You didn't have to bring a gift!" I said, changing the subject.

"Open it! I made it myself." I pulled out a gorgeous quilt. It was ivory with green monstera leaves on it.

"Oh my gosh, Jamie, It's gorgeous! I can't believe you made this!"

"It's in honor of Big Bertha, of course." She laughed.

"Of course," I said, admiring the quilt. She knows how much I love my monstera, Big Bertha. It was going to look perfect on our bed.

Will left earlier to go pick up Mrs. Beasley. She didn't drive and he wanted to make sure she made it. He texted me and said she brought us a recipe book that she put together with her favorite crockpot recipes.

Leanne was going to bring Mimi and Pop with her. She walked in, wearing her bridesmaid's dress. I'd let her pick whatever she wanted to wear. She chose a long, navy dress with spaghetti straps and a pearl necklace that her mom gave her a long time ago. It suited her perfectly and she looked stunning.

"Sydney, I have some bad news. Pop can't come," she said, sadly.

I couldn't believe it. We'd pushed the wedding up so fast purely so he could make it. He'd wanted to come so badly. "What? Why not?" I asked her. I wanted to cry.

"He's not feeling well, and he wasn't able to even get out of his chair to get dressed. He said to tell you he's sorry."

My eyes started tearing up. Dammit, my makeup. I didn't think to wear waterproof mascara. I thought of Pop sitting at home, probably feeling terrible about not being able to come. I decided Will and I would go to his house immediately after the wedding to see him. Maybe that would help him feel better.

I stopped and rearranged a few of the tiny succulents at the wedding favor table. I'd seen the idea on Pinterest, and they came out looking absolutely adorable.

Will's friend played the acoustic guitar and as the music started, not one little inch of me was nervous, just sad about Pop not being there. I held my bouquet as I looked out of the sliding glass door and saw Will standing by the arch, next to Kip. Leanne and the kids made their way down the aisle, and it was my turn.

I looked at guests to see who was there. I saw Will's parents, Lilly, Toby, and Kayla. Both sets of my parents were there, Eric, Kennedy, Ashley, and Antonio among several other family and friends. I think people had come around to the idea more since when they first found out we were getting married. At least that's what I was going to tell myself.

I'd decided I would walk down the aisle by myself. I didn't need to be "given away" as is often the tradition at weddings. Lately, I'd thought about that tradition as old fashioned and I wanted to do things a little differently. I didn't belong to anyone, and I wasn't going to be given away to anyone, either. I was my own person. Will and I would be equal partners.

Everyone stood as the music changed and I walked alone towards the front. Will didn't take his eyes off mine. He looked so good in his crisp white shirt which made his dark tan look even darker. In only a few minutes he was going to be my husband. He and I and Micah and Elsie were going to be a family, forever.

I'd wished Pop could have been there to see it. We'd tried so hard to get things done so fast that he could be here.

Behind me, I heard Elsie's voice. "Mommy, I have to go potty." Of course we didn't remember to have her go before the wedding. I couldn't help but laugh. Luckily, Ashley came to the rescue and took her.

Will and I read the vows that we wrote ourselves. Will went first.

"Sydney, a lot of people have had their doubts about us. But the minute I met you, I knew that we were meant to be together. Before you came along, I was just existing with no reason for anything. Then I met you and all of a sudden, everything changed. I had a purpose. You gave me a reason to try and a reason to better myself. I promise to always take care of you, to be faithful to you, to protect you, and spoil you the way you deserve to be spoiled. I love you more."

Okay, I promised myself I wasn't going to tear up, but it didn't look like I was going to make it. It was my turn, and I didn't like being emotional in front of people. My non-waterproof mascara wasn't going to hold up to this.

"Will…" My voice cracked. "I always say that when you know you know. The first night that I met you, you took my hand and told the man that was hitting on me, 'she's with me,' even though I wasn't, and it was then that I knew. I may do a lot of spontaneous things that I shouldn't, but when we sat under Lupe and Felicia's bridge, and I asked you to marry me, I'd never been more positive about anything in my entire life. I promise to love you until I breathe my last breath. I love you more."

Will wiped his eyes with his hand. "You're going to have to forgive me, you've got me all choked up now and this isn't going to sound as good as it could," Will said and smiled. I looked at him confused.

He took the microphone from the minister and sang directly at me. It was a song that I'd told him I loved, and it couldn't have been more perfect. I had no idea he was planning that. I tried to keep it together but geez, this was too much. There probably wasn't a dry eye in the whole yard, including Will's.

The minister pronounced us husband and wife and after we kissed and turned around, my eyes went straight to the end of the last row. Dressed in jeans and a sports jacket, and smiling from ear to ear was Pop. His electric scooter was parked at the end of the back row, next to Mimi, who was also beaming.

Apparently, after Leanne left, Pop's medication kicked in and he had managed to get dressed and found a neighbor to give them a ride to the wedding. They arrived just in time, right after I made it down the aisle, which is why I never saw them.

Our wedding only lasted about an hour from start to finish, including the small reception, and our friends took candid photos to text us. Mrs. Beasley and Grammy both caught the bouquet together. I did a re-do toss, but this time Leanne caught it instead.

After Will and I cut our piece of cake, Lilly cut the rest of it.

"Do we have any guests with food allergies?" Kennedy asked Lilly.

"I don't believe so, Kennedy," she said. Afterwards, Kennedy opened her backpack and removed a package of gloves that she kept for emergencies and assigned herself the task of passing out plates of cake.

Elsie came up to me and tugged on my dress. "Mommy, I don't want any cake!" she cried.

"You don't have to have cake, Elsie," I told her.

"Mommy, I want cake, though!" she cried. The festivities must be too much for her. I took her to Kennedy who gave her a plate of cake.

Micah was given a toy tractor by Will's parents as his own wedding gift. He spent his time playing with it on the back porch away from the crowd.

We spent almost no money on our wedding. We didn't have any parties or showers. There were no bar tenders mixing diluted margaritas. We didn't have a DJ inviting drunken guests to dance the macarena. Nobody was forced to pose for a photographer or stand in a long line for a taco bar. But at 10:00 in the morning on the 4th of July, our wedding couldn't have been more perfect than if we'd had all the frills and fluff.

I've spent most of my life living by the rule that everything that has ever happened to me has been my own fault. Sure, I've done some stupid things and if something bad happened from my stupidity, then yeah, I'll own up to that. But what I've learned in the last few months is that a lot of good things have happened to me. I'm raising two amazing kids. I met the most wonderful man in the world. I asked him to marry me! I actually have done a lot of good things in my life. Will has taught me something that I never realized before. Everything good that has ever happened to me has been my own fault.

# Epilogue

## *Will*

### Ten months later

"Do you both have your gifts?" I asked Micah and Elsie.

"Yes!" they both said in unison. I'd taken them both shopping on the way and they did a great job of picking out their gifts. Elsie was so excited she could hardly contain herself.

We walked down the long hallway and finally came to her room. Micah stood back but Elsie scurried right over to the bassinet.

Sydney was out of bed looking through some options to dress the baby in. She'd already changed out of her hospital gown and had her own clothes on.

"Meet your new baby sister! Her name is Kendra Camille. Isn't she cute," she said to the kids. Both the kids peered in and looked at their new tiny sibling.

We'd chosen the name, Kendra, after Kennedy. She looked just like Sydney, but she looked a little like me as well. She was born ten months after our wedding. We liked to joke about that disproving the theory that Sydney had been pregnant when we got married.

"We brought gifts! I said, putting the vase of pink tulips down on the counter for her. We'd made pink tulips our tradition. Unfortunately, I had to buy them at the floral shop now because Mrs. Beasley no longer had her greenhouse. She slipped on ice a couple months ago and broke her hip. After that, she had to move to the Meadow View Nursing Home where Leanne works. Leanne kept close tabs on her and she was in good hands.

"Thank you! They are beautiful!"

Elsie and Micah handed over their gifts. Elsie chose a blanket with tomatoes all over it. Micah picked out a pair of pink pajamas.

"Knock, knock! It's us!" Leanne and Kip walked in with a gift bag. "Oh my goodness! She's so cute!" Leanne squealed looking at Kendra.

Leanne and Kip had been seeing each other ever since our rehearsal dinner and had recently gotten engaged.

"I wish Pop could have been here to see her," Sydney said. Sadly, Pop passed away two months ago. He'd made it longer than we thought he would, but he finally passed away during the night in his sleep. It had been devastating for Sydney, but at the same time, she didn't want him to suffer any longer than he had to.

Mimi still lived at home and Leanne and Sydney checked on her daily. We planned to take Kendra to see her as soon as we left the hospital.

"How's Mark doing?" Kip asked. He'd been out to see him a few times and I kept him updated on him.

"Sydney has him even more spoiled than you did. I've never seen anything like it," I told him. She'd decorated the barn and made a large wooden sign that read "Mark's Manor." We'd also put a chicken coup out by the barn with six chickens in it. We'd been enjoying the fresh eggs.

I'd plowed part of the property and had it ready for a garden. We thought it would be fun to grow our own vegetables. Sydney was all about "living off the land" and saving money on groceries.

After Leanne and Kip left, I remembered what day it was. "Um, it's the last Wednesday. Does Kennedy have a ride tonight?" I'd been picking Kennedy up and taking her with me. We still ran the pizza cart like a well-oiled machine. She wasn't going to like it when she had to have a different partner tonight. I'd also been taking her with me to Shell's Place sometimes. She liked to volunteer with office work while I volunteered in the back with the individuals. They let her sit in one of the case managers' offices and shred. She also passed out mail and any other odd jobs they had. We were making a good team.

"Yes, my mom told her that she's taking her tonight," Sydney said. "She's not going to be happy, but she'll be fine."

So far, I'd been able to take Kennedy to every Wacky Wednesday with me other than tonight. But that had just been lucky.

Quitting my job with Gerald had worked out for the best. I'd applied for a job with the prison system. The academy was five and a half weeks long and was a five-hour drive from home. I'd driven home every weekend during that time, but I'd been working at the prison for about six months. The benefits were incredible, much better than what I'd had before with Gerald, which were essentially none at all.

I'd always wanted to be a police officer, especially after what Jeff did to Sydney. But for right now, being employed at the prison was working out remarkably well for us instead.

Being in a prison five days a week was kind of ironic. Jeff was sentenced to ten years in prison. He wasn't at the same unit, that wouldn't have been allowed anyway. But I was able to check his disciplinary records, where he was housed at, and his parole status. He wasn't eligible for parole, so there was no reason to worry about him for a long time.

"Dad, do we still get to go to the tractor show?" Micah asked me. There was going to be a tractor show next weekend at the Coliseum and I'd promised Micah that I'd take him. He had his ear plugs ready, and he hadn't stopped talking about it.

We'd met with Sydney's attorney after Jeff was sentenced. It was a lengthy process, but I was adopting the kids. Jeff was not fit to be a father even if he had wanted to be one. We'd sat the kids down in the living room and we explained adoption to them, and I asked if I could be their dad instead of their stepdad. I told them they could call me anything they wanted, "dad", "daddy", "Will", or anything they liked. They've both been calling me "dad" since then.

I picked up our pink, six-pound little creation and set her down on Elsie's lap who had been eagerly waiting her turn to hold her little sister for the first time.

"Micah, sit next to them so we can take a picture," Sydney told him.

I knelt beside the kids as Sydney snapped a picture. Then, gathering all three of them, I arranged them in front of Sydney and me for our first family photo together as a family of five. My dream had always been to be a dad and a husband. This was everything I had ever wanted.

The End

www.ingramcontent.com/pod-product-compliance
Lightning Source LLC
Chambersburg PA
CBHW030245120726
47903CB00005B/1622